GHASTLY DEEDS OR GHOSTLY CHARMS?

Read this grim collection of stories and you may find yourself asking…what lies in store for you in the cold, dark of night…?

"The Tenant on the 13th Floor" and "That Dreadful Night" are sure to enhance anyone's spectral insight.

"On the Mountain" and "One Long Ribbon" show us that assistance from the dead can be quite overwhelming…and frightening.

What secrets from our pagan past really hold true? Find out for yourself in "The Big Bang" and "The Shadow of Saturn."

And let's not forget…the very real mental angst of such horrors revealed in "A Drink of Darkness," "Know Thy Neighbor" and "The Artist and the Door."

What say you avid reader? Are you prepared for a date with the macabre?

TABLE OF CONTENTS

Volume 5
E. HOFFMANN PRICE
and others

ARMCHAIR FICTION
PO Box 4369, Medford, Oregon 97504

For more information about Armchair Books and products, visit our website at…

www.armchairfiction.com

Or email us at…

armchairfiction@yahoo.com

KNOW THY NEIGHBOR

By Elizabeth R. Lewis

The terrors that inhabit the night may be even more awful in deceitful broad daylight!

IT BEGAN with the dead cat on the fire escape and ended with the green monster in the incinerator chute, but still, it wouldn't be quite fair to blame it all on the neighborhood...

The apartment house was in the heart of the district that is known as "The Tenderloin" that section of San Francisco from Ellis to Market and east from Leavenworth to Mason Street. Not the best section.

To Ellen's mind, it was an unsavory neighborhood, but with apartments so hard to get and this one only $38.00 a month and in a regular apartment building with an elevator and all—well, as she often told the girls at the office, you can't be too particular these days.

Nevertheless, it was an ordeal to walk up the two blocks from Market Street, particularly at night when the noise of juke boxes dinned from the garish bars, when the sidewalks spilled over with soldiers and sailors, with peroxided, blowsy-looking women and the furtive gamblers who haunted the back rooms of the innocent-appearing cigar stores that lined the street. She walked very fast then, never looking to left or right, and her heart would pound when a passing male whistled.

But once inside the apartment house lobby, she relaxed. In spite of its location, the place seemed very respectable. She seldom met anyone in the lobby or the elevator and, except on rare occasions like last night, the halls were as silent as those in the swanky apartment houses on Nob Hill.

She knew by sight only two of her neighbors—the short, stocky young man who lived in 410, and Mrs. Moffatt, in 404. Mrs. Moffatt was the essence of lavender and old lace, and the young man—he was all right, really; you couldn't honestly say he was shady-looking.

ON THIS particular morning, the man from 410 was waiting for the elevator when Ellen came out to get her paper. He glanced up at the sound of the door and stared. Quickly, she shut the door again. She didn't like the way he looked at her. She was wearing a housecoat over her nightgown, and a scarf wrapped around her head to cover the bobbypins—a costume as unrevealing as a nun's—but she felt as though he had invaded her privacy with his stare, like surprising her in the bathtub.

She waited until she heard the elevator start down before opening her door again. The boy must have aimed from the stairs; her paper was several yards down the hall, almost in front of 404. She went down to get it.

Mrs. Moffatt must have heard Ellen's footsteps in the hall. An old lady with a small income (from her late husband, as she had explained to Ellen) and little to do, she was intensely interested in her neighbors. She opened the door of her apartment and peered out. Her thin white hair was done up in tight kid curlers. With her round faded-blue eyes and round wrinkled-apple cheeks, she looked like an inquisitive aged baby.

"Good morning," said Ellen pleasantly.

"Good morning, my dear," the old lady answered. "You're up early for at Saturday."

"Well, I thought I might as well get up and start my house cleaning. I didn't sleep a wink after four o'clock this morning anyway. Did you hear all that racket in the hall?"

"Why, no, I didn't." The old lady sounded disappointed. "I don't see how I missed it. I guess because I went to bed so late. My nephews—you've seen them, haven't you?—They're such nice boys. They took me to a movie last night."

"Well, I'm surprised you didn't hear it," said Ellen. "Thumping and scratching, like somebody was dragging a rake along the floor. I just couldn't get back to sleep."

The old lady clicked her tongue. "I'll bet somebody came home drunk. Isn't that terrible? I wonder who it was."

"I don't know," said Ellen, "but it was certainly a disgrace. I was going to call Mrs. Anderson."

With the door open, the hall seemed filled with the very odd odor of Mrs. Moffatt's apartment—not really unpleasant, but musty, with the smell of antiques. The apartment itself was like a museum. Ellen had been inside once when the old lady invited her in for a cup of tea. Its two rooms were crammed with a bizarre assortment of furniture, bric-a-brac and souvenirs.

"Oh, how's your bird this morning?" Ellen asked.

In addition to being a collector, Mrs. Moffatt was an animal fancier. She owned three cats, a pair of lovebirds, goldfish, and even a cage of white mice. One of the lovebirds, she had informed Ellen yesterday, was ailing.

"Oh, Buzzy's much better today," she beamed. "The doctor told me to feed him whisky every three hours—with an eyedropper, you know—and you'd be surprised how it helped the little fellow. He even ate some birdseed this morning."

"I'm so glad," said Ellen. She picked up her paper and smiled at Mrs. Moffatt. "I'll see you later."

The old woman closed her door, shutting off the musty smell, and Ellen walked back to her own apartment. She filled the coffeepot with water and four tablespoons of coffee, then dressed herself while the coffee percolated. Standing in front of the medicine cabinet mirror, she took the bobbypins out of her hair. Her reflection looked back at her from the mirror, and she felt that unaccountable depression again. I'm not bad-looking, she thought, and young, and not too dumb. What have other women got that I haven't? She thought of the days and years passing, the meals all alone, and nothing ever happening.

That kind of thinking gets you nowhere; forget it. She combed her hair back, pinned it securely behind her ears, ran a lipstick over her mouth. Then she went into the kitchenette, turned off the gas flame under the coffeepot, and raised the window shade to let in the sun that was just beginning to show through morning fog.

A dead cat lay on the fire escape under the window.

SHE stared at it, feeling sick to her stomach. It was an ordinary gray cat, the kind you see in every alley, but its head was twisted back so that its open eyes and open mouth leered at her.

She pulled the blind down, fast. Sit down, light a cigarette. It's nothing, just a dead cat, that's all. But how did it get on the fire escape? Fell, maybe, from the roof? And how did it get on the roof? Besides, I thought cats never got hurt falling. Isn't there something about landing on your feet like a cat? Maybe that's just a legend, like the nonsense about nine lives.

Well, what do I do, she thought? I can't sit here and drink coffee with *that* under the window. And God knows I can't take it away myself. She shuddered at the thought. Call the manager.

She got up and went to the telephone in the foyer. She found the number scribbled on the back of the phone book. Her hand was shaking when she dialed.

"This is Ellen Tighe in 402. Mrs. Anderson, there's a dead cat on the fire escape outside my window. You'll have to do something about it."

Mrs. Anderson sounded half asleep. "What do you mean, a dead cat? Are you sure it's dead? Maybe it's sleeping."

"Of course I'm sure it's dead! Can't you send Pete up to take it away? It's a horrible thing to have under my window."

"All right, I'll tell Pete to go up. He's washing down the lobby now. As soon as he's finished, I'll send him up."

Ellen set the phone back on its stand. She felt a little silly. What a fuss to make over a dead cat. But really, outside one's window—and before breakfast—who could blame me?

She went back into the kitchenette, carefully not looking toward the window, even though the shade was drawn, and poured herself a cup of coffee. Then she sat at the table in the little nook, drinking coffee, smoking a cigarette and leafing through the paper.

The front page was all about a flying saucer scare in Marin County. She read the headline, then thumbed on through the paper, stopping to read the movie reviews and the comic page.

AT THE back section, she was attracted by a headline that read: "Liquor Strong These Days—Customer Turns Green, Says Bartender." It was a brief item, consciously cute. "John Martin,

38, a bartender of 152 Mason Street, was arrested early this morning, charged with drunkenness and disturbing the peace, after firing several shots from a .38 revolver on the sidewalk in front of his address. No one was injured. Martin's defense, according to police records, was that he was attempting to apprehend a pale-green, claw-handed customer who fled after eating a live mouse and threatening Martin.

"Upon questioning, Martin admitted that the unidentified customer had been in the bar for several hours and appeared perfectly normal. But he insisted, 'When I refused to serve him after he ate the mouse, he turned green and threatened to claw me to death.' Martin has a permit to carry the gun and was dismissed with a fifty dollar fine and a warning by Judge Greely against sampling his own stock too freely."

Drunken fool, thought Ellen. With fresh indignation, she remembered the disturbance in her own hall this morning. Nothing but drunks and gangsters in this neighborhood. She thought vaguely of looking at the "For Rent" section of the want ads.

There was a noise on the fire escape. Ellen reached over and lifted up the shade. The janitor was standing there with a big paper sack in his hand.

Ellen opened the window and asked, "How do you think it got there, Pete?"

"I dunno. Maybe fall offa the roof. Musta been in a fight."

"What makes you think so?"

"Neck's all torn. Big teeth marks. Maybe dog get him."

"Up here?"

"Somebody find, maybe throw here—I dunno." Pete scratched his head. "You don't worry any more, though. I take away now. No smell, even."

He grinned at her and scuttled to the other end of the fire escape where he climbed through the window to the fourth floor corridor.

Ellen poured herself a second cup of coffee and lighted another cigarette, then turned to the woman's page in the paper. She read the Advice Column and the Psychology and glanced through the

"Help Wanted—Women" in the classifieds. That finished the morning's reading. She looked at her watch. Almost ten.

She carried her coffee cup to the sink, rinsed it out and set it on the drainboard. There was still a cup or more of coffee left in the pot. That could be warmed over later, but she took out the filter and dumped the grounds into the paper bag that held garbage. The bag was almost full.

I'll throw it in the incinerator now, she thought, before I straighten the apartment.

She emptied the ashtrays—the one beside her bed and the other on the breakfast table—then started down the hall with the garbage bag in her hand.

THE incinerator chute was at the rear of the hall, next to the service stairs. Ellen could see the door standing slightly open. She hesitated. 410 might be there. It was bad enough to ride in the elevator with him, feeling his eyes on her, but there was something unbearably intimate about standing beside him, emptying garbage.

The door seemed to move a little, but nobody came out. She waited another minute. Oh, well, maybe the last person out there just forgot to shut the door tight. She opened it wider, stepped out on the stair landing. No one was there.

The chute was wide, almost three feet around. Ellen opened the top and started to throw the bag down. Something was stuck in there. Her eyes saw it, but her brain refused to believe.

What was there, blocking the chute, looked like—looked like—a chicken's foot, gnarled, clawed, but as large as a human foot—and an ugly, sickly green!

Automatically, she reached in and clutched it. Her stomach turned at the cold feel of the thing, but still she tugged at it, trying to work it loose. It was heavy. She pulled with all her strength, felt it start to slide back up the chute. Then it was free!

She gaped in sick horror at the thing she held. Her hand opened weakly and she sat down on the floor, her head swimming and her throat muscles retching. Dimly, she heard the thing rattle and bump down to the incinerator in the basement.

The full horror of it gradually hit home. Ellen stood up, swaying, and ran blindly down the hall. Her feet thudded on the carpeted floor. As she passed 404, she was vaguely conscious of Mrs. Moffatt's concerned face poking around the door.

"Is there something wrong, Miss Tighe?"

"No," Ellen managed to gasp. "It's all right—really—all right."

She kept on running, burst through the apartment door, slammed it behind her, fell on her knees in the bathroom and became thoroughly, violently ill.

She continued to kneel, unable to think, her head against the cool porcelain bowl. Finally, she stood up weakly, ran cold water, washed her face and streaming eyes. Thank God the wall bed was still down. She fell on it, shaking.

WHAT was that unbelievable ghastly, impossible thing? It was the size of a man, but thin, skeleton thin, and the color of brackish water. It had two legs, two arms, like a man...but ending with those huge, birdlike claws. Heaven alone knew what its face was like. She had let go before it was that far clear of the chute.

She thought of the story in the paper. So *that* was what the bartender saw. He wasn't drunk at all, and what happened when he told the police? They laughed at him. They'd laugh at me, too, she thought. The proof is gone, burned up in the incinerator. Why did this happen to me? Dead cats on the fire escape, dead monsters in the incinerator chute...it's this terrible neighborhood!

She tried to think coherently. Maybe the cat had something to do with it. The bartender said the thing ate a mouse—maybe it had tried to eat the cat, too. A monster like that might eat anything. Her stomach started churning again at the thought.

But what was it doing in the incinerator chute? Someone in the building must have put it there, thinking it would slide all the way down and be burned up. Who? One of *them,* probably. But there couldn't be any more green monsters around. They can't live in an apartment house, walk the streets like anyone else, not even in this neighborhood.

She remembered something else in the bartender's story. He said it looked perfectly normal at first. That meant they could look like humans if they wanted to. Hypnotism? Then any man could be...

Suddenly another thought struck her. Supposing they find out I saw—what will they do to me?

She jumped up from the bed, white with fear, her faintness forgotten in the urge to escape. She snatched her bag from the dresser, threw on her brown coat.

At the door, she hesitated, afraid to venture into the hall, yet afraid to stay inside. Finally, she eased open the door, peered out into the corridor. It was deserted. She ran to the elevator, punched the bell, heard the car begin its creaky, protesting ascent.

The elevator door had an automatic spring closing. The first time she tried it, her hands shook and the door sprang closed before she got in. She tried it again. This time she managed to hold it open long enough to get inside. She pushed the button, felt the elevator shake and grind and move slowly down.

Out into the lobby.

Out into the street.

THE FOG was completely gone now. The sun shone on the still-damp street. There were very few people around—The Tenderloin sleeps late. She went into the restaurant next door, sat down at the white-tiled counter. She was the only customer. A sleepy-eyed waitress, her black hair untidily caught into a net, waited, pad in hand.

"Just coffee," Ellen mumbled.

She drank it black and it scalded her throat going down. The waitress put a nickel in the jukebox and then Bing Crosby was singing "Easter Parade." Everything was so normal. Listening to Bing Crosby, how could you believe in things like green monsters? In this sane, prosaic atmosphere, Ellen thought, *I must be batty*.

She said to herself, "I'm Ellen Tighe, bookkeeper, and I just saw the body of a green man with claws on his feet..." No, that didn't help a bit. Put it this way: "I'm Ellen Tighe and I'm 27 years old and I'm not married. Let's face it, any psychiatrist will tell you that's enough cause for neurosis. So I'm having delusions."

It made more sense that way. I read that story in the paper, Ellen thought, and it must have registered way down in my subconscious. That had to be it. Any other way, it was too horrible, too impossible to be borne.

I'll go back to the apartment and call Dr. Clive, thought Ellen. She had the feeling, no doubt held over from the days of measles and mumps, that a doctor could cure anything, even green monsters on the brain.

She drank the last of the coffee and fished in her coin purse for change. Picking up the check, she walked over to the cash register at the end of the counter, facing the street. The untidy waitress came from the back of the restaurant to take the money.

Ellen looked out at the street through the glass front. The man from 410 was standing out there, smoking a cigarette, watching her. When their eyes met, he abruptly threw away the cigarette and started walking toward the apartment house. Again she felt that faint dread she had experienced in the hall earlier.

The waitress picked up her quarter, gave her back a nickel and a dime. Ellen put the change into her purse, got out her key chain and held it in her hand while she walked quickly next door. 410 was just ahead of her in the lobby; he held the front door open for her.

She kept her head down, not looking at his face, and they walked, Indian file, across the lobby to the elevator. He opened the elevator doors, too, and she stepped in ahead of him.

WHEN the doors clanged shut, she had a feeling of panic. Alone with him...cut off from help. He didn't pretend not to know her floor, but silently pressed the proper button. While the car moved slowly upward, her heart was beating wildly.

I'm not convinced, she thought, I'm not convinced. I saw it so plainly...I felt it, cold in my hands.

The elevator stopped. The man held the door open and for a moment she thought he was going to say something. His free hand made a swift, involuntary movement as though he were going to catch her arm. She shrank away, but he stepped back and let her through.

Ellen almost ran down the hall. Behind her, she heard his footsteps going in the opposite direction toward his apartment. She was panting when she reached her door. She fumbled for the right key—front door, office—and then she froze. There was a scratching sound in the apartment.

She put her ear close to the door, listened. There was a rasping noise, like somebody dragging a rake...or like claws, great heavy claws, moving over the hardwood floors.

Ellen backed away from the door. It was true, then. She retreated, inch by inch, silently. Get away, leave before it catches you! She turned, ready to make a dash for the elevator...and faced the man from 410.

Down at the end of the hall, in front of his apartment, he was watching her. The way he lingered outside the restaurant, the way he looked at her. One of them...maybe underneath that homely, ordinary face, his skin was green and clammy. Maybe there were long, sharp claws on his feet.

She was breathing unevenly now. Trapped! The thing in the apartment, the man in the hall. Her eyes darted to the elevator, then back down the hall, past the door marked 404...the door marked 404! She covered the few yards in a mad dash, flung herself at the door, pounding wildly.

"Please, please!" she sobbed. "Mrs. Moffatt, open, please!"

The door opened at once. Mrs. Moffatt's round, wrinkled face beamed at her.

"Come in, my dear, come in."

She almost fell over the landing. The door closed behind her.

She stumbled to the davenport, sank down, gasping. Two cats rubbed against her legs, purring. Two cats?

She heard herself say stupidly, "Mrs. Moffatt, where's the other cat?" and wondered why she said it.

Then she understood.

The old lady's face quivered, altered, melted into something...something green.

OUTSIDE in the hall, the man from 410 slowly returned to his apartment. Pushing open the door, he thought, I'll never get the nerve to ask her out.

Well, probably wasn't a chance, anyhow. What would a girl like her have to do with a lousy cop like me?

THE END

THE BIG BANG

By Gregory Luce

Harry Townsend raised his glass. "To Christina Sheppard...first woman to walk on the moon."

Three crystal glasses clinked together. The light of the full moon overhead danced reflectively off the bubbling champagne I drew to my lips. As I drank, a warm breeze blew through my hair. It rippled across the terrace from the direction of the coast and the Sargasso Sea beyond that. It was an exquisite summer night.

I lowered my glass and edged my wheelchair closer to our host. "How about a few words, Ethan?"

Ethan Sheppard looked down and smiled. "I'm not much at making speeches," he said, "but I would like to say how grateful I am to have you both here this evening. In your own different ways, each of you has had a tremendous effect on the course of my life...but I've never been so acutely aware of it until tonight." Ethan raised his glass. "To Harry Townsend and Andrew Bates."

Harry and I looked at each other and smiled. It had been a long haul for the three of us. We raised our glasses and shared in Ethan's generous toast.

I looked at the moon high overhead, then said, "Have you heard anything from the Cape this evening?"

Ethan shook his head. "Nothing since this afternoon. The landing came off without a hitch. Christina was the second one out of the lunar module." He raised his eyebrows and stared down into his glass. "The first woman on the moon...now that's quite a feat." He paused to ponder his statement for a moment, then looked at me. "The return lift-off is scheduled for Monday morning."

I shifted back in my wheelchair. "Any problems so far?"

"No...nothing they've told me about anyway."

"I'm sure everything's going to be fine," Harry said.

A reflective expression came across Ethan's face. "You know, the three of us were just kids the last time there was a moon-shot." His eyes glanced skyward at the glowing orb above. "And now *my wife's* walking around up there. Who would have ever thought she'd be picked for such an historic mission."

"She got picked because she worked her ass off," Harry replied, smiling.

"That's very nice, Harry, but…" Ethan's mouth curled downward slightly and he started shaking his head, "…I think we can chalk this one up to Mother Luck…or who knows what else."

I was somewhat startled by this statement. "Ethan, how can you say that? She's been with NASA for over ten years. For crying out loud, she's logged over 300 hours in shuttle missions."

"She was one of nearly seventy equally qualified astronauts…including twelve other women."

"Never-the-less she was deserving," Harry cut in.

I quickly agreed. "There's no doubt about it. Christina has a level of skill and dedication that most of the others are lacking. She was able to put herself ahead of the rest of the pack…that's why she was picked."

Ethan shrugged his shoulders indifferently. "Maybe…who knows."

There was something peculiar in Ethan's mood. I'd noticed it all evening. It was markedly low-key and devoid of the high spirits one would expect for such an occasion. There was even a certain degree of callousness in his tone; yet, in spite of that, he did seem pleased to have the presence of his two closest friends. I decided to try and raise his spirits.

"You're a lucky man, my friend."

"Really? In what way Andrew?"

"First of all, you're a hell of a writer," I complimented.

Ethan shrugged. "If you like reading books and articles on Haitian voodoo practices, I suppose."

"Maybe you should come back to work for the paper again," Harry remarked.

"Secondly," I continued, "you're married to a gorgeous woman who's not only beautiful, but intelligent and successful, too."

"Now that," Ethan said, raising his index finger, "is a dangerous combination."

I was again puzzled. "What do you mean?"

"The more valuable the possession, the more it's coveted by others," he replied. "And that's a fact."

"That might be true," I responded, "but you'll never have to worry about Christina."

Ethan took a drink and smiled, then said, "You're showing your naivety."

I lowered my glass. "What are you driving at?"

He leaned over and stared straight into my eyes. "What I'm driving at Andrew, is that my wife is a cold, calculating, two-timing bitch."

I was incredulous. "You're kidding, of course."

Harry seemed startled, too. "Ethan...you can't be serious."

Ethan picked up the champagne bottle and refilled his glass. "It's been going on for over a year," he replied. His eyes gazed up at the moon again. "I suppose I should have expected something like this to happen. I mean I'm not exactly around all the time...am I?" He looked at both of us with a strange smile on his face. "When the cat's away..." His voice trailed off into a soft laugh.

I was completely taken aback. "Ethan, this is—to say the least—a bit hard to believe. Are you on the level?"

He nodded slowly. "A hundred percent."

I looked for a glimmer of mischief in his eyes, hoping the whole thing was some kind of joke—there was none. Then I asked, "When and how did you find out?"

Ethan took another drink. "Oh...I started noticing little telltale signs about a year ago...shortly after I got back from one of my trips to the islands. I didn't think too much about it at the time, but later on I grew suspicious...so the next time I left for Haiti I had her watched. She and her secret lover weren't exactly secret about it."

"Well...who the hell is she seeing?" I asked.

Ethan shook his head. "That's my little secret." Then he smiled and winked. "At least for the moment."

I didn't know what to say. Ethan and Christina had been married since Ethan's exodus from the paper two years earlier, and even though they spent much of their time apart, they had always seemed genuinely happy when they were together. I was flabbergasted at the thought of any improprieties between them. Finally I spoke, "what's going to happen now? I mean...what are you going to do about all this?"

"Well...hopefully I'll be able to cut myself a nice, sweet piece of revenge before I drop dead."

"Drop dead?" Harry asked, a look of perplexity on his face. "Now what's that supposed to mean?"

"What it means, dear Harry...is that I'm dying."

I was stunned. "What in the hell are you talking about?"

Ethan got a far away look in his eyes. "I got the bad news last Friday. It's Pancreatic Cancer. I've only got a few weeks...maybe a couple of months." A strange smirk came over his face. "Quite a night for a celebration isn't it?" He smiled and downed the rest of his glass.

"Good lord, Ethan," I said, "does Christina know?"

"She's already got enough to celebrate about. Why should I give her another reason to smile?"

Harry, who had been strangely silent, looked down at the terrace, a somber expression on his face. "I'm sorry to hear about all of this, Ethan. I really, truly am."

Ethan broke out laughing. "That's real good coming from you, Harry."

"What's that supposed to mean?" I asked.

"Haven't you figured it out yet, Andrew?" Ethan answered. He closed his fist and pointed his thumb in Harry's direction. "Our dear friend Harry's the son-of-a-bitch who's been sleeping with my wife!"

I was speechless.

"You're drunk," Harry replied curtly.

I shook my head in disbelief and said, "Ethan, do you realize what you're accusing him of?"

"Oh it gets even better Andrew. You see...I'm not the only close friend Harry's ever betrayed. Isn't that right, Harry?"

Harry said nothing.

Ethan began pouring another glass of champagne. "You see Andrew, the day you went to conduct your interview with Miami drug lord Arturo Clemente, Harry knew five minutes after you left that the police were going to raid Clemente's headquarters within the hour. I was there in the office when he got the call from his informant inside the Miami PD. All he had to do was dial up your cellular number and have you return to the office. But uh-uh...that would have been too easy. Besides, think of the story. I mean how often does a major daily get to have one of its best reporters on the inside during a major drug raid?"

"You don't know what you're talking about," Harry scoffed.

Ethan walked around the table and stood face to face with him.

"Yes I do, Harry," he shot back, "and you know damn well it's all true." He started shaking his head in disgust. "A bullet in Andrew's spine and a wheelchair to go along with it...but it gave the paper a great headline, didn't it?" Ethan stepped back and took another drink. "And now this affair with Christina. That's one for the society section, isn't it?"

A look of blank resignation had crept into Harry's eyes.

Ethan continued, "I've always known you could be a ruthless bastard at times, but I never dreamed you could be so disloyal to someone so close to you."

I was bowled over by what I was hearing. I turned to Harry and said, "This has to be some kind of a joke...right? Harry?"

Harry didn't utter a word. Instead, he gazed down at the surface of the terrace, a decidedly grim look on his face.

"No Andrew," Ethan said, interrupting the awkward silence, "Harry doesn't have much to say right now. Do you Harry?"

There was a long pause. Finally, Harry responded, "Well what did you expect, Ethan?" he asked. "How much time have you spent with Christina over the past two years? Four...maybe five months? She may put in a lot of hours with the program, but at least she wasn't gallivanting all over Haiti looking for witch doctors and voodoo dolls." A slight smirk came over Harry's face. "First you leave the paper to pursue this occult research you're so obsessed with...then you leave her alone for months at a time...and now after two years what do you have to show for it?" He held his hands up as though framing a picture. "A new book on the wonders of voodoo cupie dolls." He broke into a flourish of contemptuous laughter.

"You're whole life has turned into a joke, Ethan," Harry sneered. "You're one hell of a writer when you want to be, but what do you waste your time and talent on…voodoo-hoodoo-hocus-pocus crap!"

There was a moment of silence, then Ethan responded in a very calm manner, "I'm glad you brought that up Harry…because that's part of the reason I asked you here tonight."

Ethan walked over and picked up a cardboard box that was sitting to the side of the terrace, next to the entryway to the house. He carried it over and placed it on the table we'd been sitting around, then looked down at me in my wheelchair.

"I'm sure you'll appreciate what's about to happen, Andrew. Especially after what you've learned tonight about our good friend, Harry." He looked in Harry's direction. "I'm going to give you a demonstration of one of the oldest and most effective ways of dealing with betrayal."

Ethan reached into the box and produced a small, crude-looking handmade doll. He held it up for both of us to look at.

"Quite a beauty, isn't it?"

He carefully laid the doll face up on the table, then reached back into the box and pulled out two long needles, one in each hand.

Harry put his hands on his hips. "What is this crap, Ethan?"

"Crap, Harry?" Ethan grinned for a moment, then said, "I guess I should expect a response like that from you. You've never thought too highly of my work, now have you? Of course maybe that's part of the grand rationalization you used for slam-banging my wife." He chuckled again. "I suppose for you voodoo has never been more than the silly stuff we used to watch in old horror movies. But you know, it's the damnedest thing…" he put his hands on the table and leaned forward, "…all that weird stuff about hexes and zombies…all that campy old 'pins and dolls' gibberish…all that voodoo-hoodoo-hocus-pocus crap you never believed in…well you know what?"

Ethan straightened up, smiling ear to ear.

"It's *all* true."

He laughed sardonically for several seconds. A crazed expression was coming over his face. He continued, "In fact...not only is it all true, but it's a hell of a lot worse than you could ever imagine."

A sickening premonition of horror suddenly came over me. "Ethan, I think I'd like you to take me home now."

"Be patient Andrew, we're going to wind this whole thing up in just a few mo—"

"If you think I'm going to stand around and listen to any more of this supernatural drivel, you're crazy," Harry finally cut in. He turned to leave and briefly looked down at me, an apologetic expression on his face. "I'm sorry, Andrew. I'm really sorry." He began walking toward the entryway to the house.

As Harry walked across the terrace, Ethan raised the two needles—one in each hand—high over his head.

"You're not walking out on me, Harry..."

A second later he jammed them down forcefully into the legs of the crude-looking doll...

At that instant, Harry Townsend's legs literally exploded...

In mid-stride the flesh on Harry's lower legs burst outward with such terrific force that it ripped right through his trouser legs. His body went careening forward, smacking face first onto the hard tile surface of the terrace.

Ethan smiled, "...try crawling instead."

I was completely paralyzed with horror; my eyes practically bulged out of my head. It appeared all that was left of Harry's lower legs was shredded material and bones, like a skeleton in ragged pants. The terrace around him was covered with a spray of crimson and numerous chunky bits of flesh.

Harry managed to roll himself over. The evening air suddenly reverberated with his screams. Then I realized...

I was screaming, too.

"Calm, calm, Andrew," Ethan said in a consoling manner. "Nothing to get excited about. Harry's debt to you is now squared." He crossed over and stood over Harry's wriggling body. "How'd you like to have a box seat in a wheelchair for the rest of your life, Harry?" Ethan laughed.

Harry didn't reply, he just kept screaming. Although blood was gushing out of his trousers, he actually managed to sit up. Then his screams stopped for a moment and a look of befuddlement came over his face. He appeared to be trying to comprehend what had happened to him, staring at the tattered remains of his lower pant legs for a good three or four seconds.

Then he started screaming again.

Ethan moved back over to the table and took another drink of champagne. "Music to my ears, Harry." He placed his glass back on the table and picked up the needles, once again holding them high over his head.

"And now you can square your debt to me." He briefly looked at the shining lunar body above. "Full moon and empty arms, eh?"

I screamed, *"Ethan, No!"*

Ethan plunged the needles down forcefully again, this time into the doll's arms.

"Give her a hug now, Harry."

The same eruption of flesh and blood followed as Harry's arms detonated into an explosion of flying crimson matter. His body went flopping backward, the back of his head hitting the terrace with a distinct thud.

I was nearly overcome by abrupt physical and emotional shock. My body was literally shaking with horror. I gripped my armrests and tried to raise myself up.

"Ethan...what have you done!"

"Something that should have been done over a year ago," he replied calmly. His eyes looked down on the convulsing body that lay dying in front of us. "Still conscious, Harry?" he said with a smile, "don't worry, you won't be for long."

Some gurgling noises came from deep down in Harry's throat, but I had no idea if he was actually trying to talk (or scream for that matter), or whether they were just the garbled, involuntary sounds emitted by the throat cavity of a dying man.

My body was still trembling violently as I collapsed back down into my wheelchair—then I saw Ethan raise one of the needles again.

"I won't let you suffer any longer, Harry. That's the one act of mercy I *will* show you tonight."

"Ethan!"

I closed my eyes as Ethan drove the needle down into the head of Harry's death-doll. I didn't see the explosion of skull and brain matter that splattered across the terrace, but I could hear its sickening sound. I could also hear Ethan laughing softly. But no more sounds came from Harry's direction. It was over.

By now I was weeping. I put my head down in my lap and sobbed for the next minute or two. Ethan, on the other hand, simply stood behind the table staring at his handiwork, saying nothing, just staring. There was a dull look of morbid satisfaction on his face.

Finally he spoke, "I left a letter for the police, Andrew...explaining...all this. Don't know whether they'll believe it or not...but I don't think you'll have any trouble with them."

My voice was choked with distress, but somehow I managed to speak. "What—in heaven's name—have you done, Ethan? How is this—possible?"

He pondered the question for a moment or two. "Let's just call it super voodoo," he responded in a casual manner, "a form of black magic lost over the eons of time. That is...until it was rediscovered by yours truly." He paused and gave a quick bow of his head. "It's a force so terrific, so volatile, that it completely destroyed the Haitian cult that once guarded its secret. I estimate I'm the first person in nearly a thousand years to know the secret of its power, and...as you can see..." he gracefully waved an arm in Harry's direction, "...it's definitely not something one should fool around with. That's why its secret will die with me tonight."

"Die? Tonight?"

"Yes, Andrew. I'm afraid so. Not much fun waiting for cancer to eat your insides out while being cooped up in a jail cell." Ethan reached down into the box on the table and produced a small vile of fluid. He uncapped it and poured it into his glass of champagne.

"Bottoms up, old friend," he said with a smile, then downed the rest of his glass. He glanced at his watch. "It won't be long now."

"What about me Ethan? How could you subject me to all this? I'll have to carry this nightmare with me for the rest of my life."

"My deepest apologies, Andrew...truly. I suppose I thought vengeance might be as sweet for you as it is for me. I can see I was wrong, though. But unfortunately…I'm afraid it isn't over…quite yet. There's one last thing I have to attend to."

Out of the box Ethan lifted a pasty-looking, off-white colored globe that he laid on the table in front of him. It was about the size of a basketball and had a crusty, pockmarked surface.

I looked at the globe on the table, then glanced skyward at the glowing orb that still hung high overhead. A wave of mind-numbing realization suddenly shot through my brain.

"Dear lord, Ethan. Don't do it! Not Christina…*not like that!*"

His hand had already risen above his head. I saw the shaft of the needle sparkle in the moonlight.

"I always wanted to go out with a bang," he said…

…*then plunged the needle down!*

THE END

THE UBIQUITOUS PROFESSOR KARR

By Stanton A. Coblentz

A blameless man, the Professor…everybody thought!

"WHAT would you say, Chief, was your most baffling experience in all your years with the force?"

Larry Finch, until recently Chief of Police in our hometown of Coleton, leaned back among the amply upholstered pillows of the Antelope Club. His square, ruddy face, marked by the bald head, the pugnose, and the little blue-gray eyes that squinted shrewdly from above their wrinkles of fat, wore a sort of vague, tantalizing smile.

"Well, you know, boys," said he, while the four or five of us gathered closer on the club chairs and sofas, "nobody can hold down a job like mine for thirty years without having some hard nuts to crack. Just the same, I don't think any case ever came to near driving me crazy as the Emerson J. Karr affair. It had elements in it that went way beyond a regular police case. In fact, I can't say I understand it entirely even now. Any of you fellows remember Emerson J. Karr?"

"Seems to me there was something about him once in the papers, wasn't there, Chief?" I asked, for the name did strike a faint echo.

"You bet there was!" Finch affirmed, as he knocked out the ashes from a fat cigar. "However, that was all of twenty years back—yes, nearer twenty-five. Emerson J. Karr was a pretty well known man in his field. He was the head of the Department of Sanskrit at Newlands University, and he'd written some highbrow books and made some translations that they say were in every college library. All in all, he was about the last man you'd ever have connected with organized crime."

"Organized crime?" several of us gasped; while, leaving our Martinis half-finished, we leaned closer in tingling excitement.

"If you'd ever seen the guy," went on the Chief, after he had slipped down the remains of his Old-fashioned and taken another puff or two at his cigar, "you'd have expected him to be as proper as a parson. He was a sort of walking beanpole, with a huge head perched on top. I never saw another such a head; it looked big enough for two, a monstrous bald bulb, with great yellowish teeth, like a hallowe'en goblin's, and two pale green eyes that seemed to stare out at you from some sort of a dream-world of his own. His face was always pasty-pale, and the big Adam's apple on his thick neck wobbled up and down, but what made him look queerest of all was a long twisted gray scar running down from the left corner of his lips."

"Not exactly a beauty, was he?" remarked Fred Mayfield, from over my shoulder.

"BELIEVE me, he wasn't! Maybe that was one reason no woman had ever taken to him. He was sixty-one or two, and had never married; lived with his eighty-three-year-old mother in a dilapidated two-story house in the suburbs. At the college he was a sort of an institution, having been at the place longer than most folks could remember; everybody respected him, but he was the sort of guy that has a crowd of acquaintances and no friends. His habits were as regular as a monk's; he never went out anywhere, and I doubt if he'd been seen for years anywhere much except on the half-mile stretch between his home and the campus. A story went the rounds that you could set your watch by his goings and comings, and I believe it, too—which was why I just couldn't take it seriously when the reports seemed to connect him with the Nich Rocco gang."

"Nich Rocco gang?" I burst forth. "Wasn't that the one that—"

"Yes sirree, worst gang this part of the country ever saw. Sure did more than anything else to turn me gray," stated Finch, with a growl, as his fingers ranged over the few grizzled hairs that remained at the sides of his head. "Their specialty was robbing safes in banks, stores and factories, and they got away with so many crack-ups they took to leaving a big R, painted in red, out of sheer bravado whenever they finished a job. I tell you it was maddening, and for a while it looked like I'd lose my own job if I couldn't outwit them. Just about this time, Emerson J. Karr began to stick his nose into things."

"What could Emerson J. Karr have to do with a thug like Nich Rocco?"

"That's the question that worried us all. When the first stories began coming in, I called them pipe dreams. I remember when Officer Pete Kelly, who was pretty new on the force, said he saw Professor Karr standing on the street, just in front of the Seaboard National Bank at 3 a.m., right before its safes were blown open. He swore he knew Karr by sight, because his first assignment had been to the University beat. But he couldn't tell me what in blazes a man like Karr would be doing at 3 a.m. at the Seaboard National Bank."

"Simply doesn't seem reasonable," muttered Joe Tracy, just to my left.

"You're telling me, are you? But just as sure as I'm a man, and not a monkey, I didn't feel quite so positive two days later, when I heard from Captain O'Donnell, one of our veterans. He rushed with a squad of men down to the Coddings Lumber Mills right after the alarm came in. They almost nabbed two of the crooks, but they got away somehow over a fence, and he swore one of them was a tall rambling stake of a fellow, with a huge head and a big Adam's apple, and a twisted gray scar running down from the left corner of his lips."

"Must have been Karr's double," I suggested. "I've sometimes seen two men look so much alike you could take them for twin brothers."

The Chief leaned far forward in his chair, while one pudgy hand fondled his bony chin.

"Tell the truth, I thought it was something like that, too. Even the detail of the scar—after all, in his excitement, a man mightn't really see what he thinks he sees. So I let things rest for another week, until officers Muzzio and Olsen—two men I really trusted—described a fellow with exactly the same features, who'd been seen running away after a street robbery."

"If he was seen so often," I argued, "I should think he'd have been caught."

FINCH shook his great square head ruefully; his face seemed even redder than usual by the light of the overhead lamps.

"That was just what puzzled us most of all. Before the month was up, he was reported again four or five times. More than once the boys came within an inch of getting him, but suddenly he would slip away—whisk around corners, or through windows or over walls, they couldn't ever explain just how, except that he was gone like a shot."

"Sounds weird to me."

"Weird? Wait till you hear the rest! Of course, being pretty hard-boiled, none of us supposed we were up against anything but a specially clever crook. I know I expected to clear up the mystery the day I went to visit Professor Karr. I didn't think any dry-as-dust bookworm could put anything over on me. But I still had some things to learn. Believe me, I had some things to learn."

The Chief called for a second Old-fashioned; and having hastily consumed it, went on in a wry, hesitant manner.

"You know, boys, I'm not a guy that embarrasses easy—couldn't, in my line of work, if I wanted to get along. Just the same, I was like a school kid reciting his first piece when I let myself in there with the professor. I'd trumped up some sort of phony excuse, about maybe wanting him to appear as a witness—it was still a police secret what about. He was so damned polite you would have thought I was the King of England: 'Won't you kindly step in, Officer,' 'Make yourself comfortable, Officer,' and that kind of junk, all in a deep burring bass you'd never forget. He led me upstairs to his study, which was lined with books from floor to ceiling—God, I don't see how I any man could ever read all that stuff. I sure began hemming and hawing, when I found myself opposite his desk, where he had a portable typewriter open; he looked at me with such a peculiar steady stare of those big round pale-green eyes that I sort of felt I was the one that was under inspection. However, I did manage to jerk my questions out.

"'Professor, do you remember where you were last Thursday night?'

"He didn't give even a second's thought. 'Thursday—why, yes, Thursday I remember being busy all evening writing my paper on

'Some Aspects of the Philosophy of Sankara' for *The International Scholar.*'

"Anyway, I think that was what he said, and it had me sort of stumped, so I went on to ask, 'And Tuesday evening?'

"There still wasn't the faintest hesitation as he answered, 'Why, yes, Tuesday evening—Tuesday evening I always prepare my lecture for my advanced course on the Sutras of Patan'—Patanjali, I guess it was, or something like that anyway.

"Believe me, boys, that had me cornered. He answered every other question right off, too; let out he hadn't been away from home any evening the whole blasted month. What's more, he looked so damned honest I couldn't in my heart believe he was lying, especially as his story was confirmed by his mother. She was a birdlike lovely little thing, with such clear blue eyes that looked you straight in the face you felt like a louse for having any suspicions. This lady—she didn't look at all like eighty-three— came in at about nine with a pot of tea. 'Emerson always has his tea at this time,' she said. 'Won't you join us, Officer?' Just imagine, boys, me having tea! Just the same, you have to submit to pretty near anything in my line, so I took it with a perfectly smooth face.

"Got the mother to chat, too; said, 'Well, Ma'am, what does your son do about his tea the evenings when he's out?'

"'Oh, but he's never out!' she answered. 'Why, I don't believe Emerson's been away one evening since he gave his lectures over to Clinton College, a year ago last May.'

"I've interviewed lots of men and women in my day, boys, and caught 'em in packs of lies, but I'd have staked my reputation there wasn't even the chance of a lie in the pure, sweet eyes of that old lady. No, somehow we'd made a dreadful mistake.

"I stuck around a while after the mother went out, just for the sake of appearances, while the professor showed me some of the books he'd written. There was some highfalutin thing, a study of some old Hindu poem or other, and others with jaw-cracking names I don't even begin to know what about. That was why it gave me a whale of a surprise, as I was leaving, to see a strip of gaudy color peeping out at me from under a pile of highbrow magazines on the rack. Jerking it out, I sure got a shock to see a copy of *'Stirring Crime Stories.'*

"I GAVE a low whistle, and could see the professor's face going from white to red. 'Lord bless me, but I'm getting careless!' he burst out, looking like a schoolboy who's been caught red-handed stealing something. 'Please push it back, Officer, so my mother won't see it. I wouldn't have her know—you see, in my work, I sometimes need relief from tension, and have been finding it of late in crime and detective stories. Of course, it's only a sowing of intellectual wild oats, so if you'll just help me keep it from Mother—'

I knew that brainy men sometimes did turn to blood-and-thunder thrillers so as to sort of let off steam. Still, I wondered if I mightn't be running into a clue. But before I had time to ask questions, somebody rapped at the door, and a lean tall man with a black face and black moustache and hair came in and took the professor's hand in a familiar sort of way. 'Officer, meet my friend Mr. Rasmani,' he introduced us. 'He used to be my student, but I'm his student now; he's instructing me in the practice of Yogi.'

"This was a little beyond my depth, and I was getting uncomfortable as hell in the presence of that Hindu, who gave me a look that seemed to go through me like a bullet. So I snatched my cap and left. God! but was I glad to be out of that house!"

The Chief reached for another cigar, and passed half a minute in lighting it.

"Well, I don't see that you were getting anywhere," I filled in the interval. "You came away without any evidence, so far as I can see."

"So far as I could see, either," Finch resumed, sitting back with a smile as of one who enjoys a good joke on himself. "Just try to imagine how befuddled I was when a call came that very night. The Firestone Jewelers had been robbed at 2:30, and the same walking beanpole, who resembled the professor even to the scar under his lips, had been seen directing the robbers just before they made their get-away."

"Well, my theory," contributed Fred Mayfield, "is that it was a case of split or dissociated personality. You've heard, haven't you, of men with a sort of Dr. Jekyll-Mr. Hyde division inside themselves, so that they act like two men, one of whom doesn't know what be other is doing. Thus, old Karr might have been chumming with gangsters part of the time, without his normal self having any notion of the crimes."

"Well, don't you ever think we overlooked that bet, boys. In fact, it was the only theory that looked halfway sound. If Karr really was a divided personality, maybe he did go out nights and get mixed up with thugs. On that supposition, I set two plainclothes men to guarding the house every night, hiding in the shrubbery so that no one could come or go without their knowing. But for the next three nights, nothing happened. It looked like the Rocco gang was laying low. Then, on the fourth night, it was the old story again. Hawley's Cash Market, down on Main Street, had been broken into, and several hundred dollars taken from the tray. Two guys who happened to be passing just before the crime took place, said they'd seen a tall, lean man with a huge head, tortoise-shell glasses and a scarred lip, prowling in front of the Market. But Officers Ryan and Benton, who'd been guarding Karr's house, swore a blue streak nobody could have possibly left.

"I gave special orders then for the boys to concentrate on that skinny daredevil. Whoever he was, Karr or his twin brother, we'd have to catch him damned quick. Well, can you believe it, it was just like he was playing with us all. He kept on being reported, and was almost caught time after time. Take what happened to Patrolman Pat Mulligan. 'Sure, an' the dirty loafer was hangin' roun' Jefferson Square at two in the mornin',' Pat reported. 'Well, muh boy, ye'll come with me,' he said, and reached out to handcuff the fellow. 'By the oly Mother, Chief,' he swore, 'ye'll think I'm dreamin', but when I stuck my hand out he just wasn't there no more. I say there's somethin' spooky about it, Chief. Sure looks like he's been a-flirtin' with the Evil One.'

"'Mulligan,' I answered, severely, 'looks like you've been flirting with the bottle. You'll have to steer clear of it when you're on duty, if you want to stay with the force.'

"Just the same, I knew Mulligan wasn't much of a boozer. I was all the more knocked off kilter since there'd been a big fur theft at Jefferson Square sometime between two and two thirty that morning. A few nights later I was still befuddled when Officer Kelley, along with Swensen and McGrath, reported they'd cornered

Professor Karr right at the entrance of the blind alley leading from East Fifth Street toward the Athens Grill. 'Take my word for it, Chief, I knew him, all right!' Kelley insisted. 'We came across him just under the street lamp, and there was that funny green light coming from his big goggle eyes—I'd have known him in a million.' The boys held back from shooting; had orders not to fire unless it was necessary, and this time it didn't seem necessary, as they ran him down that blind alley, with no way of escaping except over a ten-story brick wall. But when they got to the end of the alley, there wasn't a sign of him. Not one deuced sign! All three of them swore he couldn't have gotten out by any natural means. Later that night, the Athens Grill was robbed of nine hundred dollars."

"Were you still keeping guard around Karr's house?"

THE CHIEF nodded. He sat back in his chair, blew out several hearty mouthfuls of cigar smoke, and waited a moment, while the rest of us inched nearer.

"Of course, we kept guard, never skipping a night. But the boys said the professor never went out any evening—went to bed at 10:30, regular as the clock. They could see him snapping on his bedroom light; then winding his watch and the clock; then pulling the covers back on his bed, then drawing the blinds, and finally putting the light out—all done so damned methodically it didn't look like one night was a hair's breadth different from the next."

"Well, maybe that was only a ruse, to put you off the track," conjectured Joe Tracy. "Maybe he sneaked out later at night?"

"We didn't overlook that bet, either, even if it wasn't easy to see how he could get by the boys. One morning at about one o' clock, I called his number. When he answered, which he did only after a long time, he sounded drowsy as the devil, but I couldn't help recognizing that burring bass of his. 'Is this Elliott 2589?' I balked into the receiver, purposely giving the wrong number. 'No, damn you, it's 2598!' he growled back at me; and I was a little surprised to learn he could swear. 'What d'ye mean, waking a man this hour of the night?' As I heard the receiver slam back into place, I was more baffled than ever.

"But that wasn't anything to the way I was mystified half an hour later, when I got a call about a robbery in the Atlas Plating Mills. Professor Karr had been seen by two of the boys as they dashed down to the scene, but he'd gotten round the side of a building and escaped."

"Well, wasn't it possible," asked Fred Mayfield, "that he rushed down there just after your phone call?"

"No, that's the hell of it. It just wasn't possible. Don't suppose you know where the Atlas Plating Mills are—over toward Dumbarton, at the extreme other end of the city from Karr. A racing car might have made it in forty-five minutes. But the robbery, remember, occurred less than half an hour after I spoke to Karr on the phone."

"Well then, obviously," I concluded, "it must have been some mistake in identity."

"Mistake in identity—my eye!" Finch argued, impatiently. "Couldn't have made any mistake in identity, not with that gink, if you'd ever had a squint at him. Besides, what happened later showed it wasn't a mistake in identity."

"Well, what did happen later?"

"Plenty, believe me! The big climax didn't come, though, till I stuck my own finger into the pudding. Ordinarily, of course, I didn't go out with the boys on any of the cases. But I swore I'd lie in wait with them for the professor, by glory if I wouldn't! By this time, you see, I was getting desperate. The robberies of that blasted gang were coming so thick and fast there was getting to be a public furore, and my job hadn't the chance of a snowflake in hell if they kept up the game. So I thought I'd better crack the case wide-open myself."

"Did you?" I asked.

"I'm telling you, I did! But not at first. Things kept going downhill fast. It only made things worse one night when the boys nabbed two of the Rocco gang just as they were getting away with the swag over at the Northern Security Company. We put them through the third degree, like we never put anybody before. But they swore up and down they'd never seen old Karr or anybody like him. I knew very well they'd both have lied a mile a minute to save their own hides, but I couldn't see why they'd lie to save the professor, especially as we promised to let them off easy for squealing. What was more, they didn't look like guys that were lying. I don't think they could have play-acted the surprise they showed when we spoke of the professor."

"Well, what about your cracking the case open?"

"I'M coming to that." With a wry smile, Finch rubbed one hand across his ruddy face. "Lord! I sure didn't know what I was bucking one night when the boys brought me a tip-off of a safe cracking coming off down at Morehouse Appliance Company. I figured that the professor wasn't likely to keep away from anything like that, and I made my mind up I'd catch him, if it was within human power . Well, I guess I had self-confidence enough, even if I was due for a jolt. Anyhow, that night is one I won't ever forget. No, not if I live to be a hundred," the Chief finished, with something between a sigh and a groan, as he dabbed at an unseen perspiration on his shiny bald pate.

"So you met your friend Professor Karr again?"

"Wait, wait, not so fast there," he held me back. "We had everything beautifully staged to take on whoever came. There were six of us ranged all about that office, which was a large rambling one—we were all well hidden behind doors, desks and cabinets. I picked a prize place behind a row of large files, with just enough space between two of them to let me peek out without being seen. All of us boys was in place before midnight—and take my word it was a long, lonely wait there in the dark, none of us even daring to smoke or speak for fear of giving ourselves away."

"But did anybody come?" popped up Joe Tracy.

"Sure did. It was just 3:15 on the radium dial of my watch when we heard a faint creaking—and believe me, we tried not to breathe aloud. Maybe it was only the damned rats. But another creaking followed, and another and we knew the rear window was being jimmied. I tell you I did admire the way those boys worked—quick and expert-like, didn't waste any time or make any unnecessary noise. It didn't seem more than a minute before we heard them coming. Luckily, the last half hour the moon, which was pretty near full, had moved far enough to shine right in through the big window opposite me; and there was enough light to see ordinary things, though the odd color of the walls, which were painted a sort of sickly blue, gave the moonlight a spooky look. Maybe it sounds queer to say it, but I felt just like somebody waiting patiently in a tomb."

"Yes, but what about those robbers? Was it really the Rocco gang?"

"Well, part of the gang. Three husky louts, looking just about as sure of themselves as the plumbers coming to fix a faucet, made a beeline for the safe. Or, rather, two of them did, and the third kept a lookout. We didn't move a muscle till they were in place. It was our luck they didn't seem to have any hunch of anything wrong. Maybe success had made them careless. But all at once, when two of them were hunched over that safe, I gave the signal.

"Everything went off just the way we'd planned. Quicker'n you could draw a breath, those three bandits found themselves surrounded by the six of us, with our guns drawn. We didn't need to tell them to throw their hands up. They could see that the game was up, and anybody who made a move was a dead man."

"But Professor Karr? So Karr wasn't there?"

JUST give me a chance, and you'll find out," Finch reassured me, as he took time to light another cigar. "As I was saying, we'd covered all those three thugs. Everything happened so fast we didn't even have time to switch a light on. So here we had them cornered in that queer bluish moonlight, and two of the boys was about to slip on the handcuffs. But just at that moment I saw another figure. Swear to God I don't know where he came from; all the boys said afterwards they hadn't seen him come in. But there he was sure enough, motioning to the robbers as if trying to warn them; he was just across a wide desk from me, so near I couldn't help making out his features: his large bald head, his big eyes leering under their tortoise-shell glasses, his thin neck with the Adam's apple standing out from it.

"Well, I didn't waste any time letting my surprise bind and gag me. I leveled my pistol straight at the fellow. 'Hands up!'

"He didn't even seem to hear. In the most matter-of-fact way he started drifting—yes, drifting was how it looked to me—straight toward the hall door, about fifteen feet away.

"'Halt!' I yelled. 'Or I'll shoot!'

"You'd have thought he was plumb deaf. He didn't hurry like a man who was trying to get away; he just kept on toward the door, like somebody walking in his sleep. In another second, his hand was lifted to the knob; a second more, and he'd have been out of reach…

"I'll take my oath, boys, I don't know just how it happened. I'm mortally sure, though, I hadn't meant to fire—not at least, the way I did. But I guess my fingers were shaky and my excitement got the best of me—you can picture it all for yourselves, with the blue moonlight filling that office, three men covering the three crooks with guns, and two others just about to clap the handcuffs on, when this lanky devil pops up, God knows where from, and starts making his getaway as if he didn't give a damn for anybody. No wonder my gun went off.

"There was a bang that seemed louder than any pistol shot I ever heard before; a puff of smoke aimed right at the man's heart; and a terrible shuddering cry that I still remember in my nightmares, though to this day I can't be sure if it came from the struck man or heaven knows who else. Anyhow—and this was what pretty near bowled me over—when the smoke cleared away, old Karr wasn't anywhere in sight. What was more, we didn't find his slumped dead body. There wasn't even a trace of blood. The door was closed, showing he couldn't have gotten out; the bullet, stuck deep in the wood, was proof that the door couldn't have been open when the shot was fired."

The Chief paused, heaved a long sigh, and called for another drink.

"Maybe you only imagined you saw him," Mayfield dared to suggest.

"Imagined? Like hell!" denied Finch, giving his thigh a resounding slap with one plump hand. "All the other boys swore they saw him, too. Besides, I had another proof before the night was over—yes, one that sends the cold waves running down my spine every time I think of it. We'd hardly got back to headquarters, taking those three gangsters in tow, when I was told there was a phone call—something urgent. It was Officer Ryan, who'd been guarding the Karr home; his voice shook so you'd have thought he was scared of an invasion from Mars.

"'Chief—Chief, for Christ's sake, Chief, jump into your car and beat it up here like hell!'

"'What in the devil's name is it all about?' I bawled back.

"Like a man who's been taken with delirium tremens, he'd already put the receiver down, without seeming to hear me. So there wasn't anything for me to do but dash over to the Karr house, growling and cursing like a soused sailor, and swearing I'd demote Ryan if he'd called me on a wild-goose chase."

"But was it a wild-goose chase?"

"No, by God, it wasn't!"

Finch bit his thick lower lip, shook his head grimly, and slowly went on.

"When I got to the Karr house, the whole cursed place was blazing with lights. Ryan met me as I jumped out of the car, and his face looked white in the glare of the street lamp. I followed him up to the professor's bedroom, and even before I got there I heard a woman sobbing. As we rushed in, the first thing my eyes fell on was that Hindu, Rasmani, who looked at me a little like a cat that's about to spring. In a second, I'd taken in the rest of the scene: poor old Mrs. Karr, all hunched up in one corner, crying like she wouldn't ever stop; and a heavy-set mustached fellow that I recognized as Dr. Edmunds, as he used to be my married sister's family doctor. But what really glued my eyes to the spot was someone else that lay on the bed, as motionless as a rock. He wasn't wearing his tortoise-shell glasses now, and his glazed eyes were wide open, with a look of the most awful pain and terror—"

"God in heaven! Was he—was he—"

"WHEN I pushed my way in," Larry continued, ignoring my interruption, "the doctor turned from the thing on the bed. 'Glad you're here, Chief. I've done about all I can, but it looks like it's no use.'

"'What was it, Doctor? Heart failure?'

"'Well, you can call it that. We'll have to call it that in the report.' But it was plain as day he had some reservations in the back of his mind. 'Anyhow, I don't think you'll find any evidence of foul play.'

"Then, for the first time, the mother looked up. I was surprised at what blazing strength and fury she could show. 'Oh, but there must have been foul play! Emerson's heart was all right, I know it was! Why, you remember very well, Doctor, you examined it only last summer and said he ought to live to be a hundred!'

"'Yes, but sometimes hidden complications, Mrs. Karr—'

"'Oh, but the way he called out in the night! I'll never forget that scream—like a man being murdered! And then—then, when I got to his room, I found him—I found him—like you see him now—on the bed—'

"It was pitiful the way that poor woman struggled with her feelings, then broke down again and sobbed. Just the same, there were some questions I had to put to her. And so, as soon as she'd quieted down a bit, I asked her, as gently as I knew how, 'About what time, Ma'am, have you any idea, did this thing occur?''

"'Yes, I have a very good idea,' she answered, as soon as she could control herself. 'I slept wretchedly, and had just gone for some sleeping tablets in the bathroom cabinet. I happened to notice the time: exactly three-eighteen.'

"'Three-eighteen?' I threw back at her, knocked right off my base. 'But it couldn't be! Why, that was just when I saw him down at Morehouse's. That was just when I fired at him!'

"I was amazed at the way those remarks were taken up. No, not by Karr's mother—by Rasmani, who'd been standing darkly in a corner. 'Oh, so you fired at him?' he burst out, in a fierce, accusing way I'd never have stood from ally man if I hadn't been about shot to pieces. 'So you fired at him?'

"Well, what if I did? He was in the place, along with those safe-cracking thugs—'

"Rasmani muttered something I couldn't understand, probably an oath in his native jargon. But his next words were almost yelled at me. 'I see now! I see! From the moment I got that hysterical phone call from Mrs. Karr, I suspected something of the kind. So you fired at poor Emerson! Do you know what you've really done?'

"I can't begin to tell you how powerfully these words were hurled at me. There was a weird force about them, something that backed me into a corner, while Rasmani stood before me, pointing one finger at me like a condemning judge.

"'Maybe you don't know,' he went on, 'that Karr was studying Yogi, under my care?'

"'Yes, he mentioned that to me.'

"'Then mark this: he was still in the first stages. He'd only advanced far enough to release his astral part—his spirit, as you westerners would call it—while he lay asleep. This might travel wherever his desires would take it, and might actually be seen, since it was a real entity—'

"'But in that case,' I forced out, getting more and more confused, 'why in perdition was he getting mixed up with all kinds of bandits—'

"WITH a savage swift motion, Rasmani reached under the bed, and drew out a pile of brightly covered magazines: '*Banner Crime Stories,*' and the like. 'Because he'd been secretly feeding on stuff like this, as a relief from routine and monotony—gratifying his suppressed impulses for adventure, which had been starved all his life. Naturally, in these early Yogi stages, when the soul was let loose in sleep, it took the road of least resistance—the road of its day-dreams—in this case, connected with crime and detectives. The lower astral, we Orientals would call it. Just the same, he'd have risen in time—if it hadn't been for your shot.'

"'My shot?'

"'Yes, your shot. Don't you see now what you did? When you fired at him in your blundering ignorance, you sent a terrific shock to his astral part. This shock in turn was transmitted to the physical body, which lay at home in deep sleep. It is well known that any man, even the most healthy, can be killed by a severe enough nervous jolt. Well, this jolt was more than our friend could stand. He awoke to one moment of intense horror, which caused the scream Mrs. Karr heard—and that was all. Maybe you don't know it, Chief Finch, but you are a murderer. *You are a murderer!*'

"While the eyes of Rasmani and old Mrs. Karr followed me accusingly, I left the room. I told myself that that Hindu fakir was crazier'n a bat, but just the same in my heart I did feel like a murderer... And after some time had gone by and that goggle-eyed beanpole hadn't ever shown up again near a night crime but the Rocco gang had been broken up like a rotten squash, I knew

Rasmani had been right. Karr had done more than hang around when the Rocco boys did a job. Remembering how he'd been motioning to them just before I fired the shot, I knew he'd been their guide, their secret captain. Maybe some of them didn't see him or know anything about him, but I'm mortally sure some of them did follow him, not knowing he wasn't flesh and blood. He'd showed them where to find the loot; showed them how to get around our nets. And that's why, when I think things over, I'm glad I fired that shot. Because even if I did get old Karr, I ended the Rocco gang too. And put a stop to the worst crime wave this city ever had."

THE END

THE ARTIST AND THE DOOR

By Dorothy Quick

I bought the door—even though the auctioneer warned of evil.

THE advent of the artist and the door was almost simultaneous. I have always wondered if the one would have been as sinister without the other. Of course, the evil was in the door, but if the artist hadn't come along just then perhaps it might never have been released. I say that to comfort myself, but I know it isn't true. Evil is evil. It is a power and its strength is beyond mortal knowledge. Even without the artist there would have been horror. He only served to give it speedier expression.

But I am ahead of myself. The story goes back to my desire to have a carved door for my Elizabethan farmhouse.

I had rescued the cottage from demolition. It was just a frame when I first saw it, but the Tudor structure was there and two of the old tiny-paned glass windows had miraculously survived. The old beams were still in place and one linen fold panelled room, which I visioned for my study. There was a gap, like a missing tooth, where the front door had been.

I bought the house and restored it tenderly into the lovely place it now is. I did it with care and devotion, but my entrance door was modern and an anachronism. I hated it, but I told myself someday I would find an old one in keeping with the rest of Little Tudor—the name I had bestowed on my home.

I moved in, made friends with my neighbors, particularly the ten-year-old daughter of the people who owned the Manor house of which the farm had originally been a part. Anne was old for her years and bookishly inclined. When she heard I was an author, she read my historical novels and accorded me a kind of hero worship that was good for my lonely spinster's heart. She was always under foot and my brother, Weston, who lives with me and looks after my affairs, said, "She's good for you, Tansy. She keeps you from too much work and loneliness."

Weston was right. He had to be in London a good deal attending to my contracts, for my novels are done in the cinema and on the wireless, and there are quite a lot of details to look after for which I have no head. I wouldn't be half the moneymaker I am without Weston' s pushing. As it is, we do very well.

When he was away I welcomed Anne's society. We grew very close and her parents were delighted. They were busy enough, Sir Richard with his bird raising and Lady Salter with her young. She had five children younger than Anne. So all in all, Anne was with me a good deal of the time.

I was alone, however, the day I found the door. It had been a day I intended to devote entirely to work, so I'd told Anne not to come over. The morning's writing had gone very well, but after lunch I struck a snag. Katherine Howard, my current heroine, proved difficult, the facts about her too obscure to fit into my plot. "You need air" I told myself sternly, and went out to the barn for my car.

As I drove the Bentley past the road leading to the Manor I slowed up, but Anne wasn't in sight, so I rode on, thoroughly enjoying the Kentish countryside. It was in springtime blossom and the apple trees in full flower provided such breath-taking beauty I could hardly keep my eyes from them long enough to do justice to my driving.

As a matter of fact, it was fortunate there was no traffic on the back roads I had chosen or anything might have happened. I gave myself up to the season and wove in and out and around every orchard I could find. All at once I noticed a group of cars and carriages, even a riding horse or two, standing by an old stone fence. I stretched my neck and saw at the end of a long lane a dark, forbidding stone house with a sign hanging from one of the windows announcing "Sale Today." There were people going in and I realized it was an auction.

I added my Bentley to the cluster of cars and walked up the lane. Auctions have always fascinated me, and a country one is usually something special. When I saw the door I knew why I was here. I had been led. There it was, just what I needed for Little

Tudor, The Farm, Aldringham, Kent. It was of oak polished by centuries of wind and rain, carved by the hand of man in Tudor times—just what I wanted.

I went inside, sharp-eyed for London buyers who might prevent my getting it. Antiques and period pieces are hard to come by now-a-days. But so far as I could see, the people were local. There was no one well dressed enough for London. It was a country crowd.

I looked around. The large room, drawing room I supposed, was quite crowded with people and the strangest assortment of furniture I'd ever seen—of all kinds and periods from a Gothic bench through a wonderful Queen Anne chest to some pieces that must have come from Grand Rapids, U. S. A.

There was a table, complete with a pitcher of water, a glass and a gavel for the auctioneer. Presently a red-faced, jolly-looking man took his place behind it, picked up the hammer and was just about to begin when a voice rang out, "Tell the truth before you sell, man. Don't let them buy the Devil's wares unknowing."

The speaker was a wizened old woman who looked like a witch. Her were beadily bright and she with authority.

The auctioneer held up his hand. He was obviously annoyed. "If you'd given me time I was going to tell my audience," he began with a lie, for I'm sure he'd had no intention of anything but the usual patter, "that this house has had the reputation of being haunted. That's why it's to be torn down, but everyone in these parts knows that. The last owner—an artist—was supposed to have sold his soul to the devil so he could live here. He was the last of the line and the pictures he painted were passing strange."

His audience was breathless now, and a little shivery, so he warmed up to his work by adding melodramatically, "These pictures have all been burnt, and the house has been exorcised with bell, book and candle by a priest. That includes the furnishings, ladies and gents, so you can buy with a free hand. Now take this chest, genuine Queen Anne—" he began extolling the beauties of the chest I had singled out.

FROM then on everything went quickly, to "ohs" and "ahs" from the "Ladies and Gents." Bidding was brisk and the auctioneer worked even faster than most of his kind. It was as though everyone was anxious to get away before sundown.

I didn't blame them. The place had an uncanny atmosphere despite the exorcising, or maybe that had only been in the auctioneer's mind. A good many things had been sold that morning, so there wasn't so much to fall under the gavel. I edged nearer the witch-like old woman. Towards the end she grinned at me. "You're wise, dearie, not to buy. The Masserys never had no luck—not since William the Conqueror's time they didn't, and their things shared their evil with them. Hain't you noticed things do? Reflect their owners, I mean."

I told her I hadn't, but now that she spoke of it I thought she was right. I admitted I wanted to buy the door.

She looked at me and shook her head. "It's been there a long time. It had best go with the house, miss. The door now. It's evil too. Maybe it was open and the priest's words were lost on it. Let be, girl, let be."

But I bought it just the same, for three pounds. No one else wanted it, and the auctioneer was anxious to be off. As his men tied it on the roof of my car I saw the old woman shaking her head in the background, but I had no premonitions. I was overjoyed to have found just what I had always craved for Little Tudor. I had been careful to get the old hinges along with the door, and once it was in place my home would be complete. I was so happy I hummed a little tune all the way home. Even the apple trees had lost their charm.

When I drove up in front of my barn I found Anne, Weston and Old Tim, the gardener, wondering where I'd gone. They were glad to welcome me back and delighted to see my find. "It's perfect," Weston announced.

"Just like you to get the very thing, miss," contributed the gardener.

Only Anne was silent. "Don't you like it?" I asked, not wanting there to be one fly in the ointment, or one word of dissent. I had already forgotten the old woman.

Anne looked at the door, which Weston and old Tim were holding. "It's beautiful," she said reluctantly, "beautiful, but there seems something evil about it." She shuddered involuntarily.

I remembered the old woman then. I thought it strange that Anne, child as she was and miles away, should echo her words. But I spoke sharply. "It's old, all old things have seen evil, much of evil. Sometimes they can reflect what they've seen to sensitive minds."

She accepted my explanation with gravity, but she had the last word. "Yes, only—only it's as though this evil were alive."

Long before the twilight, which is so lasting in England had ended, Weston and old Tim had the door in place.

"Evil or not, it looks magnificent," Weston said.

"Does it seem evil to you?" I asked.

"No." Weston was matter of fact. "What you said to Anne is true, though. It doesn't seem just like any door."

"It isn't. It's Tudor." We laughed at the pun. Then I told Weston about the old woman. He was quiet for a little, then he shrugged. "Maybe—but it's a fine old piece and just what we wanted. Let's forget the rest." That was how we left it.

The next morning Weston went up to London in his own car— an ancient Daimler, which true to tradition, still ran like a song. I decided I'd walk to market. Aldringham wasn't far; the exercise would do me good. Anne, who had come over for breakfast, went with me. When we reached the gate we found the artist. He was lying spread-eagled on the road with a nasty bruise on his forehead. We knew he was an artist as his easel lay beside him and a box of paints with half its contents spilled was there, too. He was quite unconscious, evidently the victim of a hit and run driver.

I sent Anne to ring up the doctor and when she'd done that to return with old Tim. I felt the artist's pulse. In view of the tools of his trade there was no doubt of his profession. The beat under my fingers was faint but steady. I knew enough about fractures and concussions not to disturb him, so I began picking up the tubes of paint and putting them in his box. I was just aware of the doctor's car in the distance when I found him awake and regarding me.

"So you're better," I said.

He smiled ruefully. "I guess so. Is anything broken?"

"You should know." I told him and watched him flexing his arms and legs. Apparently there was nothing wrong with him. He grinned as the doctor came over. After a hasty examination the doctor said he was suffering from shock. He should be quiet for a day or so. The M.D. looked at me so I invited him to stay at Little Tudor. After all, he'd practically been injured on my ground. I really had no choice.

The doctor and old Tim helped him in. I put him in the guestroom. He slept most of the day. The doctor had seen to that—but by night he was up and insisting on being no trouble. He finally came to dinner in a robe of Weston's.

HE LOOKED very young and handsome with blond, waving hair and deep blue eyes the color of turquoise. There was something open and ingenuous about him that made him most appealing. He was a charming talker too. Actually he was an artist only on the side. He had a regular job on a newspaper. Painting was his hobby and he was on a two weeks' vacation walking tour indulging it. He had only a few days left before he had to be back at Fleet Street. He showed me his sketchbook. The things in it were good. He certainly knew how to draw and paint. Maybe some day he could illustrate a book of mine, I suggested.

He'd like that, he told me. By now Mrs. Tim had cleared the table and I was sitting by the fire. The artist, his name was Sandy Gordon, was moving up and down the big room. But he'd like to do something now to pay his way. How about painting that door? It looked so plain in the room.

I explained it was Tudor and all the carving was on the outside. Inside there was only the outline of four squares, and the wood wasn't as well polished, but I told him it would be out of character to paint it.

"No, it wouldn't." He'd been to some castle on his trip, pure Tudor, which had painted doors. It was even rumored Holbein had painted them. He'd do a good job. Please let him. Otherwise he could hardly accept my hospitality.

What could I do but weaken? When I came down next morning he was at work, Mrs. Tim hovering near enthusiastically. Later in the day Anne joined Mrs. Tim. "It's a lovely color, isn't it?" she asked, but she looked worried. When I asked her why, she mumbled something about "still evil."

Sandy didn't finish the back of the door until just before it was time for me to take him to the train. Then he called me. "Do you like it?" He pointed to the door and stood back.

It was exquisite, a path outlined with a serpentine hedge of box leading off into a riot of roses. There were roses all along the side, across the top, bower-like. Mammoth roses, incredibly full blown. The colors were gorgeous. One could almost smell them.

"It's wonderful," I told him with enthusiasm, and it was. Then, because he was obviously waiting for more, I added, "It makes one want to find out where the path goes."

He turned away. "I shouldn't try to discover if I were you. It's a funny thing," he went on with a rush as though the words were forced out of him. "It isn't what I meant to do at all. I'd planned a Persian sort of thing, a princess in a flowery field with a prince on horseback. But when I started to paint it was as though another hand seized mine and this is the result. Those exotic colors aren't me at all. I usually deal in muted shades. These are stronger than I ordinarily use, and I never saw a rose like any of these. Oh, well, I suppose it's genius. Anyway, it's more vivid than anything I've ever done. Actually I'm quite proud of it."

"I shall be too." I told him. Then we rushed for the train. As it pulled out he leaned from the window and called, "Don't walk down that path." Then the train took him off to London.

WHEN I got back to Little Tudor, Anne was sitting, watching the door. I thought she was looking out for me, but such it developed was not the case. She was looking at Sandy's mural.

"Isn't it funny how those lovely roses take all the evil away, Aunt Tansy!" She called me that. "I've never seen such pretty flowers and that path—where do you suppose it goes? I'd like to find out."

"You mustn't," I broke in sharply, remembering what Sandy had said.

She raised her brown eyes to my slate gray ones and laughed childishly, "As though I could! But I'm sure it's somewhere lovely—like the flowers. Perhaps Sandy knows."

"When he comes back to visit we'll ask him." I looked at the door myself and once again it seemed as though I could smell the roses and that they moved as if swept by some slight breeze.

Anne slipped her hand in mine. "The roses dance. I'm sure at the end of the path there's a carnival—a carnival of roses."

I wondered where she'd heard the word carnival. It was an odd word for a child to know. Perhaps she'd picked it up from Sandy. "Such a lovely scent." She half whispered. "There were never such roses in this world." She wasn't really aware of what she was saying. It was curious that she seemed to have taken the words right out of my mind.

"Come on." I cried, sweeping her up. "Let's go for a walk." Instinctively we went out the side door leading onto the terrace. It was only then that I realized since I had brought home the new door no one, not even Weston, had used it.

THE next morning I was doing much better with Katherine Howard when suddenly Anne rushed into the room. "Surprise, surprise," she cried and dropped a yellow rose on my manuscript. It was the most perfect flower I have ever seen, much larger than most. It looked like a sequined star and the dew on it glistened like diamonds.

"Why, Anne, wherever did you get this? It looks like one of Sandy's roses."

She giggled. "It is! I found it lying in front of the door. Do you suppose it dropped off?"

"Don't be silly, Anne. You know that's impossible." I was sharp again, hating myself and the hurt look in her eyes. "Did you pick it in your mother's garden?"

"No rose is blooming yet." She told me gravely. "Not even in the conservatory. Besides, I've never seen a rose like this, not even at the Flower Show in London."

I knew she'd been taken for a treat last year, and I knew she was right. I had never seen such a rose either.

"Perhaps it comes from the end of the path," she suggested.

"Anne, you mustn't say such ridiculous things, or even think them. Probably Sandy sent the rose down from London. It's most likely a new kind he knew and that's why he drew them on the door. He told old Tim to put it there for me to find." I made my tones convincing, although I was remembering what Sandy had said about his painting. It wasn't like him and I never saw a rose like any of these. Maybe he had found one and sent it as I'd told Anne.

Anne didn't argue. She only looked hurt. "Don't you want it?" she asked, her lip quivering.

"Of course, dear. Let's put it in one of the best vases. I'll keep it here on my desk. It will inspire me." We made quite a thing of putting it in water and a ceremony of placing it on my desk.

It didn't inspire me. It worried me, for it lasted as no flower has any right to last. After a week it was as fresh as the day Anne brought it. Its yellow unfaded, dew still nestling at its heart. Anne worried me, too. She was always sitting, looking at the door. When I asked her why she said she saw so much in the picture. "Some day I'll know what's at the end of the path. I have to." She was serious and I was frightened. I tried to discourage her visits, but it was no use. She was always there and now she was no longer interested in being with me. It was only the door that fascinated her. I was beginning to wish I'd never found it. I wished Weston would come home, but he was detained in London with a big cinema contract for my last book. "Even with the tax you're going to have some money to spend." he told me on the telephone.

I was too worried, and too afraid to care. Anne was changing before my vision, growing thin and pale. Her eyes, great pools of mystery, and her hands when they touched mine were like claws. I tried to talk to her mother, but she wouldn't take it seriously, "just growing," was her comment on her child, "and working her imagination overtime. If it wasn't your door it would be something else. Don't worry."

But I couldn't help it. There came a rainy day and between the wind and storm I knew Anne wouldn't get over to Little Tudor. I made up my mind I'd watch the door myself, to see if I could discover what she saw. I suggested to Mrs. Tim that she take a nap, and when I knew she was settled I went into the long room. There, in front of the door, lay another rose. A red one this time, as beautiful and as unreal as the yellow one Anne had brought me. I knew now Sandy hadn't sent it. I'd written and asked him and he'd denied it heartily. "Couldn't be a real rose like those products of my imagination—" he'd put on paper.

I took the red rose and put it in the vase with the yellow one, which was so strangely unwithered. I left it, glad to be free of the over-powering scent, but when I returned to the long room the perfume was still there, heavy as pure attar of roses, permeating the entire room. I sat in the deep chair facing the door where Anne always sat, with the sweet, cloying odor of the rose in my nostrils growing stronger every second. I watched the door. Once again the roses seemed to sway as though moved by some, to me, unfelt breeze. They seemed to be leaning towards me, beckoning me to come to the path, and the patch stretched endlessly and invitingly before me. What a picture it was. Genius, Sandy had said, it was more. It was a masterpiece, living as some pictures do.

I grew more and more enthralled. Now I could understand Anne's feelings. No wonder she liked to sit here with such sheer beauty before her, with endless, inviting vistas opening to her eyes. Carnival of roses—roses in riotous confusion, the epitome of beauty urging me to be a part of it.

The heady aroma of the roses' perfume must be affecting my brain. But I was like one compelled. I had to touch the flowers, to feel their velvety petals, to be a part of them. I was out of the chair without my knowledge, moving towards the door. The scent was stronger now, more alluring, and the path more inviting. I knew if I opened the door I could step onto the path and I knew, too, that I desired that more than anything in the world. I put my hand on the door handle. I turned it, opened the door. There was sunshine and roses outside, a riot of roses, red, pink, yellow and white rustling roses, moving towards me, touching my hands with velvet, my cheeks with dew, while the path sparkled like diamonds, and a bright, unnatural sunshine flooded everything like a spotlight.

I was dizzy with the redolence of the flowers. I took a step forward. I was on the threshold. Now, in another minute, I would be on the path. I would know such beauty as was not in the world.

Crashing through the sunlight and the roses came Sandy's voice, "Don't walk that path," and then suddenly the cloying scent was gone and instead I smelt that foul odor of decay that is part of yellow roses just before they begin to wilt.

Shocked, I drew back, though there were hands, strong, masculine hands, trying to pull me forward through the door. I exerted my will and stepped back again into my long room. The path, the sun and the roses were gone. There was only wind and rain outside as the door slammed shut. I fell back into the chair and covered my face with my hands.

The door *was* evil. I knew now Anne was right. The old woman had known. She had been right too. Tomorrow I would have it removed. I could run no risks with Anne.

I remembered now what Sandy had said about it was as though someone else had seized his hands, and it wasn't his kind of painting. It was that of the last owner of the house. He had been an artist, the auctioneer had said so, who had sold his soul to the devil so he could stay in the house, and that his pictures had been burned. The roses were his pictures, not Sandy's—his. They would have to be destroyed, know the cleansing of fire. They were utterly evil, like the door, which, as the old woman had said, probably had been open and escaped the exorcising by the priest, so the evil spirit of the artist could cling to it and come to Little Tudor, bringing his evil with him. This was all strange and shattering to me, but I did not question it. I somehow knew it was so, knew too that I must cleanse the evil with fire, tomorrow. I could do nothing while the storm raged. Now I was shaken and unnerved. Work would be my best medicine. I went back to my study. I ignored the roses on my desk. I couldn't bear to touch them. I started to write. My pencil took no note of time, but suddenly I was aware of movement on my desk. I looked up. The sun was shining in my windows. I had been too absorbed in Katherine Howard's love scene with the king to notice the storm was over, but that wasn't what had disturbed me. It was the roses. They were swaying and moving as though dancing with joy.

"Anne!" I cried, clasping my throat. The rain was over. She could have come to Little Tudor. I rushed into the long room. She was there, her hand on the door knob, just as mine had been a short time ago. "Anne," I called. "Anne, come back." There was all the fright and horror I felt in my voice.

It didn't stop her. She only called out over her shoulder "I can't stop, Tansy. I've got to find out where the path goes."

I rushed forward toward Anne and the moving roses but I was too far away. She swung the door open. I saw again the carnival of roses, the path, the sunshine so different from that visaged from my study window.

"Anne, Anne, no, no." I was screaming, but it was no use. She was over the threshold; when I reached the door it was shut, the painted roses on it rustled mockingly.

I opened the door. There was no sign or Anne, no path, no roses, no unnatural sunshine.

Anne was never seen again. She had found the path and vanished completely. Her disappearance made a nine days wonder in the neighborhood. I said I had last seen her go through the door. There was no use telling the rest. No one but I ever knew the truth—or what I thought was the truth.

The next day we burned the door. Old Tim and I. We chopped it up first, in small pieces, and what a bonfire it made!

As it burned wildly I heard, or thought I heard, two voices. One was a man's screaming with frustration, the other was Anne's. "Thank you, Tansy," was what she said. I like to think the fire freed her soul from Evil.

When the door was completely ashes and I got back to my study I looked for the roses. They were gone. Only around the vase were little seared petals that resembled the ashes of the door.

THE END

A DRINK OF DARKNESS

By Robert F. Young

All peoples have their myths of wanderers through time…who, though they may not end their own sufferings, have the power to help others save themselves… Such a one was the gaunt man.

YOU'RE walking down Fool's Street, Laura used to say when he was drinking, and she had been right. He had known even then that she was right, but knowing had made no difference; he had simply laughed at her fears and gone on walking down it, till finally he stumbled and fell. Then, for a long time he stayed away, and if he had stayed away long enough he would have been all right; but one night he began walking down it again—and met the girl. It was inevitable that on Fool's Street there should be women as well as wine.

He had walked down it many times since in many different towns, and now he was walking down it once again in yet another town. Fool's Street never changed no matter where you went, and this one was no different from the others. The same skeletonic signs bled beer names in naked windows, the same winos sat in doorways nursing muscatel; the same drunk tank awaited you when at last your reeling footsteps failed. And if the sky was darker than usual, it was only because of the rain, which had begun falling early that morning and which had been falling steadily ever since.

Chris went into another bar, laid down his last quarter and ordered wine. At first he did not see the man who came in a moment later and stood beside him. There was a raging rawness in him such as even he had never known before, and the wine he had thus far drunk had merely served to aggravate it. Eagerly he drained the glass, which the bartender filled and set before him. Reluctantly he turned to leave. He saw the man then.

THE man was gaunt—so gaunt that he seemed taller than he actually was. His thin-featured face was pale, and his dark eyes seemed beset by unimaginable pain. His hair was brown and badly in need of cutting. There was a strange statuesqueness about him—an odd sense of immobility. Raindrops iridesced like tiny jewels on his gray trench coat, dripped sporadically from his black hat. "Good evening," he said. "May I offer you a drink?"

For an agonizing moment Chris saw himself through the other's eyes—saw his thin sensitive face with its intricate networks of ruptured capillaries; his gray rain-plastered hair; his ragged rain-soaked overcoat; his cracked rain-sodden shoes—and the image was so vivid that it shocked him into speechlessness. But only briefly; then the rawness intervened. "Sure I'll have a drink," he said, and tapped his glass upon the bar.

"Not here," the gaunt man said. "Come with me."

Chris followed him out into the rain, the rawness rampant now. He staggered, and the gaunt man took his arm. "It's only a little ways," the gaunt man said. "Into this alley here...now down this flight of stairs."

It was a long gray room, damp, and dimly lit. A gray-faced bartender stood statuesquely behind a deserted bar. When they entered he set two glasses on the bar and filled them from a dusty bottle. "How much?" the gaunt man asked.

"Thirty," the bartender answered.

The gaunt man counted out the money. "I shouldn't have asked," he said. "It's always thirty—no matter where I go. Thirty this, or thirty that; thirty days or thirty months or thirty thousand years." He raised his glass and touched it to his lips.

Chris followed suit, the rawness in him screaming. The glass was so cold that it numbed his fingertips, and its contents had a strange Cimmerian cast. But the truth didn't strike him till he tilted the glass and drained the darkness; then the quatrain came down from the attic of his mind where he had stored it years ago, and he knew suddenly who the gaunt man was—

So when at last the Angel of the Drink Of Darkness
finds you by the river-brink,
And, proffering his Cup, invites your Soul
Forth to your Lips to quaff it—do not shrink.

But by then the icy waves were washing through him, and soon the darkness was complete.

Dead! The word was a hoarse and hideous echo caroming down the twisted corridor of his mind. He heard it again and again and again—*dead...dead...dead*—till finally he realized that the source, of it was himself and that his eyes were tightly closed. Opening them, he saw a vast starlit plain and a distant shining mountain. He closed them again, more tightly than before.

"Open your eyes," the gaunt man said. "We've a long ways to go."

Reluctantly Chris obeyed. The gaunt man was standing a few feet away, staring hungrily at the shining mountain. "Where are we?" Chris asked. "In God's name, where are we?"

The gaunt man ignored the question. "Follow me," he said, and set off toward the mountain.

Numbly Chris followed. He sensed coldness all around him but he could not feel it, nor could he see his breath. A shudder racked him. Of course he couldn't see his breath—he had no breath to see. Any more than the gaunt man did.

The plain shimmered, became a playground, then a lake, then a foxhole, finally a summer street. Wonderingly he identified each place. The playground was the one where he had played as a boy. The lake was the one he had fished in as a young man. The foxhole was the one he had bled and nearly died in. The summer street was the one he had driven down on his way to his first post-war job. He returned to each place; played, fished, swam, bled, drove. In each case it was like living each moment all over again.

Was it possible, in death, to control time and relive the past?

He would try. The past was definitely preferable to the present. But to which moment did he wish to return? Why, to the most precious one of all, of course—to the one in which he had met Laura. Laura, he thought, fighting his way back through the hours, the months, the years. "Laura!" he cried out in the cold and starlit reaches of the night—

And the plain became a sun-filled street—

HE and Minelli had come off guard duty that noon and had gone into the Falls on a twelve-hour pass. It was a golden October day early in the war, and they had just completed their basic training. Recently each of them had made corporal, and they wore their chevrons in their eyes as well as on their sleeves.

The two girls were sitting at a booth in a crowded bar, sipping ginger ale. Minelli had made the advances, concentrating on the tall dark-haired one. Chris had lingered in the background. He sort of liked the dark-haired girl, but the round-faced blonde who was with her simply wasn't his cup of tea, and he kept wishing Minelli would give up and come back to the bar and finish his beer so they could leave.

Minelli did nothing of the sort. He went right on talking to the tall girl, and presently he managed to edge his stocky body into the seat beside her. There was nothing for it then, and when Minelli beckoned to him Chris went over and joined them. The round-faced girl's name was Patricia and the tall one's name was Laura.

They went for a walk, the four of them. They watched the American Falls for a while and afterward they visited Goat Island. Laura was several inches taller than Minelli, and her thinness made her seem even taller. They made a rather incongruous couple. Minelli didn't seem to mind, but Laura seemed ill at ease and kept glancing over her shoulder at Chris.

Finally she and Pat had insisted that it was time for them to go home—they were staying at a modest boarding-house just off the main drag, taking in the Falls over the weekend—and Chris had thought, *Good, now at last we'll be rid of them.* Guard duty always wore him out—he had never been able to adapt himself to the two hours on—two hours off routine—and he was tired. But Minelli went right on talking after they reached the boarding house, and presently the two girls agreed to go out to supper. Minelli and Chris waited on the porch while they went in and freshened up. When they came out Laura stepped quickly over to Chris's side and took his arm.

He was startled for a moment, but he recovered swiftly, and soon he and Laura were walking hand in hand down the street. Minelli and Pat fell in behind them. "It's all right, isn't it?" Laura whispered in his ear. "I'd much rather go with you."

"Sure," he said, "it's fine."

And it was, too. He wasn't tired any more and there was a pleasant warmth washing through him. Glancing sideways at her profile, he saw that her face wasn't quite as thin as he had at first thought, and that her nose was tilted just enough to give her features a piquant cast.

Supper over, the four of them revisited the American Falls. Twilight deepened into darkness and the stars came out. Chris and Laura found a secluded bench and sat in the darkness, shoulders touching, listening to the steady thunder of the cataract. The air was chill, and permeated with ice-cold particles of spray. He put his arm around her, wondering if she was as cold as he was; apparently she was, for she snuggled up close to him. He turned and kissed her then, softly, gently, on the lips; it wasn't much of a kiss, but he knew somehow that he would never forget it. He kissed her once more when they said good night on the boarding house porch. She gave him her address. "Yes," he whispered, "I'll write." "And I'll write too," she whispered back in the cool damp darkness of the night. "I'll write you every day…"

EVERY day, said the plain. *Every day,* pulsed the stars. *I'll write you every day…*

And she had, too, he remembered, plodding grimly in the gaunt man's wake. His letters from her were legion, and so were her letters from him. They had gotten married a week before he went overseas, and she had waited through the unreal years for him to come back, and all the while they had written, written written; *Dearest Chris* and *Dearest Laura,* and words, words, words. Getting off the bus in the little town where she lived, he had cried when he had seen her standing in the station doorway, and she had cried too; and the years of want and of waiting had woven themselves into a golden moment—and now the moment was shreds.

Shreds, said the plain. *Shreds,* pulsed the stars. *The golden moment is shreds…*

The past is a street lined with hours, he thought, *and I am walking down the street and I can open the door of any hour I choose and go inside. It is a dead man's privilege, or perhaps a dead man's curse—for what good are hours now?*

The next door he opened led into Ernie's place, and he went inside and drank a beer he had ordered fourteen years ago. "How's Laura?" Ernie asked. "Fine," he said. "And Little Chris?" "Oh, he's fine too. He'll be a whole year old next month."

He opened another door and went over to where Laura was standing before the kitchen stove and kissed her on the back of the neck. "Watch out!" she cried in mock distress. "You almost made me spill the gravy."

He opened another door—Ernie's place again. He closed it quickly. He opened another and found himself in a bar full of squealing people. Streamers drifted down around him, streamers and multicolored balloons. He burst a balloon with his cigarette and waved his glass. "Happy New Year!" he shouted. "Happy New Year!" Laura was sitting at a corner table, a distressed look on her face. He went over and seized her arm and pulled her to her feet. "It's all right, don't you see?" he said. "It's New Year's Eve. If a man can't let himself go on New Year's Eve, when can he let himself go?"

"But darling, you said—"

"I said I'd quit—and I will, too—starting tomorrow." He weaved around in a fantastic little circle that somehow brought him back to her side. "Happy New Year, baby—Happy New Year!"

"Happy New Year, darling," she said, and kissed him on the cheek. He saw then that she was crying.

He ran from the room and out into the Cimmerian night. *Happy New Year,* the plain said. *Happy New Year,* pulsed the stars. *Should auld acquaintance be forgot, and never brought to mind...* The gaunt man still strode relentlessly ahead, and now the shining mountain occulted half the sky. Desperately Chris threw open another door—

HE was sitting in an office. Across the desk from him sat a gray-haired man in a white coat. "Look at it this way," the gray-haired man was saying. "You've just recovered from a long bout with a disease to which you are extremely susceptible, and because you are extremely susceptible to it, you must sedulously avoid any and all contact with the virus that causes it. You have a low alcoholic threshold, Chris, and consequently you are even more at the mercy of that 'first drink' than the average periodic drinker.

Moreover, your alternate personality—your 'alcoholic alter ego'—is virtually the diametric opposite of your real self, and hence all the more incompatible with reality. It has already behaved in ways your real self would not dream of behaving, and at this point it is capable of behavior-patterns so contrary to your normal behavior-patterns that it could disrupt your whole life. Therefore, I beg you, Chris, not to unleash it. And now, good bye and good luck. I am happy that our institution could be of such great help to you."

He knew the hour that lay behind the next door, and it was an hour in which he did not care to relive. But the door opened of its own accord, and despite himself he stepped across the dark threshold of the years...

He and Laura were carrying Friday-night groceries from the car into the house. It was summer, and stars glistened gently in the velvet-soft sky. He was tired, as was to be expected at the end of the week, but he was taut too—unbearably taut from three months of teetotalism. And Friday nights were the worst of all; he had always spent his Friday nights at Ernie's, and while part of his mind remembered how poignantly he had regretted them the next day, the rest of his mind insisted on dwelling on the euphoria they had briefly brought him—even though it knew as well as the other part did that the euphoria had been little more than a profound and gross feeling of animal relaxation.

The bag of potatoes he was carrying burst open, and potatoes bounced and rolled all over the patio. *"Damn,"* he said, and knelt down and began picking them up. One of them slipped from his fingers and rolled perversely off the patio and down the walk, and he followed it angrily, peevishly determined that it should not get away. It glanced off one of the wheels of Little Chris's tricycle and rolled under the back porch. When he reached in after it his finger's touched a cold curved smoothness, and with a start he remembered the bottle of whiskey he had hidden the previous spring after coming home from a Saturday-night drunk—hidden and forgotten about till now.

Slowly he withdrew it. Starlight caught it, and it gleamed softly in the darkness. He knelt there, staring at it, the chill dampness of the ground creeping up into his knees. *What harm can one drink do?* his tautness asked. *One drink stolen in the darkness, and then no more?*

No, he answered. Never. *Yes,* the tautness screamed. *Just one. A sip. A swallow. Hurry! If it wasn't meant to be the bag would not have burst.* His fingers wrenched off the cap of their own volition then, and he raised the bottle to his lips...

When he returned to the patio Laura was standing in the doorway, her tall slenderness silhouetted softly against the living-room light. He knelt down and resumed picking up the potatoes, and perceiving what had happened, she came out, laughing, and helped him. Afterward she went down the street to her sister's to pick up Little Chris. By the time she got back, the bottle was half empty and the tautness was no more.

HE waited till she took Little Chris upstairs to put him to bed, then he got in the car and drove downtown. He went to Ernie's. "Hi, Chris," Ernie said, surprised. "What'll it be?"

"Shot and a beer," he said. He noticed the girl at the end of the bar then. She was a tall blonde with eyes like blue mountain lakes. She returned his gaze coolly, calculatingly. The whiskey he had already drunk had made him tall; the boilermaker made him even taller. He walked down to the end of the bar and slipped onto the stool beside her. "Have a drink with me?" he asked.

"Sure," she said. "Why not?"

He had one too, soaring now after the earthbound months on ginger ale, all the accumulated drives finding vent as his inhibitions dropped away and his drunken alter ego stepped upon the stage. Tomorrow he would hate what he was tonight, but tonight he loved what he was. Tonight he was a god, *leaping upon the mountains, skipping upon the hills.* He took the blonde to her apartment and stayed the night, and went home in the small hours, reeking of cheap perfume. When he saw Laura's face the next morning he wanted to kill himself, and if it hadn't been for the half-full bottle under the porch, he would have. But the bottle saved him, and he was off again.

It was quite a spree. To finance it, he sold his car, and weeks later, he and the blonde wound up in a cheap rooming house in Kalamazoo. She stayed around long enough to help him drink up his last dollar, and then took off. He never went back to Laura. Before, when he had walked down Fool's Street, it had been the booze and the booze alone, and afterward he had been able to face her. But he could not face her now—not Laura of the tender smile, the gentle eyes. Hurting her was one thing; destroying her, quite another.

No, he had not gone back; he had accepted Fool's Street as his destiny, and gone on walking down it through the years, and the years had not been kind. The past was not preferable to the present after all.

THE shining mountain loomed death-tall against the star-flecked sky. He could face it now, whatever it was meant to be; but there was still one more door to open, one final bitter swallow remaining in the cup. Grimly he stepped back across the bottomless abyss of time to the little tavern on School Street and finished the glass of muscatel he had bought six years ago. Then he walked over to the window and stood looking out into the street.

He stood there for some time, watching the kids go by on their way home from school, and after a while the boy with Laura's eyes came into view. His throat constricted then, and the street swam slightly out of focus; but he went on watching, and presently the boy was abreast of the window, chatting gaily with his companions and swinging his books; now past the window and disappearing from view. For a moment he almost ran outside and shouted, *Chris, remember me?*—and then, by the grace of God, his eyes dropped to his cracked shoes and his mind remembered his seedy suit and the wine-sour smell of his breath, and he shrank back into the shadows of the room.

On the plain again, he shouted, "Why didn't you come sooner, Mr. Death? Why didn't you come six years ago? That was when I really died."

The gaunt man had halted at the base of the shining mountain and was staring up at the snow-white slopes. His very aspect expressed yearning, and when he turned, the yearning lingered in his eyes. "I am not death," he said.

"Who are you then?" Chris asked. "And where are we going?"

"*We* are not going anywhere. From this point you must proceed alone. I cannot climb the mountain; it's forbidden me."

"But why must *I* climb the mountain?"

"You do not have to—but you will. You will climb it because it is death. The plain you have just crossed and upon which you still stand represents the transition from life to death. You repeatedly returned to moments in your past because the present, except in a symbolic sense, no longer exists for you. If you do not climb it, you will keep returning to those moments."

"What will I find on the mountain?"

"I do not know. But this much I do know: Whatever you find there will be more merciful than what you have found—or will ever find—on the plain."

"Who are you?"

The gaunt man looked out over the plain. His shoulders sagged, as though a great weight lay upon them. "There is no word for what I am," he said presently. "Call me a wanderer, if you like—a wanderer condemned to walk the plain forever; a wanderer periodically compelled to return to life and seek out someone on the verge of death and die with him in the nearest halfway house and share his past with him and add his sufferings to my own. A wanderer of many languages and much lore, gleaned through the centuries; a wanderer who, by the very nature of my domain, can move at will through the past... You know me very well."

CHRIS gazed upon the thin-featured face. He looked into the pain-racked eyes. "No," he said, "I do not know you."

"You know me very well," the gaunt man repeated. "But through words and pictures only, and a historian cannot accurately describe a man from hearsay, nor can an artist accurately depict a face he has never seen. But who I am should be of no concern to you. What should be of concern to you is whether or not there is a way for you to return to life."

Hope pounded in Chris's brain. "And is there? Is there a way?"

"Yes," the gaunt man said, "there is. But very few men have ever traveled it successfully. The essence of the plain is the past, and therein lies its weakness. Right now you are capable of returning to any moment of your life; but unless you alter your past while doing so, the date of your death will remain unchanged."

"I don't understand," Chris said.

"Each individual, during his life span," the gaunt man went on, "arrives at a critical moment in which he must choose between two major alternatives. Oftentimes he is not aware of the importance of his choice, but whether he is aware or not, the alternative he chooses will arbitrarily determine the pattern, which his future life will follow. Should this alternative precipitate his death, he should be able, once he is suspended in the past, to return to the moment and, merely by choosing the other alternative, postpone his death. But in order to do so he would have to know which moment to return to—"

"But I do know which moment," Chris said hoarsely. "I—"

The gaunt man raised his hand. "I know you do—and having relived it with you, I do too. And the alternative you chose *did* precipitate your death: you died of acute alcoholism. But there is another consideration. Whenever anyone returns to the past he automatically loses his 'memory' of the future. You have all ready chosen the same alternative twice. If you return to the moment once more, won't the result be the same? Won't you betray yourself—and your wife and son—all over again?"

"But I can try," Chris said. "And if I fail, I can try again."

"Try then. But don't hope too much. I know the critical moment in my past too, and I have returned to it again and again and again, not to postpone my death—it is far too late for that—but to free myself from the plain, and I have never succeeded in changing it one iota." The gaunt man's voice grew bitter. "But then, my moment and its consequences are firmly cemented in the minds of men. Your case is different. Go then. Try. Think of the hour, the scene, the way you felt; then open the door. This time I will not accompany you vicariously; I will go as myself. I will have no 'memory' of the future either; but if you interpret my presence in the same symbolic way you interpreted it before, I may be of help to you. I do not want your hell too; my own and those of the others is enough."

The hour, the scene, the way he had felt. Dear God! ...*It is a summer night and above me stars lie softly on the dark velvet counterpane of the sky. I am driving my car into my driveway and my house is a light-warmed fortress in the night; secure stands my citadel beneath the stars and in the womb of it I will be safe—safe and warm and wanted... I have driven my car into my driveway and my wife is sitting beside me in the soft summer darkness...and now I am helping her carry groceries into the house. My wife is tall and slender and dark of hair, and she has gentle eyes and a tender smile and much loveliness... Soft is the night around us, compassionate are the stars; warm and secure is my house, my citadel, my soul...*

THE bag of potatoes he was carrying burst open, and potatoes bounced and rolled all over the patio. "Damn!" he said, and knelt down and began picking them up. One of them slipped from his fingers and rolled perversely off the patio and down the walk, and he followed it angrily, peevishly determined that it should not get away. It glanced off one of the wheels of little Chris's tricycle and rolled under the back porch. When he reached in after it his fingers touched a cold curved smoothness, and with a start he remembered the bottle of whiskey he had hidden the previous spring after coming home from a Saturday-night drunk—hidden and forgotten about till now.

SLOWLY he withdrew it. Starlight caught it, and it gleamed softly in the darkness. He knelt there, staring at it, the chill dampness of the ground creeping up into his knees. *What harm can one drink do?* his tautness asked. *One drink stolen in the darkness, and then no more?*

No, he answered. Never. *Yes,* the tautness screamed. *Just one. A sip. A swallow. Hurry! If it wasn't meant to be the bag would not have burst.* His fingers wrenched off the cap of their own volition then, and he raised the bottle to his lips—

And saw the man.

He was standing several yards away. Statuesque. Immobile. His thin-featured face was pale. His eyes were burning pits of pain.

He said no word, but went on standing there, and presently an icy wind sprang up in the summer night and drove the warmth away before it. The words came tumbling down the attic-stairs of Chris's mind then, and lined up on the threshold of his memory:

So when at last the Angel of the Drink
Of Darkness finds you by the river-brink,

And, proffering his Cup, invites your Soul
Forth to your Lips to quaff it—do not shrink.

"No," he cried, "not yet!" and emptied the bottle onto the ground and threw it into the darkness. When he looked again, the man had disappeared.

Shuddering, he stood up. The icy wind was gone, and the summer night was soft and warm around him. He walked down the walk on unsure feet and climbed the patio steps. Laura was standing in the doorway, her tall slenderness silhouetted softly against the living-room light. Laura of the tender smile, the gentle eyes; a glass of loveliness standing on the lonely bar of night—

He drained the glass to the last drop, and the wine of her was sweet. When she saw the potatoes scattered on the patio and came out, laughing, to help him, he touched her arm. "No, not now," he whispered, and drew her tightly against him and kissed her—not gently, the way he had kissed her at the Falls, but hard, hungrily, the way a husband kisses his wife when he realizes suddenly how much he needs her.

After a while she leaned back and looked up into his eyes. She smiled her warm and tender smile. "I guess the potatoes can wait at that," she said.

THE gaunt man stepped back across the abysmal reaches of the years and resumed his eternal wandering beneath the cold and silent stars. His success heartened him; perhaps, if he tried once more, he could alter his own moment too—

Think of the hour, the scene, the way you felt; then open the door... *It is spring and I am walking through narrow twisting streets. Above me stars shine gently in the dark and mysterious pastures of the night. It is spiritual and a warm wind is blowing in from the fields and bearing with it the scent of growing things. I can smell matzoth baking in earthen ovens... Now the temple looms before me and I go inside and wait beside a monolithic table... Now the high priest is approaching...*

The high priest upended the leather bag he was carrying and spilled its gleaming contents on the table. "Count them," he said.

He did so, his fingers trembling. Each piece made a clinking sound when he dropped it into the bag. *Clink...clink...clink.*

When the final clink sounded he closed the bag and thrust it beneath his robe.

"Thirty?" the high priest asked.

"Yes. Thirty."

"It is agreed then?" he replied.

For the hundredth, the thousandth, the millionth time, he nodded. "Yes," he said, "it is agreed. Come, I will take you to him, and I will kiss his cheek so that you will know him. He is in a garden just outside the city—a garden named Gethsemane."

THE END

RAPPORT

By Mary Elizabeth Counselman

...No matter what happened the door wasn't to be opened till the time appointed.

MARCO the Mentalist was seated before his dressing-room mirror, cold-creaming the grease paint from his long bony face, when the note was delivered. He glanced at it, idly at first—for he was always receiving mashnotes from some fluttery female in his audience, fascinated by him because he had "read her mind" during his usual three-a-day performance. Nor was he bad-looking; glancing back at his reflection in the mirror, he frowned slightly, aware of a pouchy dissipated sag beneath his eyes and under his chin. Not that forty-eight was too old for a stage and nightclub mentalist with the arrogant good looks of a fallen Lucifer—but it wasn't young, either. Another five years, of this, eating hurriedly in one-arm joints across from the theatre, moving from one town to another as his novelty in the present locality began to wane...

His thoughts broke off sharply as his piercing black eyes focused again on the note. *Elias Rutherford,* it was signed. A man, not a woman; and from the cramped old-fashioned handwriting, a rather elderly man. Marco, still rubbing cold cream into his face, read the first few lines more carefully—and sat up straight.

Dear Sir: (the note said formally, with a slight tone of amused condescension).

I attended your last performance tonight, and have decided that you are either a great psychic—or a very great fraud. I am a wealthy man, but not a happy one—the latter state due largely to the loss of my wife and our unborn child several years ago. If I had then believed in the power of one human mind to transmit thought to another, my wife and baby might now be alive... But I did not then, and do not now, believe in such a psychic phenomenon beyond the realm of mere coincidence. However, I am willing to accept proof of anything that modern science has not as yet disproved. The possibility haunts me.

If you can give me indisputable proof that a normal human being of your choice can transmit or receive thoughts, from me or from some person of my choosing, I will give you my personal check for $20,000. Will you call at the above address tomorrow at ten, if you elect to accept this challenge? If you decline, I shall assume that you are an ordinary stage-trickster, honest enough to admit it. If you try to fool me, however, I shall feel obligated to expose you to the press, and to the American Society for Psychic Research whose genuine efforts to separate the true from the false are not fully appreciated by the layman.

Sincerely, your servant, Elias Rutherford

Marco sucked in a long breath, his eyes narrowing as they lingered on that $20,000. Some old crackpot, he mused. Lonely and bored, brooding over the death of his wife—which, obviously, he half-believed he had "sensed" in time to warn her. He was always running into people like that; Marco laughed shortly. Naive, wide-eyed innocents with long-winded tales of a "dream" they had had of some relative at the very moment of his death. One would think they could recognize a coincidence for what it was—but, no! People worried about their loved ones dying a hundred times a day, but when it finally happened, and happened the very way they feared it was going to, nobody could convince them that they had not experienced a moment of "clairvoyance" or "telepathy."

This Rutherford, Marco decided with a wry smile, was just such a fool; perhaps a bit more intelligent than the average, but nagged by regret that he had not given the idea more thought. It might be easy to convince him of something he wanted to believe, anyhow, the mentalist told himself, narrow-eyed. Just another rich old codger who had more of the worldly goods than he deserved— Marco scowled bitterly. Fat soft capitalist...! Probably never had worked a day in his life. Never sweated to warm up a cold audience. Never lived on hamburgers between bookings, or slept in a railroad station because he didn't have the price of a hotel room.

THE mentalist stood up, mouth twitching slightly like that of a hungry cat stalking an unsuspecting bird on the garden walk. With swift hands that trembled a little in their eagerness, he wiped the cream from his face and strode out into the night-shrouded city. A way of collecting that $20,000 had just occurred to him—a hole-proof way of proving that "telepathy" is a scientific fact, if one first puts the cart before the horse...

Hurrying down the dark street to the little hotel where he was staying this week, Marco stopped by a little bookshop, open all night for the convenience of late-abeds like himself. For some time he browsed about, then slipped a small volume under his coat. Paying for a second book, which he tossed into a trashcan on his way, the mentalist almost ran the rest of the way to his hotel, and locked himself in. There, assured of a complete privacy, he opened the book he had bought: a treatise on medical hypnotism and suggestion.

He read all night, committing much of the book to memory. And when, as the dingy light of dawn seeped in through his window, he drifted off to sleep, Marco was smiling...

Promptly at ten o'clock, the great brass knocker on Elias Rutherford's front door boomed hollow notice of his arrival. Marco, in the only good suit he had, was ushered into a great paneled study, furnished in deep red leather. A fire was burning in the ornate fireplace, and a shriveled little man, with the cold gray eyes of a fish and a nose and pointed chin that almost met, was poking at the blazing logs peevishly.

As Marco entered, he turned and regarded him with the shrewdest expression the mentalist had ever encountered. He fidgeted, trying to smile and look at ease as the old man waved him to one of the deep chairs. But when, moments later, Elias Rutherford was still staring at him without uttering a word, Marco began to wish he had not come.

This, he realized abruptly, was not going to be an easy customer to fool. He swallowed twice, then in a matter-of-fact tone, began the spiel he had decided upon as a build-up. He had gone to some trouble to look up theories on telepathy, in order to sound convincing.

"Mr. Rutherford... May I trouble you for a pack of cards? A new pack, if possible. I am not," he smiled, "going to show you any magic tricks, believe me. I should merely like to give you the ESP test perfected by Dr. Rhine of Duke University. You are familiar with it, perhaps? Cards are turned by one person, while another tries to receive the impression of their color or number. Thirty-seven right out of 52 tries is so far beyond mathematical chance as to indicate extra-sensory perception..."

The old man nodded, to his dismay. With a shrug, he produced a sealed pack of cards from a small buhl cabinet and handed them to the mentalist with a manner as matter-of-fact as Marco's own.

"Oh, yes," Rutherford grunted. "Rhine. Dr. P. K. McCowan, of Dumfries. And Dunne, the English philosopher. I've studied all their pet theories. But, Mr. Marco, I may as well tell you that I have subjected myself to every known ESP test. Ever since...since my wife, Nadja..." The old man's voice broke slightly, betraying the grief that seemed as poignant now as on that day years ago. "I... She was in a department store, buying me a small present for my birthday. She...she entered a self-service elevator—at precisely 3:15, I later learned. I was at home with a slight cold, dozing by the fire here in this same chair.

"Suddenly I...I began dreaming that I saw her walk through a small sliding door. There was a sign hanging on that door, a sign Nadja could not read because she was Polish and knew very little English. But...I am sure she sent me an *impression* of that sign, puzzled by it and by the fact that nobody else seemed to be using the elevator...

"*She* took it, however." The old man brought out the words harshly. "And it fell five stories with her the moment she pressed the release button. The sign, of course, said: 'OUT OF ORDER, TAKE STAIRS.' Tell me," he broke off, fixing Marco with his cold eyes, "is it possible that my wife could read a sign without knowing what it said, and yet project its meaning to someone who could—to me? I...I *saw* that sign, you see. Let's say I *dreamed* I saw it, and I could have phoned the store in time to warn her not to take that elevator...*Or could I?*" Rutherford smiled drily. "That, Mr. Marco, is what I am willing to pay $20,000 to find out. The balance of my estate will then be bequeathed to the American

Society for Psychic Research—to find out *how* and *why* the transmission of thought is possible, and perhaps save others from the tragedy that I might have averted."

MARCO suppressed a smile. Then the old hellion was suggestible! He already half-believed in, or wanted to believe in, something that his logic told him could not be so. Also, he was obsessed with that "acid test" which, at some later date, he planned to give this charlatan who claimed to be able to broadcast and receive "thought-waves." Like a walkie-talkie set. (Which, actually, was the gimmick Marco and his pretty blonde assistant used, to "transmit thoughts" from aisle to stage.) The rest of it was done with a clever system of signals: "*And* guess *w*hat? *G*uess…?" The answer was: *A* gold *w*atch, girl's. Then Marco, still blindfolded, "read minds" from the stage as his assistant picked up the written questions handed her by those who had "problems." She held them to her forehead, then read them aloud in a whisper to some third person seated in the audience, who then dramatically was allowed to tear up the paper. Up on the stage, Marco, hearing it read through walkie-talkie earphones set into his phony black-velvet blindfold, then answered the question, such to the mystification of all concerned.

He grinned now, eyeing Elias Rutherford warily. If he could fool a whole audience for cakes-and-coffee money, surely he could trick this senile old codger into believing that he, Marco, was possessed of a sixth sense. It all hinged on the old magician's trick of misdirection.

Smiling, more at ease now, he settled back in the deep chair and put his fingertips together in a pedantic manner calculated to impress even the most scientific-minded.

"Really, sir," Marco went into the act he had planned last night in his shabby hotel room, "there is nothing supernatural about telepathy and clairvoyance. We know that sounds and pictures can be transmitted by means of electrical waves broadcast by man-made machinery…yet we are unwilling to credit this same power to that most intricate of all machines, the human mind."

MARCO'S voice, casually, had sunk to a monotone. His piercing eyes were fixed on Rutherford's, holding them—while between his fingers he swung a small silver pencil. Back and forth it swung, back and forth, until the old man's eyes were impelled to follow its rhythmic motion. Intent on Marco's learned discourse, he did not seem to be aware of what the stage trickster was trying to do…

"…a radio, a human radio, that's what the mind is," the mentalist droned on. "It is simply a matter of finding someone whose mind operates on the same frequency as one's own; the same wave-length, let us say. Many of us think in *words*, and can therefore transmit our thoughts only in words, or groups of syllables, or letters. Only another such mind could, therefore, be expected to receive its telepathic message. Other minds project *pictures*, rather than words; let us say, a television broadcast, to be picked up only by similarly trained minds…"

Back and forth, the silver pencil swung. *Back, forth, back, forth…* Old Mr. Rutherford blinked at it drowsily—and Marco suppressed a grin of triumph. But his soothing voice did not alter its monotone:

". . . very simple, if we could only grasp the principle as we now understand the principle of radio-reception and transmission. We have at least invented a machine for measuring the wave-impulses of the mind; I refer to the encephalograph, used in tests for epilepsy and certain other types of insanity. Why is not such a machine used to experiment with psychic, as well as medical, phenomena of the mind? It well may be, and in the very near future. Insanity itself used to be considered a supernatural thing. A man was 'possessed of devils' when the electrical process called *thought* went awry… Do you hear me, Mr. Rutherford?" Marco threw in softly. "Do-you-hear-me…?"

The old man swayed slightly, eyes fixed glassily now on that swinging pencil. He nodded with the mechanical obedience of a marionette.

"I…hear…you…"

Marco leaned forward, fixing the glazed eyes of the old man with his own compelling gaze.

"Repeat after me," he commanded softly. "Repeat: 'Tom, Tom, the piper's son... Stole a pig and away he run...'"

"Tom...Tom...the piper's..." Elias Rutherford, in a dull voice like a sleepwalker, repeated the nursery rhyme.

"Now," Marco said quietly. "You will remember that—do you understand? Remember those words. They are the words you will use in the test, when you send them as a telepathic message to me. Understand?"

"I...understand..." Rutherford droned.

"Tomorrow night, at nine," Marco commanded.

"At...nine..." the old man repeated, like an obedient child.

Then Marco made a small sharp sound, by snapping his fingers. The other blinked and started, rubbing his eyes. The mentalist smiled.

"Am I boring you?" he asked politely, as though nothing had occurred to break the trend of his conversation. "I mean, about the mind being a radio. It is quite possible that our minds are in tune—or *en rapport,* as the French say, Mr. Rutherford. If it so happens that my thinking-apparatus operates on the same frequency as yours, I am confident that you could send me a thought-message...oh, tomorrow night, let's say. At eight?" Marco suggested slyly.

"At nine," said the old man firmly, with a slight frown of puzzlement as he said it. "I...feel, for some reason, that it should be at nine."

"As you wish," Marco agreed smoothly—trying not let a gleam of triumph in his eyes betray that his plan had worked.

Elias Rutherford had been hypnotized, neatly and completely. He had been given a post-hypnotic suggestion, which he would follow now without ever understanding why he did so.

TOMORROW night, promptly at nine, the old man would 'project' that nursery rhyme as his test-message, believing it to have originated in his own head—not that of the receiver. And $20,000 would change hands—because old Rutherford could not help but be impressed by this startling proof of mental telegraphy. There might even be, Marco considered with a half-smile, ways to get the millionaire to bequeath *him* the balance of his estate, rather than some idiotic Society for Psychic Research. Crackpots. Seekers after sensation and bizarre amusement. These metaphysical groups went all-out to kid themselves, the mentalist thought wryly; but he himself, for all that he made his living with the so-called "black arts," was a materialist.

"Very well," he agreed now pleasantly, as though humoring Elias Rutherford in some whim, "nine it shall be. But...for your own sake, and for mine, sir, I must ask that you enforce certain test-conditions while the experiment is going on. Remember," his dark eyes twinkled, "I am a professional magician. There might be ways, other than through telepathy, that I could get hold of your message."

The millionaire smiled coldly. "I thought of that," he said drily. "There are many tricksters in the field. Oh, I know all about these table-tapping devices and cheesecloth ectoplasm, used by professional mediums. And I have read that the great Houdini himself had a standing offer of one thousand dollars to anyone who could produce psychic phenomena, which he could not duplicate by scientific means. You may consider me the same sort of hard-boiled skeptic."

"Splendid," Marco said smoothly. "I was hoping you would take that very attitude, sir. How shall we work it, then? In separate rooms? And under guard?"

"In separate rooms...across town," Rutherford snapped. "I will remain here in this library, with someone you can trust. A member of the police?" he suggested slyly, his keen old eyes fixed on Marco's bland countenance. "You would not object—since you say there is to be no question of fraud?"

Marco's expression did not waver. He bowed graciously, accustomed to eyes that were critical and observant of his every facial tremor.

"As you wish," he agreed. "And I shall be confined to, say, my own hotel room across town? I am not a wealthy man," he gestured apologetically. "It is a very small dingy hotel—with no fire-escape at the single window of my fifth-story room. You may station a police guard outside the door if you like, and tie or handcuff me to my bed. The phone will be in the hall, so there is no question of my conferring with any accomplice who might get hold of your message. But I must request that you write it down on a piece of paper, at the hour we agreed upon. Write it, reread it to yourself, concentrate on the word-picture it presents. That way, perhaps I can receive your message in letters, words, or pictures—whichever type of thought-projection is most suitable as a means of communication between your mind and mine."

Rutherford chuckled, eyeing the mentalist with, almost, a grudging respect—the respect of one hard-headed realist for another of the same caliber.

"You certainly have your...your patter down to perfection," he commented, amused. "One would think we were planning an actual scientific test in, say, wireless communication..."

"Perhaps we are," Marco answered him simply. "Perhaps we are, Mr. Rutherford... Tomorrow night, then. At nine. I shall expect your...ah...friends from the police at my hotel promptly, a short time before that hour. I suggest, too, that you seal the doors and windows with paraffin, as an added precaution. They say," he drawled, "every man has a price—and how do you know your police guard could not be bribed?"

"I intend to pick one who can neither be bribed nor tricked," the old man said. "You will not find me an easy man to hoodwink, sir. Not for $20,000," he chuckled good-humoredly, "which it took me a great many years of hard work to acquire."

Marco laughed, and bowed himself through the door of the great paneled room. Outside on the street again, as he signaled for a passing cab, his face hardened. Damned old miser! Well, tomorrow night he would shake him loose from some of that "hard-earned" cash—$20,000 of it—as easily as one could take candy from a baby.

AT EIGHT-THIRTY the following night, Marco the Mentalist was absent from his usual nightly performance of standing, blindfolded, on a spot-lighted stage and reading "thought-messages" sent by those in his audience.

Instead, pleading sickness to the annoyed stage manager of his second-rate theatre, he waited in his room, heart pounding with excitement.

A knock on the door roused him. He opened it quickly, to find two plainclothesmen from the bunco squad standing there, grinning at him. One dangled a pair of handcuffs, whistling cheerfully, while the other went carefully over every inch of Marco's cheap little room, looking for mechanical devices such as a short-wave radio or wireless outfit.

The mentalist lounged against the cracked plaster wall while they searched, smoking lazily—and looking more than ever like a fallen Lucifer in his ornate dressing gown, with the smoke drifting up past his half-closed eyes and enigmatic smile.

One of the officers glanced at him. "What's this all about, Marco? The Chief sent us, but he didn't say what was the gimmick. Publicity stunt?"

Marco shrugged. "Something like that, Reilly. You'll know after it's over. Just be sure to seal me up in this room so even a termite couldn't get in. *And don't open the door, whatever happens.* Not until ten o'clock. Understand? One hour."

"We got our orders," the detective grunted.

Some minutes later, Marco the Mentalist sat smiling on his unmade bed, with his wrists handcuffed to the iron head—alone with his thoughts. Or Elias Rutherford's, he mused, laughing silently.

The tiny room, with its now-sealed and locked door and window, had become stifling in the short time he had been waiting. Sweat beaded Marco's forehead and upper lip, but he leaned back patiently against the head of the bed, smoking and thinking.

Twenty grand! Just for sitting here, waiting for an old fool to "think" of a nursery rhyme his skillful hypnotism had already planted in his mind. The mentalist chuckled, dreaming of Monte Carlo, of the Riviera; of sleek blond women who would never give a second-rate vaudeville artist a second glance; of sunlight, and leisure, and long amusing hours that he could never have afforded, as a four-a-day entertainer. And it need never end!

Because, his thoughts leaped ahead eagerly, this need not be the only fraud he would perpetrate on some gullible, wealthy old coot... Why, he could establish a cult! The idle rich went for psychic nonsense, hook, line, and sinker. Telepathy! Why hadn't he thought of the hypnotic angle before? It was a natural, a lead-pipe cinch to pick from some idiot's mind a few words that had already been planted there!

The mentalist laughed softly, eyes half-closed as he lay on his bed, waiting and looking with amusement at that paraffin sealed door behind which two minions of the law were waiting also. Thoughts. Nothing but thoughts—invisible, inaudible little electric waves, according to his spiel to Rutherford—could penetrate this fort of his own cleverness. Twenty thousand bucks! Twenty thousand... Marco's eyes closed drowsily, dreaming of a ridiculous scene that was taking place in a big paneled library across town. An old man, earnestly scribbling a nonsense rhyme on a piece of paper. Concentrating on it, his withered lips moving, his will focused on the idea of projecting the words through space to...

MARCO stiffened, wrinkling his thin arched nose. He sat up painfully, spread-eagled against the bed-head by his handcuffed wrists. For, quite suddenly, to his horror, he had smelled something...

Smoke!

With a sharp intake of breath he glanced down at the bedclothes and saw a tiny tongue of flame licking hungrily at the sheets, at his wool overcoat recently cleaned with...Gasoline! He smelled the fumes of it now, as the flame reached it and glazed higher where the coat lay carelessly flung across the bed at his feet. He tried to kick it off, struggling to reach it, with his wrists straining against their steel shackles... But the movement only served to fan the blaze.

It leaped higher, ate deeper, finding sudden food in the cotton mattress. Marco coughed and cried out hoarsely, drawing up his feet.

"Help!" he yelled. "Hey! You cops out there—my bed's on fire! Get me out of here...!"

For answer, the two plainclothesmen in the hall outside laughed lightly.

"No kiddin'?" one of them drawled.

"Yeah! The Chief said you might try to pull something like that," the other jeered. "No dice, Marco—we don't open this door till ten o'clock. And it's only nine-thirty five..."

"No, listen!" Marco shouted, half-laughing. "This is no gag. I set fire to the bed with my cigarette. Get me out of this!"

Laughter. A few jesting catcalls from the men outside his door.

Marco's smile vanished. Sweat that was half from the mounting heat, half from horror at his predicament, popped out on his face and ran down his quivering mouth. The wicked little flames were ringing him in now, creeping toward his drawn-up feet. Smoke billowed from the charred bedclothes, stinging his eyes and nose so that he could hardly see. Coughing and gagging, straining at his handcuffs, Marco screamed.

"Please. For God's sake! I'm not kidding…! I…I'm burning to death! I…can't breathe…!"

Laughter, ribald and derisive. One of the men was even going away. Going downstairs for a drink; a cool bubbling drink… Marco gagged, swallowing smoke. His throat was raw now, his eyes streaming. The tiny sealed room had filled to the ceiling with black, stifling clouds. And the mattress blazed, scorching his shoes now, singeing the hairs on his legs. Like a mocking red-and-yellow demon, the fire reached for him with graceful hands that blistered his face…that…that seared his staring eyes…!

"Rutherford!" he screamed, insanely. *"Rutherford—help me! I'm…burning! I'm…burning…Rutherford, help! Help…!"*

The fire reached, enfolding him in its red arms. Marco screamed, a long tearing sound of agony…through which, it seemed, somewhere that he could hear a bell ringing. A phone… A telephone bell…ringing and ringing, with frantic insistence…

HE AWOKE, painfully, in a hospital bed; awoke to darkness, and the pungent smell of antiseptic, and the low murmur of a doctor's voice conferring with a nurse. There was, he dimly recognized, also another voice—an old man's treble, sharp and sour.

"Doctor, will he…How much of the body surface was burned?"

"About a third. Oh, he'll live, I think. But…even with plastic surgery…Well, he won't be a pretty sight."

"What a pity." The nurse's voice. "He was...awfully good-looking. I...I saw his act on the stage last week. Wonderful, isn't he? I mean, golly, the way he just reads your mind...?"

AT HER thrilled tone, gullible and utterly mystified, Marco the Mentalist almost smiled through his agony and tried to stir. Why...why, he was a mass of bandages! What...where....? Who was the gauze-swaddled mummy?

He remembered, groaning. The hoax, the great hoax by which he was to have fleeced an old man of twenty thousand dollars. It was gone now. And...and his face; his arrogant good looks, his charm, his stage magnetism—all that was gone, too! Marco whimpered deep in his throat, cursing himself, cursing his own avarice.

And then:

"Wonderful?" old Rutherford's voice was murmuring, oddly, in answer to the young nurse. "Why...yes, my dear. I believe Marco was genuinely able to transmit and receive thought. I shall, of course, pay all his hospital expenses—since, in a way, his disfigurement is my fault. And he will receive my check for twenty thousand as agreed. Tell him that the moment he awakens, will you, Doctor? It...it might console him. And I owe it to him. A...sort of bet."

"Twenty thousand?" the nurse gasped. "He *won* it, Mr. Rutherford?"

"Yes. Marco proved that telepathy is possible...and practical, even under test conditions," Elias Rutherford answered softly. "I...I am convinced, personally. And...I shall leave my fortune to the ASPR for further research into...what well may be a new branch of science, rather than a mere superstitious theory. Marco and I did send and receive a telepathic message," the old man muttered. "Although...in reverse. I was transmitting to him a silly bit of nursery rhyme, which I intended using as a test-message...when all at once, very clearly, there came into mind a picture of Marco handcuffed to his bed, *surrounded by flames! I...I...* It was so vivid an impression that I could not restrain an impulse to phone his hotel—and thereby saved him from a horrible death. So, we did succeed in establishing...*a rapport.*"

Under the bandages Marco's burned face contorted. Muffled sounds came through the gauze that covered his blistered mouth.

He was laughing, wildly...

THE END

ONE LONG RIBBON

By *Florence Engel Randall*

From beyond the grave, her husband had given her this house. But as she slowly went mad in it, she wondered if it were a gift, or a vengeance.

FRAN moved into the house with all the possessions she and Chris had accumulated over the years, all the things they had chosen with such care, with such love. They had been sure that, someday, they would have a home. Chris would stop flying and she would call for him each evening at some suburban station with Jamie watching for the train and yelling, "There's Daddy, Mommy. I can see him."

She directed the moving men: "Put the piano over there, please. That easy chair goes next to the fireplace."

She directed Jamie: "Go out and play, darling. There must be lots of children here. You can help me later."

Then, when the furniture was in place and the men had left, she sat down in the living room and stared numbly into space, wanting to cry, waiting for the tears to come. Now, she was sure, they would flow easily and bring peace, release. But nothing happened. She just felt drained and weary, more tired than she could ever remember, more exhausted than she had felt that night almost a year ago when the telegram had come.

She had known what it contained the moment it had arrived. She hadn't opened it for a long time; just held it in her hands, as if by not opening it, she could negate its contents, deny the facts, bring Chris back again.

And then, months after the telegram, the lawyer had given her Chris' letter.

"I COULD NEVER GIVE YOU A HOME," it had said, the handwriting strong and bold like Chris. "WE WERE ALWAYS ON THE MOVE—ONE AIR BASE AFTER THE OTHER. I HAVE REQUESTED THAT THEY WAIT A WHILE BEFORE

GIVING THIS TO YOU, BUT NOW THE TIME HAS COME WHEN I THINK YOU'LL BE ABLE TO MAKE THE MOVE. THIS HOUSE IS YOURS WITH MY LOVE. LIVE IN IT FOR ME. LIVE IN IT FOR JAMIE AND FOR YOUR OWN FUTURE."

She had memorized his words. She had read and reread the letter so often that it had become almost devoid of meaning. There had never been a house for them before, yet, now that Chris was gone, he expected her to live in this one.

The lawyer had been firm. "It was what he wanted, Mrs. Holden," he had said, the sunlight reflected in his glasses. "He was most explicit. He made all the arrangements about two years ago. He said that if anything happened to him, you must live in this house." He took off his glasses and polished them. "I do hope," he added thoughtfully, staring into space, "that you won't be too lonely there."

THIS was the house! White-shingled, red-roofed, the first house on a winding lane; a lane, curving, rambling, meandering as if it couldn't make up its mind where it was supposed to go. This was the house, the house Chris had chosen, his gift to her. She fell in love with it at once. There was something almost fey about it; a sense of instant recognition that this was home, that this was where she and Jamie belonged.

Searching for Jamie, she stood up and peered out of the window. The lane had been empty, deserted, but it was as if her appearance was a signal. It was as if her presence at the window had caused the curtain to roll up, the play to begin. Little boys pedaled bicycles; roller skates scraped the sidewalks; the trees waved to the sky and, just next door to her, two women stopped to talk, their voices clear in the spring air.

The lawyer had said, "I do hope, you won't be too lonely there."

This wasn't a street for loneliness and grief. This was a street for happiness with the houses like a child's colored blocks set neatly side by side. Chris had seen its life, its happiness and had wanted her to be a part of it. That was why he had bought this house and no other.

She wouldn't disappoint him. She wouldn't withdraw from the life around her. She would join it, become a part of it, give Jamie the home he needed.

Fran put up a pot of coffee just in case someone dropped by to welcome her. She had almost emptied two of the cartons when Jamie came in.

"Hi, darling," she said, rumpling his hair. Jamie, at seven, was a small edition of Chris; wide, brown eyes, light brown hair and a few freckles trailing across the bridge of his nose. "Thought you were going to help me unpack," she said. "Have fun?"

"It's all right, I guess," he said politely, "if you like a lot of trees."

She grinned at him. "City boy," she teased. "You'll have to get used to living in the country."

"Sure," he said. "It's fine." Without protesting, he rested after lunch. Fran sat at the table alone, the aroma of the coffee still filling the kitchen. The house was very still. Even the electric clock didn't tick, but moved silently, counting out the minutes, the hours. Outside of her window, outside of her quiet house, the children played and laughed; the women visited back and forth.

Fran felt a little unreal. She hadn't expected a brass band to draw up, the trumpets gleaming in the sunlight, the drums rolling a greeting. She certainly hadn't expected her neighbors to jump up and down, shouting, "Welcome to the Holdens!" But still, it was as if no one had noticed the moving van at all; no one had seen them, no one wanted to see them.

FRAN thought: I'm being foolish. Probably everyone's just being considerate. They may feel it's much too soon to call. Jamie and I will go for a walk this afternoon and surely, someone will stop and greet us.

Feeling more cheerful, she ran up the stairs and paused at the door to Jamie's room. He was lying across the bed, his eyes open, staring at the ceiling.

"Jamie, what's wrong?" She was suddenly anxious. She touched his forehead with her lips. "Are you feeling well?"

"Sure," he said. "Honest, Mom. I'm fine."

"How about taking a walk with me? We can go down the lane and explore a bit."

"There's not much to see," said Jamie. "Just a lot of trees and bushes and rocks. It's going to be pretty lonely here, Mom."

Fran bit her lip. "How can you say such a thing? There are so many beautiful houses. I can hear the children playing and having a marvelous time. I saw them roller-skating just a little while ago. Why don't you unpack your skates?"

He sat up and stared at her. He touched her hand. "I'll go if you want me to," he said, but his eyes were frightened.

She was puzzled. "Jamie—"

"I'm ready right now." He stood up. "Let's go," he said and ran down the hall, down the steps.

She followed him slowly, wondering why he suddenly seemed so strange, so remote. Was he thinking of Chris too, missing him, longing for him?

She closed the front door behind them and they walked down the path together. They turned to the right. Three little boys playing marbles blocked the sidewalk.

"Excuse me, please," said Fran.

"No quitsies, no changies," said the snub-nosed boy.

"No back fires, no side fires," chanted the second.

"Hello," said Fran, smiling. "We've just moved in."

"No ricochets," said the third boy, ignoring her.

Jamie tugged at her hand. "Please, Mom."

"It's all right, darling," said Fran. "I'm sure they'll become more friendly after a while."

"Who?" said Jamie.

"The children," said Fran, impatiently. "Really, Jamie."

"Mom," he whispered, "I don't see any children."

She stared at him. "Darling, what are you saying? They're right over there. Can't you see?"

"Oh, sure," he said, his voice quivering. "I didn't at first but now I do." He patted her arm with a strangely adult gesture of reassurance. "Maybe we ought to go home," he said.

"I want to walk," said Fran stubbornly. She was suddenly, inexplicably very frightened.

The boys never looked up. They behaved as if she and Jamie didn't exist, as if they neither saw nor heard them, their eyes intent on their game, their litany.

What rude children thought Fran. Perhaps, that's why Jamie was behaving so oddly, he had never encountered rudeness before. He didn't know what to do except pretend it didn't exist.

WHAT rude grown-ups, she thought a moment later. Two women had passed, their eyes staring through her, ignoring Fran's friendly nod.

She felt a sudden chill although the day was warm and sweet with May. Magnolias were in bloom and a crab apple splashed pink against the sky. In the distance a lawn mower whirred. Jamie blinked in the sunlight.

I must be imagining this, thought Fran, it couldn't possibly be real. It was as if the entire street was determined to ignore her, as if the entire street had banded together, united in their snub.

But why? What had they done?

She turned back without a word, still holding Jamie's hand, finding comfort in the firm clasp of his fingers.

There was a man on the lawn of the house next door to hers. He was painting, his canvas propped against a rock. He stared into the distance, his back toward her.

It would be quite simple. She would walk right up to him and say, "I'm Fran Holden. I just moved next door to you and I wanted to say, 'hello.'"

She tugged at Jamie's hand but he broke away and ran toward their house. She watched him go, startled, moved uncertainly in his direction, and then, turned and walked resolutely across the lawn.

Fran cleared her throat.

THE man kept on painting, absorbed. His dark hair was cropped short, his ears lay flat against his head, his hands were brown and strong. She peered over his shoulder with the feeling of unreality flooding through her again. He was finishing, with quick brushstrokes, the portrait of a woman; a woman who stood erect against the backdrop of the sky, her skirt blowing in the breeze, her eyes slitted in the sun.

Fran took a deep breath and ran away, ran after Jamie, running, seeking, searching for the cool safety of her house. She had recognized the portrait; had stared at it unbelievingly and then, had done the only thing left to do. She had fled.

The woman on the canvas with the red lips smiling, the blue eyes shining with happiness, had been Fran.

No," she said aloud, shutting the front door behind her. "No, it's impossible." She leaned against the door, braced against it, her legs trembling.

It had been someone else. Someone who resembled Fran; someone who looked enough like Fran so that a slip of the brush, a touch of color in the wrong place, gave the illusion that it had been Fran, herself, who had posed for the picture.

Was it because she was so tired that everything was so strange, so disoriented? She just wasn't seeing things in their proper perspective. They would have an early dinner and go to sleep, and, in the morning, everything would be normal and usual. They would become part of the street. They would belong there. The faces would be friendly; they would be made welcome. Chris would never have chosen a house, would never have chosen a *street* that would hurt them in any way.

"LIVE IN THIS HOUSE," he had written, "FOR YOUR FUTURE."

For her future. She thought of the years still ahead of her, the interminable years without love, walking alone, living alone, watching Jamie grow, always alone, never to share the joy of him.

They ate their dinner in silence, seated at opposite ends of the kitchen table; Jamie still troubled, still frightened and withdrawn. She wanted to comfort him and fumbled, seeking, hoping for the right words.

"We'll do better tomorrow," she said, clearing the table. "It'll be much better tomorrow, Jamie. We'll shop at the stores and stock up on things and then, we'll go to the school and register you. You'll be happy here, darling, you'll see."

She tucked him in bed and then moved through the lonely house, not able to stay in one place, walking through the silent living room, the quiet hall.

Next door, the lights blazed and the sound of music drifted through the open windows. She could hear a woman laugh and then, the deep, answering murmur of the man. Those were her neighbors, living in a house that was filled with lights and laughter and music.

Fran opened her front door and moved silently across the path. She walked toward the house next door, across the wet, newly sprinkled lawn, her hands outstretched, as if she were pleading. She stood in front of their house, watching, aching with unbelievable longing, wanting to move toward it, and yet, fearful of being turned away, of being rebuffed.

IT would be so wonderful if she could press that doorbell and enter that house and feel the laughter and the music envelop her, warming her. She had never felt so cold, so set apart, so isolated.

Searching for courage, she took a deep breath and walked slowly up to the house. She reached for the doorbell, but before she could touch it, the man opened the door wide and peered into the darkness as if he were searching for someone. He stood next to her, so close that if she moved her hand, she could have touched him. She looked up at him, for he was very tall, but he didn't see her. His eyes stared through her.

She shivered. "Please," she said. "Oh, please."

"Steve," called the woman's voice. "Steve, what are you doing?"

It was a voice oddly familiar, a little distorted, a little muffled, as if Fran, herself, had spoken and this was the echo.

"I keep wondering," said the man, his face bathed in moonlight, his lips curving tenderly. "I keep wondering just when it happened. I keep wondering what I could do to help. But, at the same time, Fran, I'm afraid. I don't want to change anything. I don't want to change what we have now."

"Come in, quickly," said the voice. "Oh, please, darling, because I'm afraid too."

And there was a hand placed on his tanned arm, the long, white fingers curving gently, possessively. "Please, darling," and he went into the house and shut the door.

Fran stood frozen on the steps. She was having a nightmare. This is the way a nightmare begins; the thudding heart, the sudden terror, the legs that just won't obey. She was really lying in her bed, sound asleep dreaming.

She had dreamt this walk across the wet grass and the woman's shadow on the blinds and the strong, hard planes of the man's face. She had dreamt she had heard the sound of her own voice calling from within a strange house.

FRAN forced herself to move, to walk quietly back to her own house, to lock the door, turn out the lights and behave like any normal householder closing up for the night.

She wouldn't think about it. She wouldn't allow herself to think about it. That way lay madness and gibbering terror.

She forced herself to undress, shower and get into bed. She lay very quietly, trying to think about Chris, trying to think of Jamie, trying to think of anything but this winding lane on which her house was built, the house Chris had chosen.

Remembering Chris, she moved back through time to bring him close to her—the gentleness, the warmth and kindness of Chris. Why had he chosen this house for her? Chris had never done anything without a reason. Why this particular house? Had he known what she would feel here, experience here? Was this what he had wanted for her?

Or was she dreaming even through the daylight hours, as she had pretended she must be dreaming that night? Did the street exist? Was it really there or were she and Jamie suspended in some dreadful limbo, their only existence a swing on the pendulum of time and space, not belonging anywhere?

After a while, she fell asleep, her arm over her eyes, trying to close out the world, shut out her loneliness.

THE next morning, the sunlight sparkled, the birds sang and even Jamie seemed more like himself, eager to get into the car with her, eager to get to the school.

The school was new, red-bricked. It smelled of chalk and fresh paint.

The principal was cordial. "Mrs. Holden," she smiled. "I want to welcome you to our community. We do hope you'll be very happy here."

Fran smiled back, smiled at another human being, smiled at this friendly, plump little woman who actually saw her, who heard her, who spoke to her. Everything seemed suddenly delightful, very sharp, very clear—the shining desk, the fly buzzing at the window, the yellow roses in the white vase.

"Thank you," said Fran. "I'm sure we will."

"You live on the lane, don't you? It's so pretty out there."

"Yes," said Fran. "It is."

"Of course, you'll be rather lonely for a while."

"Why should I be lonely?" Fran asked carefully. "Do you know why?"

The principal looked startled. "Well," she said, uncertainly. "If you don't know why, Mrs. Holden, then you must be a very self-sufficient person indeed."

"Please," said Fran, leaning forward. "I wish you'd—"

"Excuse me," said the principal, picking up the phone. "I'm always being interrupted by calls just when I'd like to settle down for a nice long chat. I think it would be best to start Jamie fresh in the fall. I'm sure he'll be very happy here and we'll be very happy to have him."

Fran was dismissed.

She delayed the trip home as long as possible. She shopped in the supermarket; Jamie pushing the cart. She loaded the car and drove through the town. Finally, reassured, she started back along the rutted, country road that led to her house.

EACH person she had met that morning had been friendly. She had her identity once again. She was Fran Holden and next to her sat her son, Jamie. They lived in the first house on the lane and everyone in town who had met them had smiled at them.

If there was anything wrong, it was with the street not with her, not with Jamie.

Fran parked the car in the driveway. She worked in the house for the rest of the day, cleaning, straightening, unpacking. She ignored the street, closing her ears to the sounds of the laughing children, the voices of the mothers, the noises from next door.

Jamie followed her about, handing her things, opening cartons, making no move to go outdoors. She didn't urge him. If she couldn't face the street, what was it like for Jamie?

She turned to him suddenly, not meaning to say it but the words spilling out in spite of herself.

"Darling," she said. "What do you see when you look outdoors?"

His eyes were troubled. "What do *you* see, Mom?"

"Please, Jamie." Fran sat down and pulled him toward her. "Please tell me. You said you saw nothing but trees and rocks and bushes. Don't you see anything else?"

He shook his head.

"No houses?" asked Fran. "No people? No children?"

"I think I ought to go upstairs," said Jamie quickly. "There's something I've got to do."

"Jamie!"

He put his head on her shoulder. "You said you saw people, Mom," he whispered. "There was no one there."

Fran released him and stood up. She went to the sink. She let the cold water run and took a drink. It was icy against the back of her throat.

"Jamie, darling," she said gently. "Right now, there are people walking past our house. Right now, there's music coming from next door. And yet, you see nothing, hear nothing?" She clasped her hands. She mustn't frighten him. "Perhaps I'm mistaken," she said, keeping her voice light. "But that's what I see."

Jamie backed away. "I really have to go upstairs," he muttered, and ran.

She mustn't question him. She mustn't do that again. She would have to leave this house—for her own sanity, for Jamie's.

She saw the neat, manicured lawns, the carefully planned flower gardens. She saw children whirling past; she heard the thump of a ball slammed by a bat; she heard a mother calling her child.

He saw the woods; the trees stretching green and tall; the brown rocks, the grass growing wild.

This was no house for her. Chris had been wrong. But it had been his gift to her. How could she turn her back on Chris?

THE doorbell rang and she stood still for a moment, shocked, immobile. Someone was standing on her front steps. Someone was ringing her bell.

She opened the door.

It was the man who lived next door. He stood tall on her steps, his eyes, brown like Chris', alive with dancing lights.

"I'm Steve Marshall," he said.

Fran was filled with happiness.

A wave of it flowed through her, making her dizzy, making her weak with joy. It had been so long since she had felt this way.

"Please, come in," she said, opening the door wide. "Jamie," she called. "We have a visitor. It's our next door neighbor."

Jamie came down the steps, his hands in his pockets, his eyes alert and wary.

"Hi," said Steve, holding out his hand. "I'm glad to know you."

They shook hands gravely, soberly, studying each other. Jamie smiled.

"I'm Fran Holden," she said, holding out her own hand. "I've been meaning to call. I did want to meet your wife."

This was reality, the warmth of the sunlight on her bare arms, the way his teeth gleamed white when he smiled.

"I'd like you to meet my wife if I had one," he said. "I just wanted to stop by and tell you that your isolation is over."

"I was sure it wouldn't last," said Fran. "It was some sort of a joke, then?" She tried to laugh. "I'll have to admit I've been pretty lonely here." Then, as the full significance of his words struck her, she said, "But, I don't understand. You do have a wife. I heard you talking to her last night."

He frowned, puzzled. "I wasn't here last night," he said slowly. "I just stopped by today to tell you that the bulldozers will be ripping the place up soon. I'm the architect for the new development we're going to build."

FRAN backed away, reaching for Jamie. She touched his shoulder, and then moved uncertainly into the living room.

The two of them followed her, the tall man and the little boy.

The man spoke quietly, gently, as if he knew she was frightened, as if he knew of her confusion and wanted, somehow, to comfort her.

"It will be a beautiful street," he said gently. "We're going to follow the natural contours of the land. The street will curve and wind and we'll leave all the tall trees."

Fran stared at him. "This is the way it's going to be?"

He nodded, trying to understand.

"The house next door will be sprawling and low and you're going to live in it yourself," she said, not asking a question, simply stating the fact.

"It will be sprawling and low." He grinned. "I didn't know I was going to live in it, though. Are you telling fortunes today?"

Fran leaned back and smiled at Jamie. "The houses will look like building blocks and there will be lots of children here." She looked up at Steve. "The house next door to you will have three children. Two boys and a girl."

He frowned. "They just bought from the plans," he said. "How could you know?"

"I can't explain right now," she said. "I just do."

Somehow, she was no longer frightened.

Exhilarated, she stood up and ran to the front door. The street still lay stolid, real before her eyes. As she watched, it shimmered and seemed to go a little out of focus.

Tomorrow, she thought, when they start to tear up the ground, it will all disappear. I won't see it again, not until it becomes real.

Standing in the doorway, she remembered, suddenly, some thing Chris had once said.

"TIME IS LIKE A WINDING ROAD. TO THE MAN ON THE GROUND, THE FUTURE LIES HIDDEN, BLOCKED BY A CLUMP OF TREES; THE PAST, BEHIND HIM, DISAPPEARING AROUND THE BEND. TO THE MAN IN THE PLANE THE ENTIRE ROAD LIES EXPOSED, ONE LONG RIBBON UNWINDING, PAST, PRESENT AND FUTURE CLEAR AND IN VIEW."

Chris had been the man in the plane watching from above, the road of time, the lane, winding beneath him.

Now, she knew why he had chosen this house. He had known. This was what he had wanted for her. Had he also known that through some miracle she would be able to see it too?

Steve touched her shoulder.

"You know," he said, his eyes thoughtful, "just the way you look right now—someday, I'd like to paint you."

She smiled at him, drawing Jamie close to her. "You will," she said, with wonder, "and it will be beautiful."

THE END

IN THE X-RAY

By Fritz Leiber, Jr.

The radiologist sees all manner of strange things…but none as strange as this!

"DO THE dead come back?" Dr. Ballard repeated the question puzzledly. "What's that got to do with your ankle?"

"I didn't say that," Nancy Sawyer answered sharply. "I said, 'I tried an ice pack.' You must have misheard me."

"But…" Dr. Ballard began. Then, "Of course I must have," he said quickly. "Go on, Miss Sawyer."

The girl hesitated. Her glance strayed to the large, gleaming window and the graying sky beyond. She was a young woman with prominent eyes, a narrow chin, strong white teeth, reddish hair, and a beautiful, doe-like figure, which included legs long and slim—except for the ankle of the one outstretched, stockingless on the chair before her. That was encircled by a hard, white, somewhat irregular swelling.

Dr. Ballard was a man of middle age and size, with strong, soft-skinned hands. He looked intelligent and as successful as his sleekly furnished office.

"Well, there isn't much more to it," the girl said finally. "I tried the ice pack but the swelling wouldn't go down. So Marge made me call you."

"I see. Tell me, Miss Sawyer, hadn't your ankle bothered you before last night?"

"No. I just woke up from a nightmare frightened because something had grabbed my foot, and I reached down and touched my ankle—and there it was."

"Your ankle didn't feel or look any different the day before?"

"No."

"Yet when you woke up the swelling was there?"

"Just as it is now."

"Do you think you might have twisted your foot while you were asleep?"

"No."

"And you don't feel any pain in it now?"

"No, except a feeling of something hard clasped snugly around it and every once in a while squeezing a bit tighter."

"Ever do any sleepwalking?"

"No."

"Any allergies?"

"No."

"Can you think of anything else—anything at all—that might have a bearing on this trouble?"

Again Nancy looked out the window. "I have a twin sister," she said after a moment, in a different voice. "Or rather, I had. She died more than a year ago." She looked back quickly at Dr. Ballard. "But I don't know why I should mention that," she said hurriedly. "It couldn't possibly have any bearing on this. She died of apoplexy."

There was a pause.

"I suppose the X-ray will show what's the matter?" she continued.

The doctor nodded. "We'll have it soon. Miss Snyder's getting it now."

Nancy started to get up, asked, "Is it all right for me to move around?" Dr. Ballard nodded. She went over to the window, limping just a little, and looked down.

"You have a nice view, you can see half the city," she said. "We have the river at our apartment. I think we're higher, though."

"This is the twentieth floor," Dr. Ballard said.

"We're twenty-three," she told him. "I like high buildings. It's a little like being in an airplane. With the river right under our windows I can imagine I'm flying over water."

There was a soft knock at the door Nancy looked around inquiringly. "The X-ray?" He shook his head. He went to the door and opened it.

"It's your friend Miss Hudson."

"Hi, Marge," Nancy called. "Come on in."

THE stocky, sandy-haired girl hung in the doorway. "I'll stay out here," she said. "I thought we could go home together though."

"Darling, how nice of you. But I'll be a bit longer, I'm afraid."

"That's all right. How are you feeling, Nancy?"

"Wonderful, dear. Especially now that your doctor has taken a picture that'll show him what's inside this bump of mine."

"Well, I'll be out here," the other girl said and turned back into the waiting room. She passed a woman in white who came in, shut the door, and handed the doctor a large, brown envelope.

He turned to Nancy. "I'll look at this and be back right away."

"Dr. Myers is on the phone," the nurse told him as they started out. "Wants to know about tonight. Can he come here and drive over with you?"

"How soon can he get here?"

"About half an hour, he says."

"Tell him that will be fine, Miss Snyder." The door closed behind them. Nancy sat still for perhaps two minutes. Then she jerked, as if at a twinge of pain. She looked at her ankle. Bending over, she clasped her hand around her good ankle and squeezed experimentally. She shuddered.

The door banged open. Dr. Ballard hurried in and immediately began to re-examine the swelling, swiftly exploring each detail of its outlines with gentle fingers, at the same time firing questions.

"Are you absolutely sure, Miss Sawyer, that you hadn't noticed anything of this swelling before last night? Perhaps just some slight change in shape or feeling, or a tendency to favor that ankle, or just a disinclination to look at it? Cast your mind back."

Nancy hesitated uneasily, but when she spoke it was with certainty. "No, I'm absolutely sure."

He shook his head. "Very well. And now, Miss Sawyer, that twin of yours. Was she identical?"

Nancy looked at him. "Why are you interested in that? Doctor, what does the X-ray show?"

"I have a very good reason, which I'll explain to you later. I'll go into details about the X-ray then, too. You can set your mind at rest on one point, though, if it's been worrying you. This swelling is in no sense malignant."

"Thank goodness, Doctor."

"But now about the twin."

"You really want to know?"

"I do."

Nancy's manner and voice showed some signs of agitation. "Why, yes," she said, "we were identical. People were always mistaking us for each other. We looked exactly alike, but underneath…" Her voice trailed off. There was a change in the atmosphere of the office, a change hard to define. Abruptly she continued, "Dr. Ballard, I'd like to tell you about her, tell you things I've hardly told anyone else. You know, it was she I was dreaming about last night. In fact, I thought it was she who had grabbed me in my nightmare. What's the matter, Dr. Ballard?"

IT DID seem that Dr. Ballard had changed color, though it was hard to tell in the failing light. What he said, a little jerkily, was, "Nothing, Miss Sawyer. Please go ahead." He leaned forward a little, resting his elbows on the desk, and watched her.

"You know, Dr. Ballard," she began slowly, "most people think that twins are very affectionate. They think stories of twins hating each other are invented by writers looking for morbid plots.

"But in my case the morbid plot happened to be the simple truth. Beth tyrannized over me, hated me, and…wasn't above expressing her hate in a physical way." She took a deep breath.

"It started when we were little girls. As far back as I can remember, I was always the slave and she was the mistress. And if I didn't carry out her orders faithfully, and sometimes if I did, there was always a slap or a pinch. Not a little-girl pinch. Beth had peculiarly strong fingers. I was very afraid of them.

"There's something terrible, Dr. Ballard, about the way one human being can intimidate another, crush their will power, reduce to mush their ability to fight back. You'd think the victim could escape so easily—look, there are people all around, teachers and friends to confide in, your father and mother—but it's as if you were bound by invisible chains, your mouth shut by an invisible gag. And it grows and grows, like the horrors of a concentration camp. A whole inner world of pain and fright. And yet on the surface—why, there seems to be nothing at all.

"For of course no one else had the faintest idea of what was going on between us. Everyone thought we loved each other very much. Beth especially was always being praised for her 'sunny gayety.' I was supposed to be a little 'subdued.' Oh, how she used to fuss and coo over me when there were people around. Though even then there would be pinches on the sly—hard ones I never winced at. And more than that, for…"

Nancy broke off. "But I really don't think I should be wasting your time with all these childhood gripes, Dr. Ballard. Especially since I know you have an engagement for this evening."

"That's just an informal dinner with a few old cronies. I have lots of time. Go right ahead. I'm interested."

NANCY paused, frowning a little. "The funny thing is," she continued, "I never understood why Beth hated me. It was as if she were intensely jealous. Yet there was no reason for that. She was the successful one, the one who won the prizes and played the leads in the school shows and got the nicest presents and all the boys. But somehow each success made her worse. I've sometimes thought, Dr. Ballard, that only cruel people can be successful, that success is really a reward for cruelty…to someone."

Dr. Ballard knit his brows, might have nodded.

"The only thing I ever read that helped explain it to me," she went on, "was something in psychoanalysis. The idea that each of us has an equal dose of love and hate, and that it's our business to balance them off, to act in such a way that both have expression and yet so that the hate is always under the control of the love.

"But perhaps when the two people are very close together, as it is with twins, the balancing works out differently. Perhaps all the softness and love begins to gather in the one person and all the hardness and hate in the other. And then the hate lakes the lead, because it's an emotion of violence and power and action—a concentrated emotion, not misty like love. And it keeps on and on, getting worse all the time, until it's so strong you feel it will never stop, not even with death.

"For it did keep on, Dr. Ballard, and it did get worse." Nancy looked at him closely. "Oh, I know that what I've been telling you isn't supposed to be so unusual among children. 'Little barbarians,' people say, quite confident that they'll outgrow it. Quite convinced that wrist-twisting and pinching are things that will automatically stop when children begin to grow up."

Nancy smiled thinly at him. "Well, they don't stop, Dr. Ballard. You know, it's very hard for most people to associate actual cruelty with an adolescent girl, maybe because of the way girls have been glorified in advertising. Yet I could write you a pretty chapter on just that topic. Of course a lot of it that happened in my case was what you'd call mental cruelty. I was shy and Beth had a hundred ways of embarrassing me. And if a boy became interested in me, she'd always take him way."

"I'd hardly have thought she'd have been able to," remarked Dr. Ballard.

"You think I'm good-looking? But I'm only good-looking in an odd way, and in any case it never seemed to count then. It's true, though, that twice there were boys who wouldn't respond to her invitations. Then both times she played a trick that only she could, because we were identical twins. She would pretend to be me—she could always imitate my manner and voice, even my reactions, precisely, though I couldn't possibly have imitated her—and then she would...do something that would make the boy drop me cold."

"Do something?"

Nancy looked down. "Oh, insult the boy cruelly, pretending to be me. Or else make some foul, boastful confession, pretending it was mine. If you knew how those boys loathed me afterwards...

"But as I said, it wasn't only mental cruelty or indecent tricks. I remember nights when I'd done something to displease her and I'd gone to bed before her and she'd come in and I'd pretend to be asleep and after a while she'd say—oh, I know, Dr. Ballard, it sounds like something a silly little girl would say, but it didn't sound like that then, with my head under the sheet, pressed into the pillow, and her footsteps moving slowly around the bed—she'd say, 'I'm thinking of how to punish you.' And then there'd be a long wait, while I still pretended to be asleep, and then the touch...oh, Dr. Ballard, her hands! I was so afraid of her hands! But...what is it, Dr. Ballard?"

"Nothing. Go on."

"There's nothing much more to say. Except that Beth's cruelty and my fear went on until a year ago, when she died suddenly—I suppose you'd say tragically—of a blood clot on the brain. I've often wondered since then whether her hatred of me, so long and so cleverly concealed, mightn't have had something to do with it. Apoplexy's what haters die of, isn't it, doctor?

"I REMEMBER leaning over her bed the day she died, lying there paralyzed, with her beautiful face white and stiff as a fish's, one eye bigger than the other. I felt pity for her (You realize, doctor, don't you, that I always loved her?) but just then her hand flopped a little way across the blanket and touched mine, although they said she was completely paralyzed, and her big eye twitched around a little until it was looking almost at me and her lips moved and I thought I heard her say, 'I'll come back and punish you for this,' and then I felt her fingers moving, just a little, on my skin, as if they were trying to close on my wrist, and I jerked back with a cry.

"Mother was very angry with me for that. She thought I was just a selfish, thoughtless girl, afraid of death and unable to repress my fear even for my dying sister's sake. Of course I could never tell her the real reason. I've never really told that to anyone, except you. And now that I've told you I hardly know why I've done it."

She smiled nervously, quite unhumorously.

"Wasn't there something about a dream you had last night?" Dr. Ballard asked softly.

"Oh yes!" The listlessness snapped out of her. "I dreamed I was walking in an old graveyard with gnarly gray trees, and overhead the sky was gray and low and threatening, and everything was weird and dreadful. But somehow I was very happy. But then I felt a faint movement under my feet and I looked down at the grave I was passing and I saw the earth falling away into it. Just a little cone-shaped pit at first, with the dark sandy earth sliding down its sides, and a small black hole at the bottom. I knew I must run away quickly, but I couldn't move an inch. Then the pit grew larger and the earth tumbled down its sides in chunks and the black hole grew. And still I was rooted there. I looked at the gravestone beyond and it said 'Elizabeth Sawyer, 1926-48.' Then out of the hole came a hand and arm, only there were just shreds of dark flesh clinging to the bone, and it began to feel around with an awful, snatching swiftness. Then suddenly the earth heaved and opened, and a figure came swiftly hitching itself up out of the hole. And although the flesh was green and shrunken and eaten and the eyes just holes, I recognized Beth—there was still the beautiful reddish hair. And then the ragged hand touched my ankle and instantly closed on it and the other hand came groping upward, higher, higher, and I screamed…and then I woke up."

NANCY was leaning forward, her eyes fixed on the doctor. Suddenly her hair seemed to bush out, just a trifle. Perhaps it had "stood on end." At any rate, she said, "Dr. Ballard, I'm frightened."

"I'm sorry if I've made you distress yourself," he said. The words were more reassuring than the tone of voice. He suddenly took her hand in his and for a few moments they sat there silently. Then she smiled and moved a little and said, "It's gone now. I've been very silly. I don't know why I told you all I did about Beth. It couldn't help you with my ankle."

"No, of course not," he said after a moment.

"Why did you ask if she was identical?"

He leaned back. His voice became brisker again. "I'll tell you about that right now—and about what the X-ray shows. I think there's a connection. As you probably know, Miss Sawyer, identical twins look so nearly alike because they come from the same germ cell. Before it starts to develop, it splits in two. Instead of one individual, two develop. That was what happened in the case of you and your sister." He paused. "But," he continued, "sometimes, especially if there's a strong tendency to twin births in the family, the splitting doesn't stop there. One of the two cells splits again. The result—triplets. I believe that also happened in your case."

Nancy looked at him puzzledly. "But then what happened to the third child?"

"The third sister," he amplified. "There can't be identical boy-and-girl twins or triplets, you know, since sex is determined in the original germ cell. There, Miss Sawyer, we come to my second point. Not all twins develop and are actually born. Some start to develop and then stop."

"What happens to them?"

"Sometimes what there is of them is engulfed in the child that does develop completely—little fragments of a body, bits of this and that, all buried in the flesh of the child that is actually born. I think that happened in your case."

Nancy looked at him oddly. "You mean I have in me bits of another twin sister, a triplet sister, who didn't develop?"

"Exactly."

"And that all this is connected with my ankle?"

"Yes."

"But then how——?"

"Sometimes nothing happens to the engulfed fragments. But sometimes, perhaps many years later, they begin to grow—in a natural way rather than malignantly. There are well-authenticated cases of this happening—as recently as 1890 a Mexican boy in this way 'gave birth' to his own twin brother, completely developed though of course dead. There's nothing nearly as extensive as that in your case, but I'm sure there is a pocket of engulfed materials around your ankle and that it recently started to grow, so gradually that you didn't notice it until the growth became so extensive as to be irritating."

Nancy eyed him closely. "What sort of materials? I mean the engulfed fragments."

HE HESITATED. "I'm not quite sure," he said. "The X-ray was...oh, such things are apt to be odd, though harmless stuff— teeth, hair, nails, you never can tell. We'll know better later."

"Could I see the X-ray?"

He hesitated again. "I'm afraid it wouldn't mean anything to you. Just a lot of shadows."

"Could there be...other pockets of fragments?"

"It's not likely. And if there are, it's improbable they'll ever bother you."

There was a pause.

Nancy said, "I don't like it."

"I don't like it," she repeated. "It's as if Beth had come back. Inside me."

"The fragments have no connection with your dead sister," Dr. Ballard assured her. "They're not part of Beth, but of a third sister, if you can call such fragments a person."

"But those fragments only began to grow after Beth died. As if Beth's soul... And was it my original cell that split a second time?—or was it Beth's?—so that it was the fragments of half her cell that I absorbed, so that..." She stopped. "I'm afraid I'm being silly again."

He looked at her for a while, then with the air of someone snapping to attention, quickly nodded.

"But doctor," she said, also like someone snatching at practicality, "what's to happen now?"

"Well," he replied, "in order to get rid of this disfigurement to your ankle, a relatively minor operation will be necessary. You see, this sort of foreign body can't be reduced in size by heat or X-ray or injections. Surgery is needed, though probably only under local anesthetic. Could you arrange to enter a hospital tomorrow? Then I could operate the next morning. You' d have to stay about four days."

She thought for a moment, then said, "Yes, I think I could manage that." She looked distastefully at her ankle. "In fact, I'd like to do it as soon as possible."

"Good. We'll ask Miss Snyder to arrange things."

When the nurse entered, she said, "Dr. Myers is outside."

"Tell him I'll be right along," Dr. Ballard said. "And then I'd like you to call Central Hospital. Miss Sawyer will take the reservation we got for Mrs. Phipps and were about to cancel." And they discussed details while Nancy pulled on stocking and shoe.

Nancy said goodbye and started for the waiting room, favoring her bad leg. Dr. Ballard watched her. The nurse opened the door. Beyond, Nancy's friend got up with a smile. There was now, besides her, a dark, oldish man in the waiting room.

As the nurse was about to close the door, Dr. Ballard said, "Miss Sawyer."

She turned. "Yes?"

"If your ankle should start to trouble you tonight—or anything else—please call me."

"Thank you, doctor, I will."

Dr. Ballard nodded. Then he called to his friend, "Be right with you." The dark, oldish man flapped an arm at him.

The door closed. Dr. Ballard went to his desk, took an X-ray photograph out of its brown envelope, switched on the light, studied the photograph incredulously.

He put it back in its envelope and on the desk. He got his hat and overcoat from the closet. He turned out the light. Then suddenly he went back and got the envelope, stuffed it in his pocket, and went out.

THE dinner with Dr. Myers and three other old professional friends proved if anything more enjoyable than Dr. Ballard had anticipated. It led to relaxation, gossip, a leisurely evening stroll, a drink together, a few final yarns. At one point Dr. Ballard felt a fleeting impulse to get the X-ray out of his overcoat pocket and show it to them and tell his little yarn about it, but something made him hesitate, and he forgot the idea. He felt very easy in his mind as he drove home about midnight. He even hummed a little. This mood was not disturbed until he saw the face of Miss Willis, his resident secretary.

"What is it?" he asked crisply.

"Miss Nancy Sawyer. She..." For once the imperturbable, graying blonde seemed to have difficulty speaking.

"Yes?"

"She called up first about an hour and a half ago."

"Her ankle had begun to pain her?"

"She didn't say anything about her ankle. She said she was getting a sore throat."

"What?"

"It seemed unimportant to me, too, though of course I told her I'd inform you when you got in. But she seemed rather frightened, kept complaining of this tightness she felt in her throat..."

"Yes? Yes?"

"So I agreed to get in touch with you immediately. She hung up. I called the restaurant, but you'd just left. Then I called Dr.

Myers' home, but didn't get any answer. I told the operator to keep trying.

"About a half hour ago Miss Sawyer's friend, a Marge Hudson, called. She said Miss Sawyer had gone to bed and was apparently asleep, but she didn't like the way she was tossing around, as if she were having a particularly bad dream, and especially she didn't like the noises she was making in her throat, as if she were having difficulty breathing. She said she had looked closely at Miss Sawyer's throat as she lay sleeping, and it seemed swollen. I told her I was making every effort to get in touch with you and we left it at that."

"That wasn't all?"

"No." Miss Willis' agitation returned. "Just two minutes before you arrived, the phone rang again. At first the line seemed to be dead. I was about to hang up. Then, I began to hear a clicking, gargling sound. Low at first, but then it grew louder. Then suddenly it broke free and whooped out in what I think was Miss Sawyer's voice. There were only two words, I think, but I couldn't catch them because they were so loud they stopped the phone. After that, nothing, although I listened and listened and kept saying 'hello' over and over. But Dr. Ballard, that gargling sound! It was as if I were listening to someone being strangled, very slowly, very, very..."

But Dr. Ballard had grabbed up his surgical bag and was racing for his car. He drove rather well for a doctor and, tonight, very fast. He was about three blocks from the river when he heard a siren, ahead of him.

NANCY SAWYER'S apartment-hotel was at the end of a short street terminated by a high concrete curb and metal fence and, directly below, the river. Now there was a fire engine drawn up to the fence and playing a searchlight down over the edge through the faintly misty air. Dr. Ballard could see a couple of figures in shiny black coats beside the searchlight. As he jumped out of his car he could hear shouts and what sounded like the motor of a launch. He hesitated for a moment, then ran into the hotel.

The lobby was empty. There was no one behind the counter. He ran to the open elevator. It was an automatic. He punched the twenty-three button.

On that floor there was one open door in the short corridor. Marge Hudson met him inside it.

"She jumped?"

The girl nodded. "They're hunting for her body I've been watching. Come on."

She led him to a dark bedroom. There was a studio couch, its covers disordered, and beside it a phone. River air was pouring in through a large, hinged window, open wide. They went to it and looked down. The circling launch looked like a toy boat. Its searchlight and that from the fire engine roved across the dark water. Shouts and chugging came up faintly.

"How did it happen?" he asked the girl at the window.

"I was watching her as she lay in bed," Marge Hudson answered without looking around. "About twenty minutes after I called your home, she seemed to be getting worse. She had more trouble breathing. I tried to wake her, but couldn't. I went to the kitchen to make an ice pack. It took longer than I'd thought. I heard a noise that at first I didn't connect with Nancy. Then I realized that she was strangling. I rushed back. Just then she screamed out horribly. I heard something fall—I think it was the phone—and footsteps and the window opening. When I came in she was standing on the sill in her nightdress, clawing at her throat. Before I could get to her, she jumped."

"Earlier in the evening she'd complained of a sore throat?"

"Yes. She said, jokingly, that the trouble with her ankle must be spreading to her throat. After she called your home and couldn't get you, she took some aspirin and went to bed."

Dr. Ballard switched on the lamp by the bed. He pulled the brown envelope from his coat pocket, took out the X-ray and held it up against the light.

"You say she screamed at the end," he said in a not very steady voice. "Were there any definite words?"

The girl at the window hesitated. "I'm not sure," she said slowly. "They were suddenly choked off, exactly as if a hand had

106

tightened around her throat. But I think there were two words. 'Hand' and 'Beth.'"

Dr. Ballard's gaze flickered toward the mocking face in the photograph on the chest of drawers, then back to the ghostly black and whites of the one in his hands. His arms were shaking.

"They haven't found her yet," Marge said, still looking down at the river and the circling launch.

Dr. Ballard was staring incredulously at the X-ray, as if by staring he could make what he saw go away. But that was impossible. It was a perfectly defined and unambiguous exposure.

There, in the X-ray's blacks and grays, he could see the bones of Nancy Sawyer's ankle and, tightly clenched around them, deep under skin and flesh, the slender bones of a human hand.

THE END

ON THE MOUNTAIN

By Dave Mayo

An old-fashioned ghost story... but one that still can send a shiver down the spine.

A TRAVELER shifted the weight of his pack and hiked along the barren mountain path. It was wide enough for only one man, and he knew that farther along there would be no path at all. Here it left the straight, gentle incline and began to take a weaving course, finding its way along ledges and threading itself between rock formations. Hundreds of feet behind him, the path trailed into the valley, became a road, and somewhere found the town that the traveler had left days before. It was lost in the mountain range now, and he stopped to plot his distance from the next village. Almost the entire region, thousands of square miles of hills and mountains, was charted, thanks to forty years of exploration. He found his position on the map. Eighteen years earlier, a Major Vernon Groves and his party of four had conquered this peak. Although Major Groves had been lost in an avalanche during the study, the group's findings had led to the establishment of practical routes over and around the mountain, as well as several that were now dangerously inadequate and therefore abandoned.

But now the mountain was safe. The traveler tucked the map between his light parka and the heavy coat that he wore over it; then he continued his hike.

* * *

Two days later, he was sitting in his small, weatherworn tent while a blizzard piled snow against its windward side. The trail had tapered away long ago, and in the snowstorm he had lost the route entirely and wandered into a no-man's land before pitching camp. Near his tent was a short segment of path leading up the mountainside, but it was nothing he had seen before and apparently was not a re-birth of the main trail. He passed the time inside, reading a twelve day-old newspaper.

That night, the blizzard began to show vague signs of letting up. Perhaps by morning the traveler would be able to set out again and find his way back to the charted route. He lighted his small portable stove in preparation for the long night ahead. Then, with his feet wrapped in a heavy blanket, he huddled by the stove and waited.

Hours passed. He dozed occasionally but never for long because of the wind that whipped through the flapless open end of the old tent. He finally reconciled himself to watching and listening to the storm.

Shortly after midnight, he was startled by what he saw. Through the snow and darkness that stretched between him and the mountain's upper slopes, a small red light flickered faintly, disappeared, and flickered again. Soon it grew stronger and steadier. It became a sharp dot that remained still on the mountainside and seemed to study the small, battered tent. The traveler felt his flesh begin to tingle as he watched it. Who could be on the mountainside with him? He thought of the three days' journey up the mountainside and of the miles that separated him from the last human being he had seen. He thought of the desolate mountains that surrounded him: the trap of solitude that he had set for himself. There was a revolver in his pack, but he knew that he had no dry ammunition. He held his breath and waited. The red light kept its position for several minutes. Then it moved. It began to advance down the mountainside toward the tent. The traveler impulsively clenched a portion of his coat in one fist and recoiled into the corner of the tent. The light was definitely approaching. It never rose or wavered, but progressed steadily over the rocks. The traveler's face was contorted with fear; the sudden, mysterious danger was quickly beginning to prey on his sanity. He watched it come and he thought again of his isolation. There could be no one else on the mountain—no one who could glide across boulders and crevices in a blizzard. The light pressed on. He gripped a knuckle tightly between his teeth. On came the light, the unearthly red light. It was too close. He leaped to his feet and burst out of the tent; he dashed up the mountainside, stumbling and picking himself up as he went. The snow blew straight into his face, but he ran on, following the path as far as it could take him and then clambering madly over the rocks.

AT a sheltered ledge 20 yards above the path, his knees buckled and he unwillingly sank to the ground; now he was at the mercy of the red beast. He was gasping and coughing and was barely conscious when he heard a faint rumbling sound in the distance. Then scattered showers of gravel and snow began to fall from the overhanging cliff and there was a growing vibration in the stone around him. An avalanche was coming. He pulled himself as close as possible to the cliff and waited; the rumbling grew louder until it became a roar and the sturdy ledge trembled. A moment later, tons of snow and rock careened off the cliff in a dense curtain; it crashed past the ledge and out of sight, leaving only a fine white spray that hung in the air for a few seconds and then settled. The blizzard itself was tapering off. When the noise had faded into the distance, the traveler propped one shoulder against the cliff and waited, but he saw no more of the strange red light. After several minutes, he closed his eyes and slept.

* * *

Dawn was breaking when he awoke; he had been asleep only a few hours. The shelter and warmth of the overhanging cliff had kept him from freezing during that time, and now the sun was rising. He rubbed most of the numbness out of his flesh and stretched his muscles. Then he stood at the edge of the shelf and looked down on the rubble that lay in the wake of be avalanche. His former campsite—tent, gun, stove, and everything else—was gone, either buried or swept away. The strange red light had saved him.

Since he had no gear to pack or camp to break, he made his way off the ledge and immediately began climbing; he could not afford to spend another night in the snow. The mountain was not a high one and was not unusually rough; the remaining hike to the top would have been almost a day's trip with the burden of a pack, but he was able to make it in considerably less time.

As he stepped onto the uppermost level, he got his first look at the shorter, gentler side of the mountain. A village lay at its foot, within several hours' descent, and others were scattered throughout the long valley. This was the road back to civilization.

The traveler was about to start down from the windy peak when he noticed a weathered inscription in the stone. He stooped to read it. Although the lettering was nearly worn away, he was able to read the words: "Memorial. Major V. L. Groves." And nearby, nailed firmly into the rock with two spikes, was a rusty lantern with a red shield.

As a reflex, he spun and faced the rubble of the avalanche. "Major Groves!" he called. But of course there was no answer. It had been eighteen years.

THE END

MIRRORS OF MADNESS

By Don Wilcox

It seemed a mad thing when Buffler had his offices transformed into a maze of mirrors. But he had a sinister motive.

THE elevator reached the top floor of the Buffler Tower, my Uncle Jonathan Buffler's skyscraper, and I stepped out. I had come at the urgent and mysterious request of my uncle's doctor, Merrill Ramsell.

"What the devil—!" I gasped as my eyes swept the octagonal hallway.

I whirled to the elevator boy for an explanation, but he only shrugged his shoulders and went down. My eyes turned back to the walls that faced me. Each wall was a mirror, and each mirror turned gently from side to side on a vertical axis. In each mirror was a reflection of me, facing myself with a dizzy expression, swaying back and forth like a clown on a tight rope.

I glanced at my multiple self once more to make sure my several suits of new college-cut clothes were right for this momentous visit, and then struck off down the narrow avenue of mirrors. Dr. Ramsell had advised me to see him first.

In a cluttered office heaped with books and walled with medicines I met Dr. Ramsell. First I saw a pair of black slender shoes propped on a corner of the table; next, the thin grayish fingers that held a massive black book with bold white letters on the cover, "Schizophrenia." *

----

*Schizophrenia—A form of mental derangement, characterized by the simultaneous presence in the mind of contradictory ideas, resulting in inaction or the simulating of qualities which one does not possess.—Ed.

Up from behind the book came a high bald head and a yellowish white face, with a sharp thin nose and spectacled eyes that shone black and lively.

"I'm Dr. Ramsell," he said in a good voice that was much younger than his face.

"I'm Jim Olin, Buffler's great-nephew," I said. "You wired for me to come."

"Yes." He put the book down solidly and shook hands with me. "I sent for you on my own initiative. You needn't tell your uncle. He'll think you've just dropped in of your own accord. He may be glad to see you. I say *may* because I've found he's never predictable.

"But you, as one of the few inheritors to his fortune, should have a personal interest in his welfare while he lives. Maybe you can do him some good—both mentally and physically. Frankly, I'm getting nowhere. He insists on keeping me, but he resents my efforts to probe into his case."

"Is there something seriously wrong with him?" I asked.

"Has anything ever been right with him?" the doctor retorted, tapping his thin fingers nervously along the white letters of the word "Schizophrenia."

I turned his question over in my mind and didn't find any very positive answer. I had never had many contacts with Uncle Jonathan Buffler. Several years had passed since I had last seen him.

"He's made his wad of money," I answered. "I've heard that he imports the finest oriental rugs in the world, and that his own rug designs are tops. I always supposed he was a sort of genius."

"There. *That's* fine," Doctor Ramsell exclaimed. "Run right in and give him the glad hand, and make him out to be as wonderful as you can. It won't do any harm. Maybe you'll get next to him if you're willing to stay a few days."

"He'll be surprised. He doesn't know I'm coming—"

"Never mind that. You're his great-nephew and you've come to visit for a week or so. Mind you, not a word about me. I'll talk with you later."

I WALKED on down the hallway chuckling to myself. Likely as not Jonathan Buffler was up to something freakish, if harmless, that had set this doctor to worrying.

I recalled that Buffler used to dismay Aunt Mary by climbing up on a stepladder to throw pieces of colored cardboard down on the drawing room floor. Then he would study the effect, and if it pleased him he would have his artists copy the design for a rug.

But usually he would try for hours without getting any but the most terrible results, and his poor wife would be driven to a nervous frenzy.

Before I reached Uncle Jonathan's office I was almost in a nervous frenzy myself. The wobbling mirrors all along the hallway were, to put it mildly, disconcerting. On each side of me were regiments of myself walking abreast—not steadily, but wavering and trembling and jumping and jittery.

"Mr. Buffler—er—Uncle Jonathan?"

The large corner office was semi-dark. The mahogany Venetian blinds were nearly closed, admitting only a few hairline strips of reddish forenoon light that jumped capriciously from one swaying mirror to another.

The one person in the room sat behind the huge mahogany desk, which angled across the corner. From his humpty-dumpty silhouette, I knew that person was Jonathan Buffler. His pear-shaped head and round shoulders gave a startled jerk at the sound of my voice, and his shadowed face glared at me.

"I'm Jim Olin," I said. "I've dropped in for a visit."

Buffler's thick lips twisted into a scowl, but before he had time to snarl aloud one of his telephones rang. To my surprise his voice, which was naturally guttural, sounded off creamily.

"Yes, Jewel, this is Johnny…" His head turned so that I couldn't see his face. "I was just about to call you to say 'good morning'…Yes…Yes…But I did call you twice, only you hadn't come yet, Jewel…Angry? Of course not, Jewel…I know you were out late last night, Jewel—but you were in good company…Ha-ha-ha I…But you'd better get to work now…Those orders, you know…But I'm still your boss, you know…No, Jewel, I really didn't mean that—"

I should have walked out on this custardy talk if I hadn't been so stunned by it. There was something arresting in witnessing this bulbous, heavy-jowled man, owner of a skyscraper and head of a wealthy importing business, talk in such a lovey-dovey manner—and obviously he was enjoying himself.

Once he interrupted himself to mutter, "Damn that light!" and jerked the Venetian blind cord to cut off the lines of red light that played over his telephone hand.

Jewel, whoever she was, evidently knew exactly what to say to put him in a cheerful mood. But the conversation struck an uneasy note before it ended.

"But Jewel, don't you pay any attention to old Drizzlepuss. We're not going to let *her* stand in the way of our happiness…Yeah, why *don't* I fire her! We've been over all that before. But *just you wait*—"

Here he broke off abruptly, as if suddenly remembering that I was present.

"I'll talk with you later, Jewel. Don't forget tonight."

HE hung up and turned his eyes on me glowingly.

"That was Jewel, my Number Two secretary," he said. "Nice girl. Splendid girl…M-m-m-m—where were we? Oh, yes. You're Jim Olin. How are you? Sit down over here and tell me all about yourself."

I took him at his word. He lit a cigar and laid his head back in a listening attitude while I gave him a brief account of myself—how I had quit college and taken up a job that involved some foreign travel. He blew smoke so blissfully that I was sure his mind was still on Jewel.

I concluded my monologue with, "So I just thought I'd drop in for a few days' visit with you and Aunt Mary."

He removed the cigar with startled suddenness and shot a cold glance at me. By this time my eyes were accustomed to the dim light. There was something chilling in the glare of his protruding white eyeballs. The glare also came from eight or ten different mirrors. These, like the mirrors in the hallways, were tilting back and forth, slowly but incessantly, as if the very breathing of Jonathan Buffler made them restless.

"Light ever bother you?" Buffler asked abruptly. In the walls of mirrors the white glaring eyeballs continued to swing through gentle arcs.

"Sometimes," I said. "White light, especially."

The answer pleased him. "Excessive light is very bad for the eyes," he said authoritatively.

"Very," I said, certain that I was on the track of his friendship.

"You've noticed it?"

"Often."

"Many people suffer from too much light and don't know what's wrong. With me, the suffering amounts to Illness. A tangle of light vibrations torments me. But that damned doctor of mine, you can't tell him anything. No matter how I suffer, he just shrugs his shoulders."

By this time I had settled back in the red leather chair—but not comfortably. The mirrors were too disturbing. Even the ceiling was alive with moving mirrors—four circular ones, each with inverted Jonathan Bufflers rocking back and forth over my head. I began to feel seasick.

Tightly stretched cords were visible here and there between the mirror frames, and silent little electric motors tucked around in obscure corners tugged at the cords to give the mirrors their tireless motion.

"A sort of interesting place you've got here," I ventured noncommittally.

"I like it."

"Plenty of mirrors all around."

"As far as they go. But I'm having more installed in some of the other offices. They're a great scheme to reduce the tangle of light vibrations your eyes have to contend with."

"Tangle?" I asked. He had used that term before.

"And *what* a tangle! What a helluva tangle!"

He moved his chair closer to me, as if to confide something dear to his heart.

"I'm telling you, Olin, when you stop to figure it out mathematically, it's enough to drive you mad. The way light waves crisscross—"

He paused to answer a telephone. "New rugs to inspect?" His voice was all business. "Never mind, I'll get to them later. I'm in conference...No, I'm not to be disturbed!"

BUFFLER hung up and resumed his confidential manner.

"See here, Olin, when you examine the facts, you suddenly wake up and realize the truth. Light is the most confusing thing in the world. It's man's deadly enemy. It stabs him from all directions. It's merciless. Every second it bombards his most sensitive organs, the eyes. Undoubtedly it causes half the world's fatigue. Maybe three-fourths. I've got some mathematicians at work on that. Look, I'll show you..."

His plump hand reached for a desk pen filled with white ink, and he made a tiny white dot on a scratch pad of brilliant purple.

"Now you take a simple point of light," he said, "the finest point you can imagine. It's shooting into your eye at the rate of one hundred and eighty-six thousand miles a second, isn't it?"

"I suppose it is."

"You *know* it is. Oh, they may dope out some variations, but that figure is close enough. In other words"—he tapped me on the knee—"for every full second you look at a tiny white point, how much light does it poke into your eyes? A hundred and eighty-six thousand miles of it! In *one* second."

I grunted helplessly and decided this lecture had gone far enough. I was getting seasick or light-sick or Jonathan-Buffler-sick, I wasn't sure which.

"Pardon me, Uncle—"

"Wait, here's the point," Buffler commanded, tapping white ink dots on the purple paper. "Every smidget of white light from a rough surface, like this paper, diffuses in a million directions. Look, I make rugs—"

Here he rose and tossed a colorful oriental rug sample onto the desk. The sample was a foot square, with hundreds of silky threads stringing out from every edge.

"I make *big* rugs." He filled his humpty-dumpty frame with a proud breath. "Big rugs that contain thousands and millions of colored fibers woven together. *But*—the most intricate rug ever made is *simple* compared to the tangle of light waves that comes from these few white dots. Now, do you get it?"

"Yes," I said, "but I'd better—"

"No, you don't get it," he said in a wise and patient manner. "The point is that these mirrors cut down the tangle to something simpler. They don't diffuse. They reflect the light directly. Oh, it's still complicated enough to drive the average person distracted, but at least it's *some* simpler."

"It's the darned wobbling of those mirrors that drives *me* distracted," I said.

Buffler drew back in horror, and I realized too late that I must have crushed his pet idea to the earth.

"I'm surprised, Olin," he said in quiet injured tones. "You're as bad as my office help. *You'd* rather have shafts of light burning into your eyes from a single direction. Not *me!* I learned my lesson from the rolling seas, from racetracks, from movies, from prizefights. Our eyes hate monotony. They love motion—action—rhythm. But how can you have it in an office? I have found the answer: moving mirrors."

"I'm sorry," I apologized. "I didn't realize—"

"*You* may not appreciate my discovery. The doctor doesn't. Old Drizzlepuss Becker doesn't, nor the rest of them. But *Jewel—*" His harsh voice softened.

"Pardon me, Uncle Jonathan," I said, walking determinedly to the row of telephones, "but I must call Aunt Mary and tell her I'm here."

AGAIN the quick glare of those two protruding white eyeballs shot at me from a score of mirrors.

"Your Aunt Mary is dead," Buffler snapped.

"Dead? Since when?"

"Nearly a year ago." He tapped his puffy fingers nervously. "Heart failure. I supposed you knew."

I apologized for not keeping in closer touch with family happenings and expressed my sympathies as best I could. But plainly he was impatient to get on with his discussion.

"About these light waves," he resumed. "I've bought some new calculating machines and hired some mathematicians—"

An office boy interrupted with a message from a mirror salesman.

"He's in the lobby waiting for the order you promised him for today."

"Good," said Buffler. "Tell him I'll be ready in a few minutes."

The boy went, and Buffler picked up a telephone.

"Drizzlepuss?" he growled. "Come in and pick out your mirrors…I don't give a damn what you want or don't want. I'm putting tinted mirrors in your office. If you want to pick the tint, come in."

The receiver clicked down and an instant later "Drizzlepuss" stormed in. She was tall and angular and thoroughly belligerent. Her black eyes snapped and her thin nostrils flared.

"Buffler, if you call me Drizzlepuss again—"

"You'll what?" Buffler snarled.

"I'll *expose* you! That's what I'll—"

"*Shut up, dammit!*"

The high-pitched rage in Buffler's voice must have made her realize that someone else was in the room. She caught me in the corner of her eye and for an instant she froze. Then she reached out and jerked the cord to a Venetian blind.

"Why don't you get some light in here?"

She made the rounds of the windows and the noon light blazed in. Buffler's eyes narrowed and I expected him to blow into an explosion of fury. But he didn't. He turned to me calmly.

"This is Becker, my Number One secretary," he said, and with rankling sarcasm added, "a pleasant little person. Becker, my great-nephew, Jim Olin. Now, Drizzlepuss, about these tinted mirrors for your office—"

I ducked out and strode down the corridor to find the doctor. It was high time he and I had a confidential talk.

CHAPTER TWO
Jonathan's Jewel

REENTERING Dr. Ramsell's room, I carefully closed the door behind me.

"All right, Doctor, I've seen him," I said. "I'll admit he gave me plenty of pains I couldn't locate. What does it all add up to?"

"Maybe murder," said the doctor enigmatically, without looking up. "Maybe insanity. I'll discuss it with you shortly."

He remained engrossed in a book for several minutes. I sauntered to an open window and I looked down toward the wealthy residential section of the city.

From this height I could pick the Buffler estate in the bend of the river that passed the edge of the city. The red tile roof of the mansion, almost two miles distant, stood out distinctively from this vantage.

"Come," said the doctor. "We'll go to lunch and thrash this thing over. Oh, by the way, here's an interesting volume on symbolism."

From his numerous books dealing with different types of psychoses, he picked up one and opened it to a picture—a reproduction of an Intricate pen and ink drawing.

"A bit of art done by a patient at a mental hospital," he said.

I studied the picture and praised it. It was a Spanish market scene with a wealth of carefully etched detail. But not until the doctor pointed it out did I see the skull cunningly hidden among the shade-covered cobblestones. Then I saw the mark of the Spanish Loyalist that adorned the skull.

"The artist," said Dr. Ramsell, "went to infinite pains to draw that picture, just so he could plant that one symbol. His particular mental disorder happens to be based on a fear of his enemies. His fight against the Rebels came to a bitter defeat, and he saw many of his comrades shot down. But here he gets a secret feeling of victory out of representing his enemy as a death's-head being trodden underfoot."

"An elaborate lot of art for one small trick," I commented.

"Exactly. That's a curious but typical thing about many such cases," the doctor mused. "Incidentally, Jonathan Buffler's mirrors are a pretty elaborate lot of art, too. I only hope they may serve as a safety valve, in his case."

We went down the elevator a few floors to a cafeteria, where we found a suitable corner for carrying on our discussion. By this time my thoughts seemed as crisscrossed as the fibers of a rug—or even the light waves from mirrored walls.

"Then you think," I ventured, "that all these mirrors have a purpose other than saving Uncle Jonathan's eyes?"

"Uncle Jonathan's eyes—rot! His eyes are as healthy as anyone's when new rugs come in to be looked over. His suffering is just a front. So are the mirrors. Like the picture of the Spanish market.

"But that secret purpose—the death's-head—the victory over the enemy—that's what I'm looking for in Jonathan Buffler's mirror mania. And I want you to help me find it. Have you seen either of the females?"

"Becker," I said. "But I noticed a plump blonde with black eyelashes when I passed a room marked 'Secretary Number 2'. Could that be Jewel?"

"That's Jewel. All play, no work. Both eyes on your uncle's money. All right—here's how the jigsaw fits together. Your aunt died not long after Jewel came to work for Buffler. I wasn't connected with Buffler at that time, but I've heard that the coroner and a few other officials held their breaths for awhile until that incident blew over. I have reason to believe that your Aunt Mary Buffler died under strange circumstances."

RAMSELL'S tone brought my appetite to a sharp stop. I laid down my fork. I only listened. And with every word, I caught a clearer picture of Uncle Jonathan as Aunt Mary's murderer.

"Whatever those circumstances were," the doctor continued, "I'm sure, from the indications Gertrude Becker has given me, that she knows. Perhaps she has proof of that murder. At any rate, that is the source of her power over Buffler. She holds a whip hand over him. She stands in his path as solid as a prison wall."

"Prison wall," I echoed under my breath.

"And that wall has begun to frustrate Jonathan Buffler more every day. It won't let him have the one thing he craves more than anything else."

"Jewel?"

"Jewel," Ramsell replied. "Jewel expects to marry Buffler's wealth. But Gertrude Becker forbids him to marry her."

"Why?"

"Because Becker has worked for him for twenty years or more, and much of his success is due to her good business judgment, not his own. Now Gerty's just stubborn enough and proud enough to send him to prison before she'll let him dump his wealth into the lap of a cheap gold-digger."

"Is Becker in love with him too?"

"I've often wondered," said the doctor. "Whether she is or not, in *his* mind she's simply an obstruction—a wall—between him and what he wants. And Jonathan Buffler is used to having whatever he wants."

I mused over the matter, and the doctor nervously finished his lunch.

"She's a wall," he repeated, his lively black eyes snapping. "She's a wall that he hates, because walls aren't easy to dissolve. *But*—you can always make a wall *seem* to dissolve *by hanging a mirror over it!*"

I must have stared at the doctor for a full minute. All my solid thoughts on this problem suddenly jumped out from under me. I turned these last words over and over, trying to make sense out of them. Gertrude Becker was a wall. Buffler hated her. So he dissolved her—*symbolically*—by dissolving all walls. That, at least, was the doctor's theory.

Very impolitely, I laughed. Somehow I couldn't quite swallow such a theory at first taste. I felt a childish impulse to poke fun at it.

"If Gertrude Becker is the real wall he wants to dissolve," I said, "why doesn't he hang a mirror on Gertrude?"

The jibe disturbed the doctor not in the least.

"It wouldn't surprise me if he did," he retorted, swallowing the last of his coffee.

"Or," I pursued, winking to myself, "if he finds it awkward to hang a mirror on her, why doesn't he just hang *her* and be done with it?"

"You're going to be a great help," said Ramsell with a smile that stung me. "But for all your facetiousness, you've hit close to the real thing."

He looked at me steadily and I felt the perspiration break out over my body.

"In other words," he said, "whether Buffler has yet faced it consciously or not, the set-up is perfect for him to resort to another murder."

MY spine went cold. A chain of possibilities leaped through my mind. A fortune at stake. Becker fighting to save it. Murder hovering over her. The doctor plunging into the fight—and the great-nephew arriving on the scene—and what might happen to him? I tried to pull my thoughts back to something solid and tangible.

"But—but the mirrors—the safety valve—" I mumbled.

"If my theory is correct—and I'm not too confident that it is—the mirrors may act as a subconscious outlet for awhile. Buffler may even hide his worst intentions from his conscious self for a time. But sooner or later—"

The doctor rose from the table and gestured, palms outward, as if to say that anything might happen.

As we returned to the top floor I assured Dr. Ramsell that I would respect his confidence and would cooperate in every way possible.

"For the present there's nothing to do but stay around for a friendly visit," the doctor replied. "Of course you mustn't seem to be watching him. But if my suspicions are well founded you'll probably see the signs before it's too late. After all, committing a clean murder isn't as simple as purchasing rugs or installing mirrors. Keep in touch with me. We may find that my theories are groundless. I hope to God we do."

For the rest of the afternoon I loafed around the offices and the rug display rooms, letting the matter turn over in my mind. I stopped in and had a chat with Gertrude Becker about the weather and the high cost of living, and left her in a fair humor in spite of her upset over the mirrors, which were already being installed in her own office. Becker was a pretty decent sort, regardless of her ill-suppressed feud with my great-uncle.

Late in the afternoon Uncle Jonathan and I became fast friends. I listened to his pet peeves about light rays—listened my way right into his heart. He even took me through some of his offices on the next floor below, where a battery of new calculating machines was busily multiplying the number of cones in the fovea* of the human eye by the number of seconds of time, and these by the billions and trillions of light waves, which the eye must encounter going to and from work.

The review of the calculating activities, however, had a depressing effect upon Uncle Jonathan. He came away with new pains in his eyes, and he suddenly announced that he was almost too ill to be on his feet. We trudged back to his darkened office and he dropped weakly into his chair.

Then Jewel came in, her blond hair bouncing and her darkened eyes flashing with anger and her carmine lips drawn hard. I took one look at her and buried myself in a newspaper and was forgotten.

"So *that's* what you think of me," she snapped at Uncle Jonathan.

"Now Jewel," Buffler protested in his lovey-dovey voice. "Don't be that way."

"But you did it deliberately, Johnny. I'm jealous. I've got a right to be." She gored him with her sharpness. "You deliberately gave that woman her first choice of the tints—and what about poor me? Poor me gets left out in the cold."

"But Jewel, you wouldn't want pink-tinted mirrors in your office."

SHE plumped down in a chair and sulked.

"I certainly would! Pink is my color. You know that. And yet you give all the pink mirrors to old Drizzlepuss."

"Jewel, dear, be reasonable." He tried to stroke her hand but she jerked it away. "You can have any other tint you want, just so every office is different—that's the way I contracted for it."

----

*The most sensitive area on the human retina is a small *yellow spot,* which has a central depression *(the fovea centralis)* in the middle back part of the eyeball. No rods but only cones are found in this *fovea centralis.* No fibers of the optic nerve overlie it, and upon it the image at which the eye is directed is focused for acute vision.—Ed.

125

"Then change your contract!"

"You can have blue—green—amber—"

"Just because she's your Number One secretary, and I'm Number Two—"

"Jewel, stop it!"

"You don't love me, Johnny, no you don't, or you'd let me have my way."

The quarrel got worse as it went on, and I took a nod from Buffler as a sign for me to leave. I obeyed reluctantly, for the profanity was just beginning to get good, and I had never heard a female who was more of an artist at it than this Jewel.

* * *

THAT evening as the chauffeur drove Buffler and me along the river drive toward the red-roofed mansion, I perceived that my uncle was in a terrific turmoil.

"She may walk out on me," he shuddered, as if the thought filled him with deep terror.

"Then you didn't give her the pink mirrors she wanted?" I asked.

"No, dammit, the pink ones were already installed in Drizzlepuss's office. I made Jewel take green." He sighed painfully. "It's a helluva thing to break a little girl's heart over, ain't it? But that's what I've done."

CHAPTER THREE
Death in the Night

FROM all appearances my uncle was a very sick man. He had me fix a blindfold over his eyes and read the evening paper to him, while he lay on a bed and suffered. At length he said he believed he would sleep, and begged me not to waste my evening taking care of him. The yellow roadster in the garage was mine to use as long as I cared to extend my visit, and I might as well enjoy myself.

Unpredictable. That's what Doctor Ramsell had said of him, and the doctor was right. Jonathan Buffler's hospitality was so much greater than I had expected that I *should* have been suspicious.

I drove out of the garage and through the driveway with my eyes on the bright lights reflected in a pink glow over the skyline. I could see Buffler Tower, one of the nearest tall buildings, rising stately into the darkness. The majesty of that building was impressive; it made me stop and wonder whether I had the proper appreciation for its owner.

As I skimmed along the pavement, that wisp of sentiment kept tickling my mind, and it was the thing that made me turn around and go back before I had reached the city's bright lights.

"This is no way to do," I told myself, "running out on my uncle the first night of my visit, after the warm welcome he's given me. There'll be other nights to run around."

So I zipped back to the red-roofed mansion, thinking to myself what a lonely place it must be, now that Aunt Mary was gone. It was, in fact, almost a deserted place; for Jonathan Buffler had dispensed with all his servants and kept only a houseman. Perhaps he was lonely, misunderstood, in need of a companion—even such as Jewel. I could not believe he had murdered Aunt Mary.

I ran the roadster into the garage, and the doors slipped closed quietly at my touch. As I walked toward the porch steps a faint flash of light issued from along the side of the house—a curious quick flash that caught my curiosity. Impulsively I went toward it, puzzled because it had come from near the ground.

The flash did not come again, nor did I see anyone with a flashlight. All I found was a basement window with a piece of glass broken out of it. Through the break came a very faint glow of light from a basement room. I concluded that the flash I had seen must have been nothing more than an electric light switched on and off by the houseman.

The voice of Jonathan Buffler, however, rattled through the basement room. This somehow punctured my sentimental picture of him. For I had been expecting to find him still in his bed, perhaps wishing there was someone to bring him a drink of water or read a book to him. The voice I heard was vigorous and hearty, not the voice of a sick man. I bent to the window.

I couldn't see much through the aperture, for it was almost completely clogged with the ends of two tubes that pointed through the window. I had the sensation of looking down a double-barreled shotgun.

But being interested in the state of Jonathan Buffler, and not in shotguns, I paid scarcely any attention to the pair of poised tubes. I was vaguely aware that they were connected with a hodgepodge of mechanism, which cluttered a large share of the dimly lighted basement room. I was vaguely aware too, that some of that mechanism was electrical, and that all of it was new and gleaming.

But those observations were largely unconscious. It was Jonathan Buffler that I was curious about, and it was Jonathan Buffler that I saw.

"She wanted pink mirrors too, damn her!" came his voice as plainly as if I were in the room with him.

His hulking round form plodded across the floor toward the open door of an adjoining room. He was pouring out his confidences to the houseman, in whose wake he trailed.

"But I'll square things with her after we're through," he added with a bitter chuckle.

"Sure. She'll understand," said the houseman, and their voices were lost in the further room.

SO the old scoundrel wasn't sick! It made me hot in the face to think how easily he had deceived me. I walked away from the window and struck out along a river path afoot. It was high time for me to pull my slow wits together and think some of these things out.

Was Jonathan Buffler insane—or wasn't he? If he could be too sick to walk—too sick to use his eyes—too sick to keep his date with Jewel, and then within an hour could lose every symptom of that illness, he was either a superb actor or else he was mentally unbalanced. Was it possible that he had become a split personality, living alternately in two different worlds? Had he lapsed into schizophrenia?

I scuffed along the gravel path looking across toward the lights of the downtown skyline that reflected in the river. The three red lights atop the Buffler Tower and its several bright windows kept the scenes of the day turning over in my mind. A few lights on the top floor were burning.

I wondered if the doctor was still up there, pouring over his theories. I wondered if the new pink mirrors in Becker's office, and the mirrors through the hallways and in Buffler's sanctum, were still tirelessly swaying.

But most of all, I wondered why Jonathan Buffler, sane or insane, should be sick before me—and not before his houseman.

I sauntered back to the mansion and found that Buffler was again in bed with the blindfold over his eyes. He was awake and I talked with him a few minutes.

"Thank God, I can close out the devilish light with a blindfold," he muttered darkly. "I'm a sick man, Olin."

"Let me send for Doctor Ramsell," I said.

Buffler vetoed the suggestion with a pained oath.

"That damned idiot doctor! He's got no heart! I try to tell him how I suffer, but he won't hear me. He just looks a hole through me, like a hungry owl. I'd like to change eyes with him once and give him a taste of what I endure.

"But hell, you could shoot copper wires through his eyes and it wouldn't affect him any more'n every light ray that shoots through mine."

"I'm sorry you're feeling so badly," I said.

"Go to bed and forget about me,' he snapped. "And sleep late, because I'm not going to work tomorrow. I'm not going to be able."

I trudged off to bed, but not to sleep. This thing had me going now. Jonathan Buffler *was* ill in my presence. That was the thing that stuck in my mind. If he was acting, the acting itself amounted to illness, it was so intense.

Following the doctor's train of thought, I pondered over the blindfold. If this affliction was all psychological, the blindfold must be a subconscious expression of something that Buffler hated to face. But *what?* The memory of a past murder? The conception of a future one?

I snapped on a light and tried to read, but it was useless. Every news story in the paper related somehow to my troubled thoughts. Then my mind reverted to the curious apparatus I had glimpsed in the basement. I put on my clothes and tiptoed downstairs.

The clock struck eleven-thirty. Perhaps the houseman would be asleep by this time. His quarters, I had been informed, were in the rear basement room; and I had no intention of disturbing him with my prowling.

THE door between the first floor and the basement was locked. The clock struck midnight before I finally found a key, and by that time I was fairly impatient to get on with my venture, and consequently more or less reckless about the amount of noise I made. I walked down the basement stairs and turned on lights as I went.

I stopped, listened, heard nothing. At last I was in the room I had glimpsed from the outside, and a dim light showed me the mysterious mass of instruments. I gazed with an awe that was more than I can define. I felt a mysterious sense of power. Even though I had no more idea than a child as to what all these huge tubes and coils and turntables and levers added up to, I thrilled at their very beauty.

I could see the reflection of my shirt, elongated into a white saber, up the length of the largest metal tube. This brilliant metal pole sloped upward gently, and I noticed that the two small tubes I had seen from the outside—the double-barreled shotgun—were an elongation of this telescope-like piece of metal.

Perhaps the instrument was a telescope, I thought. Bending downward I tried to find an eyepiece, thinking that I might catch a glimpse of some planet or star over the skyline of the city, but my search was futile—and so was my inspiration. For after all, why should there be such a profusion of electrical equipment if this were only a telescope?

The only items I could single out as familiar were the paper-thin plates of colored glass, obviously to be used for filtering out different colors of light, and a hand switch.

My hand was on the switch, but I did not mean to snap it. However, I was suddenly shocked by the entrance of the houseman. I turned with a start, and the switch snapped beneath my hand.

Zwoom-m-m-m!

At once the room was ringing with the quiet hum of motors bedded on concrete. A purple spark sputtered across a gap—the gap widened—the spark crackled and roared—and my eyes winced under the terrific light. Blindly I groped for the switch; then in fear of the thundering delta of electric sparks, I backed away.

I knew the houseman was shouting at me, I couldn't hear a word he said, nothing but his mad roar against the clattering torrent of power.

The houseman's hand slapped the switch off. The roar died away, and the streams of sparks were now only lingering white streaks playing across my dazzled eyes. A hand clutched me across the chest and I dizzily staggered backward.

The houseman's face was the face of a demon. He shoved me against the wall, and from the look of him I believe he would have shot me down if he had had a gun. His arms reached out this way and that, expecting to grab something to club me with, but his search was cut short, for I snatched a crowbar hanging on the wall.

"Layoff me!" I yelled. "Your damned telescope's nothing to me!"

The words halted him—or perhaps the crowbar had something to do with it.

"I'm Buffler's nephew," I said, remembering that the houseman had not seen me at close range before. "If this is my uncle's telescope, I've got a right to look at it."

The houseman looked at me closely, as if trying to size up how much I knew or suspected. He relaxed a little.

"I didn't mean to start off the fireworks," I added. "If I've done any damage, I'll pay for it."

I HUNG up the crowbar and walked to the stairs, and I knew that the houseman's eyes were following me suspiciously. I glanced at the stairs to see another pair of eyes on me—and Jonathan Buffler's white eyeballs were protruding more than ever.

"Sorry if I've upset your sleep, Uncle," I said, hesitating at the foot of the stairs.

I snatched at the first lie that came to my mind.

"Aunt Mary used to keep some of my favorite books down here in the basement storeroom. That's what I came down to get...and then I saw this telescope and thought I'd look at some stars."

My uncle continued to glare at me, and the houseman stood at one side of me with his fists on his hips. Neither one seemed disposed to speak, whatever it was he might be thinking.

"Or *is* it a telescope?" I added.

"It is," said Jonathan Buffler, with a glance at the houseman.

"It's partly a telescope," said the houseman, "but it's chiefly a cosmic ray apparatus. I'll tell you about it some time when we get it working on one of the stars."

"It's out of order now," said Buffler.

"I shouldn't have messed with it," I agreed.

"Stay away from it," said the houseman. "Your uncle makes me responsible for keeping it under lock and key. If it had been anybody but you, I'd have crowned 'em."

"I shouldn't have dug up a key in the first place," I said. "Had trouble sleeping so I came down for a book."

"Get back to bed," said Buffler, and his night-shirted bulk turned and trudged up the stairs. I followed. The door between the basement and the rest of the house locked behind us.

Again I went to bed, but not to sleep. I listened for an hour or more, and at last I heard Buffler slip down the stairs, and the basement door clicked. There was no doubt in my mind that he and the houseman were having an earnest conversation.

* * *

THE thunderbolt struck home the next morning. A telephone call brought the strange news that cut through me like a knife. Shortly after midnight, a scrubwoman had died while at work in Gertrude Becker's pink-mirrored room at Buffler Tower!

CHAPTER FOUR
Shadows of Murder

THE death of a scrubwoman may seem a very small incident. There was nothing about a scrubwoman's dying while at work to give the police a headache. Nor were the coroner's talents put to any test. The coroner's verdict of death from a heart ailment was accepted without question, so far as I know, by all who knew the woman.

A second telephone call, this time from Dr. Ramsell, assured Jonathan Buffler that there was no need for him to come if he was ill, for everything was taken care of and the office force had gone back to work as soon as the body had been removed.

The death of a scrubwoman was a very small incident. But it was enough of an incident to strike a terror through me—a terror that possessed me, hypnotized me, bound me in invisible shackles.

I sat in my room with my head in my hands, looking out across the river park toward the downtown skyline. There stood the Buffler Tower, a dismal gray shaft pointing up to the leaden clouds, almost obscure in its outline, for there was a fine drizzle in the air this morning.

Lights were on, in the city's downtown offices, and I could see the top floor of the Buffler Tower as a row of dotted lights through the gray mist. Was it possible, I kept asking myself, that an electric eye from this distance could sort out those dotted lights, and choose the one that was pink?

And was it possible that a ray from this distance could leap to those swaying pink mirrors—quartz mirrors that reflected everything they could catch to every inch of surface in the room. I shuddered. In my hand there was a strange lingering feeling—the feeling of striking a lever or snapping a switch.

From Jonathan Buffler's room came a continual low hum of voices. Although my uncle remained in bed with his blindfold over his eyes, he was not too sick to converse with the houseman. This low muffled conversation was to go on for hours—today, tomorrow, the next day—and every hour of their ghastly secret talk was to leave me more and more depressed.

I must have been an ineffectual weakling during those hours. Why I did not call Dr. Ramsell and pour out my direst suspicions to him, I cannot say. I wonder if a hit-and-run driver may not experience the same terror that I felt—a terror that is blinding—a terror that says:

"I didn't do it. I don't know anything about it."

I rubbed my hand and tried to brush the memory of that accidental snap of the switch out of it. But my ears echoed with the roar of purple sparks, and the smell of humming motors was in my nostrils.

A police car moved slowly along the wet street. I thought it was going to stop, and my heart went wild. It came even with our driveway but did not turn in. It disappeared on down the street, but the scare it left upon me was as blinding as the band across Buffler's eyes.

From that moment on, the deadly instrument concealed in the basement room, together with the switch I had struck and the exhibition of deadly power I had seen, all went behind a blind spot in my consciousness. I refused to remember them. For me they were out...

"Olin!" It was Buffler's deep, suffering voice that called.

"Coming," I answered, and with hesitant step I went to his room.

"Read to me," he said. "I may have to lie here for several days, and I'll need you beside me constantly. Find a book and read to me."

I COMPLIED with his order. What I read was of no importance; indeed, I read almost without listening to myself, and I doubt whether he listened. For, as I soon realized, his only purpose was to make certain that I did not leave the house.

For three days I did not leave, nor did I talk on the telephone or have any other communications with the outside world. Not that he forbade me to use the telephone; he simply invented ways to block me. And I, seeing through his artifices, acceded to him. He watched me like a hawk, and I watched him the same way.

As for meals, he had the delivery trucks bring whatever he wanted. As for his business, he barked a few sharp orders over the telephone to Gertrude Becker each day. As for his illness, he flatly refused to have Ramsell or any other doctor meddle with him; and whenever I threatened to override this decision, he cajoled me so cunningly that I let him have his way.

Was I afraid of him? Of course I was. His acting was too superb. I knew he was insane. I knew he might murder me the first time he caught me napping. I saw plainly on that point.

For the one passion that pounded through his arteries was a plump blonde named Jewel, who had cleverly held out for marriage, and who had fed the flames of his agony by completely ignoring him for the past three days—the sickest days of his life, no doubt.

I sat beside his bed, reading to him, watching him, wondering whether he watched me through his blindfold, wondering how he expected to dispose of me. Perhaps I would never know how Aunt Mary had died; but it was clear as crystal to me now that Gertrude Becker, his Number One secretary, would die simply and easily, and that there would be no mystery. The answer would be—"heart attack."

I went to my room, adjoining his, and began a letter to my parents. I had only put down a few words when—

"Olin!" Buffler's insistent call interrupted me. "What are you doing, Olin?"

"Nothing in particular."

"Come here, Olin...Did I hear you open that stationery drawer?...Are you writing a letter?...To whom?...Read it to me."

I got up angrily and returned to his room.

"It's private," I snapped. "I don't think you'd be interested."

"Of course I'm interested. Your parents are my relatives. They're to inherit part of my wealth. What are you writing them?" He drew himself up in bed angrily. *"What are you writing them?"*

"None of your damned business!" I retorted.

Jonathan Buffler tore the blindfold off his eyes and sprang up. His bulky form bounced toward me, and his mad protruding eyes caught sight of the letter, which I'd been afraid to leave on my desk.

"Give it to me!" he roared.

I backed away from him and crumpled the letter in my fist. He came at me, reaching with his puffy fingers and yelling, "Give it to me!"

I swung my fist at his heavy jowl. I didn't mean to hit so hard, but fear and hate and physical power are all bound pretty closely together in my make-up, and there was a lot of fear turned loose in the impact. Jonathan Buffler's pear-shaped head gave under that blow, and his humpty-dumpty frame tottered backward on bent knees.

His eyes closed and he groped for the bed, groaning and coughing.

THE houseman came up the stairs, sidled past me and walked across to Buffler's bed. I started to move away.

"Just a minute," said the houseman, "till we see what's going on here. What happened, Buffler?"

The stricken man only answered with long drawn-out groans and shakings of his soggy head that made his thick lips sputter. He fumbled to get his blindfold over his eyes, and the houseman helped him. At the same time there was a quick exchange of whispers. Then the houseman turned to face me and carelessly brought a pistol out of his pocket, which he weighed in his hand.

"All right, Olin," he said in a casual tone. "The old man wants to see that letter you're writin', so cough it up. Buffler's orders are law with me. Let's have it."

I dug the wad of paper out of my pocket and tossed it over. The houseman stuck his gun in his pocket and unwadded the paper. He read aloud:

Dear Mother and Father,

If I should suddenly die and my death should be attributed to heart attack—

"Well?" Buffler demanded.

"That's all there is," said the houseman.

"The hell!" Buffler sputtered. He slipped his blindfold up on his forehead, turned on his side, and glared at me.

"What are you plotting, suicide? What the hell are you hinting at?"

"Nothing," I said.

"You lie. You're hinting at murder! A *murder!*"

He came up to a sitting position and pushed his weight up slowly with his arms. His voice had come out with a scream on the word "murder," but now as he slowly came to his feet and moved toward me, his talk came forth as a hoarse rasping whisper.

"You're accusing somebody of plotting against your life. You seem to think somebody would take the trouble to kill you.

Who the hell gives a damn about putting *you* out of the way? *Who?* Answer me, you damned traitor!"

I had no answer except to edge away from the bulbous maniacal eyes that knifed through me. But the houseman had slipped to the door ahead of me and stood in my path, tapping his pistol against the door frame.

"Answer me!" Buffler roared. "Who'd take the trouble to murder *you?* What have *you* got on anybody?"

"Nothing!" I blurted.

"Don't lie! I can see right through you. I know who you're accusing. You're accusing *me!*"

His mouth spread in a hateful grimace and he pointed his accusing finger at himself.

"You think *I'd* kill you, don't you? DON'T YOU? ANSWER ME!"

"Why should I?" I cried.

"Stalling," he hissed, and a scornful smile touched his lips. "Always stalling. But I can see through you. You think you've got something on me. You think, you'll fix up a story for the police. You think you'll get in on my dough in a hurry. You think you'll break up my little party.

"But you won't, damn you! I've had you sewed up since the night you busted in on the ray gun! And NOW—"

His furious screeching broke off at the sound of the doorbell. For a few seconds he stood almost motionless, his hands upraised, his fingers trembling, perspiration streaking down over his heavy jowls. The doorbell rang again. Slowly his hands lifted and his palms pressed over his bulbous eyes.

"I'm sick, Olin," he wailed, bowing his head. "I'm dreadfully sick. I don't know what I'm saying. Help me to bed. Get the blindfold on me."

His sudden change of mood was so complete as to pass understanding. It was baffling, and yet so convincing that the hatred and terror that had filled me a moment before softened into weakness. I helped him to bed.

The doorbell continued to ring until the houseman answered it. A moment later he came back up the stairs, to tell Buffler that Jewel was waiting to see him down in the drawing room.

CHAPTER FIVE
Jewel's Promise

THE name of Jewel was magic. The light that came into my uncle's face was wonderful to see. A reluctant schoolboy who plays sick until he hears that school is out, so he can go to the circus, could not change his mood any quicker than Jonathan Buffler.

But Buffler did not forget that he was a very ill man. He kept his blindfold on, I helped him dress, and the houseman and I escorted him downstairs.

Once in the presence of Jewel, he permitted himself the luxury of removing his blindfold; remarking, as he did so, that the light was killing him.

"You poor dear," said Jewel in luscious baby talk, stroking his eyelids. "You've just got to get well. Your little Jewel has been all sad since you walked out on her..."

"But Jewel, I didn't..."

"You got all huffy and walked out on me, and all I had asked for was pink mirrors in my office. You were an old meany." She scruffed his cheeks playfully and they laughed.

The houseman nudged me and we left them to themselves. But we stayed within hearing, for that was what the houseman wanted to do, and I had no choice in the matter. I was his prisoner.

Jewel's visit lasted for more than two hours. Buffler finally persuaded her to go back to the office. But in the course of those two hours Jewel had done most of the persuading. She had teased and pouted and cajoled; in short, she had applied all her artful wiles that had such a softening effect upon Jonathan Buffler.

It was pitiful to listen to, but in the end she had won her point. She was to have pink mirrors. Moreover, she was to be promoted from Secretary Number Two to Secretary Number One, so there would be no more occasions for her being jealous.

"Mind you," Buffler had insisted, "keep this plan under your hat until I get back to work. I know how to handle Drizzlepuss and you don't. So don't go spilling the beans. I'll be back in a few days to make the change. Until then, don't you breathe a word."

"Of course not, Johnny dear," Jewel had answered. "You know how to handle Drizzlepuss." A touch of sarcasm came into her voice. "That's why we're getting married one of these days—or are we?"

"Jewel, dear, don't start that allover again."

"Or are we?" Her voice scraped so cuttingly that Buffler might have lost his temper. But instead he had continued to fall at her feet, smoothing her ugly manners with promises and kisses born of his foolish infatuation.

"Promise me you'll forget about Drizzlepuss until I get back," he begged. "As soon as my plan works out, there'll be the sweetest little honeymoon you ever dreamed of. But you've got to sit tight until I get back to my office. Promise."

Those were Buffler's parting words, and Jewel repeated her promise as she left.

The houseman and I helped Buffler back to bed, and for the remainder of the day he was a very sick man. But back of moanings and groanings I could detect a glow of fervor. Jewel had warmed his spirit and set his scheming mind upright. I guessed that he would go through with his dastardly plan as swiftly as possible, and I guessed rightly.

I WAS now determined to break out of my inertia and blow the lid off this thing. Being followed about the house by the houseman and his gun, being denied the use of the telephone, being confined to the house by force—these things had become galling to the limit of my endurance. Moreover, the open break over my letter had brought my danger out into the open. It was high time for me to act.

"Tomorrow noon," I said to myself as I sat alone in my room.

My slow wits turned over every bit of evidence that had fallen into my hands.

"Tomorrow noon Gertrude Becker will die if I don't do something to prevent it," I told myself.

I was sure of the time Buffler would choose. For Gertrude Becker had an old-maidish habit of eating her lunch in her office every noon and allowing no intruders during that hour. Buffler had rechecked this point with Jewel in their recent visit, and I was sure he had done so for a purpose.

"When the motors begin to hum tomorrow noon," I said to myself, "where will *I* be? Buffler knows that *I* know. He let the cat out of the bag himself when he said 'ray gun'. He won't try to cover that up now. His only alternative is to get me out of the way—but how? It won't look good for him to have *two* mysterious deaths on his hands at once."

There was little comfort in that thought. I didn't eat my food for fear there was poison in it. I didn't sleep for fear I would be murdered in my bed. Whenever I had a wild inspiration to dash for a door or a window or scribble off a note to throw to a passing newsboy, I would turn to see the houseman's pistol dangling from his careless hand.

The new day came. The hours crept toward noon. Every strike of the clock struck terror through me. I was pitifully tired and exhausted from loss of sleep and nerve strain and hunger.

Now I sat languidly on the drawing room divan, almost in a stupor, my eyes resting on the gleaming pistol. The houseman seemed to be reading; he held a book of science in his hand. But if I so much as glanced at the pearl-handled extension telephone at the side of the room, his alert eyes were on me and his quick fingers twitched at the gun.

"I'll wait until eleven-thirty," I kept telling myself. "On the stroke of eleven-thirty I'll rush that telephone, gun or no gun."

My muscles grew tense. With every glance at the clock my heart quickened.

"At eleven-thirty I'll make a rush...*Or will I?*"

The demon fear must have had a deadly grip on me. I tried to close my eyes and relax, but the cold-faced houseman across the room from me had only to turn a page of his book to bring me up with a start.

The clock struck ten-thirty. On the floor above, Jonathan Buffler was stirring. The clock struck eleven. Buffler waddled down the stairs weakly. He was in his bathrobe, his blindfold was pushed high on his forehead, his flabby face was gray. He paused to look at me. His fat fingers twitched nervously.

He went to the basement door, unlocked it and disappeared down the stairs. I could hear the swish of his bedroom slippers as he toddled through the basement.

THE clock struck eleven-thirty. I sat paralyzed. The houseman looked at me sharply. He must have heard my heart pounding. My heart was a fireball beating back and forth, and my chest and throat were on fire from it. From the basement came faint clicking sounds—sounds that could only be the checking of instruments. The houseman's eyes turned toward the basement door, and in that instant I moved like a fool.

I caught the telephone, jerked it off the hook, dropped it. The houseman was coming at me. I flopped a huge overstuffed chair over myself. In my craze to get a call through, I would have dodged behind anything, even a sieve. It was folly, of course. As my hand reached for the fallen phone, a bullet went through my forearm. The low *crack!* of the pistol echoed through the house.

The houseman was upon me like a cat. I tried to kick the chair against him. He sidestepped and hovered, and the butt of his pistol swung up to strike me. I wanted to lash out with my fist. More than anything in the world I wanted to feel the crash of my knuckles against his jaw.

But nausea swept down upon me and my right hand only clamped over my wounded forearm to catch the spurting blood. Then the rap of the pistol butt caught me on the side of my skull, and spirals of blackness whirled away my consciousness.

CHAPTER SIX
Spray of Death

I AWOKE to the hum of motors and the thunder of sparks. I imagined I could even smell the hot coils and see the purple streams of power. *The death ray was at work!*

In utter horror I tried to spring from my bed, but the most I could do was roll. In my grogginess I tumbled onto the floor. My hands and feet were bound. My wounded arm was bandaged clumsily, and it was shooting with pains.

I lay on the floor listening. The electrical roar dwindled and died away. For long minutes there were no sounds. I waited. The clock struck one. Soon, I thought, there would be a telephone call from the office to bring the tragic news that Gertrude Becker had "suddenly died." But the telephone didn't ring, and an hour or more later I learned it had been disconnected.

That hour or more of waiting was uneventful, but it was by far the most excruciating uneventfulness I have ever endured. The two men came up from the basement, and Jonathan Buffler lapsed into his terrific illness. He went to bed and said he would stay there indefinitely. Under no conditions was he to be disturbed by anything or anybody.

"What about Olin?" I heard the houseman ask.

"He'll wait," Buffler grunted.

Then the doorbell rang, and to my agony of waiting was added the shattering news that I knew was coming.

"The telephone girl," began the messenger boy at the front door in a high-pitched voice, "says that Mr. Buffler don't answer—"

"The phone's cut off," said the houseman. "Buffler's awful sick. He ain't to be disturbed. What'd you want?"

"She sent me with a message," said the boy. "I'm to get word to Buffler that his Number One secretary just died. It happened this noon, so sudden that everybody's pretty much shocked, and they thought Mr. Buffler had better be told about it."

"I'll give him the message," said the houseman. "I know he'll be deeply grieved. Come back in a couple of hours and maybe he'll have a message to send back to the office."

The boy left. The houseman came up to Buffler's bedroom to report the conversation.

"I heard it," Buffler grunted, and it was a grunt of satisfaction.

"Okay," said the houseman. "There you are. The big deal's over."

"It won't take long to cover our tracks," said Buffler. "But I'd better dope out a statement about Drizzlepuss Becker. The newspapers may want something. She's been with me a long time, and she's pretty well known. The employees will expect a statement from me. Get me a pen and some paper, and I'll dope out some deepest regrets."

Two hours later the doorbell rang again. The houseman had taken the trouble to gag me in the meantime. If he hadn't, I'd have shouted to the caller at the top of my voice, for it was Dr. Ramsell. I'd have known his voice anywhere.

"No, you can't see him," the houseman barked. "He wants rest and quiet and no interviews. But here, I'll give you his statement about Gertrude Becker's death."

"Oh," said the doctor, in a curiously surprised tone.

"Well, do you want to take it or don't you?" the houseman snapped.

"I'll take it—with pleasure," came the doctor's crisp answer. "By the way, where's Olin?"

"Olin?" asked the houseman innocently. "You mean Buffler's nephew that was here a few days back? He beat it for home soon after the old man took sick. Took the train or bus, I suppose. Damfino. Maybe he flew."

RAMSELL said, "Tell Buffler I want to see him as soon as he's able. I'm stalling off the reporters and the police as well as I can, but these two sudden deaths—the scrubwoman and Gertrude Becker—both in the same roomful of pink mirrors, have naturally raised a lot of idle speculations—and some that maybe aren't so idle."

"What the hell? Ain't Buffler's lawyer on the job?"

"Yes, but the lawyer can't answer all the questions that have come up about Buffler's mirror mania. The investigators come to me about that."

"Tell them Buffler's rich enough to have things like he wants 'em," said the houseman. "Maybe he's a bit cracked, but to hell with 'em. What have mirrors got to do with a secretary's dying?"

"I hope to answer that question sooner or later," said the doctor, and with that he left.

The long evening wore on, and for a time it promised nothing but waiting. But I knew now that the only thing that would bring my waiting to an end was death.

I must have been a problem to Buffler, for I am sure that he and the houseman spent a long and earnest hour discussing how best to handle my case. Occasionally the houseman came in to look at me, and each time I felt sure that he had come for *me;* but each time he only inspected the bonds that held my hands and feet, and then went away.

Never did he pay any attention to my bullet wound, for I would soon be dead.

Now I observed that Jonathan Buffler's spirits were rising. That was another sure sign that my fate was completely sealed. Now and then a chuckle of laughter sounded from his room. I heard him get up from bed and dress. Again his illness had conveniently vanished. He went downstairs and called to the houseman to reconnect the telephone. He tried to call Jewel, but her apartment did not answer.

As a drowning man will snatch at straws, I seized at every wisp of an idea for escape that came to my mind. I even debated rolling out onto the roof. But at last I stumbled upon something—dim chance that it was—which absorbed my struggles for half the night. That something was—a heliograph message.

But not a real heliograph. My signaling instrument would have to be the little pocket mirror, which I habitually kept in the breast pocket of my suit coat. And my signaling light would be the wall lamp of my bedroom.

Squirming, I drew my rib bones up inside my jacket coat, swelled my chest with air and fought to catch the edge of the mirror against a rib. It was sweating work, desperate work, and I was sure I would never make it. But at last I felt the mirror sliding through the pocket opening.

My straining body threshed about, finally shook the mirror free. I crawled forward then, inch by inch. At last my sweaty hands felt glass. My fingers clutched at the mirror, and I maneuvered myself until the glass caught the round gleam of the lamp bulb.

Then, jerking my head up as far as possible from the cold floor, I trained the mirror so that the lamp bulb reflection on it would stream through the window opposite me and reach out in the black night to Buffler Tower.

It was almost fantastic that I should hope my "heliographed" message would attract any attention, considering what a welter of city lights filled the blackness. But the later the hour, the fewer the lights, I reasoned; and also the greater my skill.

With infinite pains to flash my dots and dashes at an angle that would catch the mirrors of Buffler Tower, I spelled out the words.

DR RAMSELL   DR RAMSELL   DR RAMSELL

On the first floor Buffler continued his efforts to telephone to Jewel. Every time the clock struck another half hour, I would hear him mutter the number of her apartment, then after a long wait put down the telephone with a splutter of impatience.

"One more job," I could hear the houseman say. "Let's get it over with. As long as he's alive we're not safe."

"I want to get Jewel first," Buffler would retort, and he would try the telephone again.

BUT between calls I could catch snatches of their conversation, enough to assure me that the houseman was impatient to take care of that "one more job" so he could unmount the ray gun. He was no mere houseman. Unimpressive as he was, he was the scientific brain that had set up this death ray apparatus. Probably he had stolen plans and equipment both. At any rate, he was scheduled to take his leave of Jonathan Buffler as soon as this job was rounded up.

All the while I listened to them, my bound wrists continued to flash dots and dashes from the wall light of my room, reflecting off the perilously fingered mirror. The process was routine by this time—a hopeless routine at that—but it was something with which to work off some of the death-cell tenseness that gripped me.

Shortly after one o'clock—and I remember that the lights were still ablaze in the top floor of the Buffler Tower—my heliographic routine came to an end. I heard the houseman coming up to get me. Quickly I tossed the little mirror under the bed.

The houseman paused in the doorway. Buffler's voice sounded from below, muttering another telephone number. This time, for some reason, Buffler called the offices of Buffler Tower. Perhaps he thought the excitement of Gertrude Becker's death had caused some of the staff to remain at the Tower discussing the strange affair, and he would find Jewel there.

"Give me the office of Secretary Number Two." His voice was tense. "Hello...Hello? Is Jewel—Who the devil is this?...*What?*...Oh, my God!"

The telephone crashed down and I could hear Buffler's hoarse breathing. I didn't know what to make of it.

The houseman, thoroughly impatient with his master's continual telephoning, went on about his business. He came into the room, and then he cursed.

"Fell out of bed, huh? What the hell you up to, Olin? Trying to escape?"

I looked him coolly in the eyes. My mouth was gagged, so I couldn't say anything, which was just as well.

He grunted sourly, picked me up in his arms, bonds, gag, bandages and all, and carried me down the two flights of stairs to the basement.

He placed me in a corner of the room on the floor. I could see the ray gun diagonally across from me, polished and gleaming under the dim light. It was a beautiful array of equipment for such an ugly purpose. But it murdered clean, without leaving a mark that any coroner or doctor would ever find. That was its beauty. I wondered what they would do with my body.

Slowly, weakly, Jonathan Buffler tottered down to the basement level. His blindfold was over his eyes again. He lifted it long enough to glance at me, then replaced it. I never saw his face so white.

"One more job," the houseman observed in his characteristically impersonal manner. "It won't take but a minute. I'll have these instruments disassembled and packed away before dawn, and our fears will be over...What's the matter, Buffler?"

"You won't disassemble it," said Buffler in a voice that was like dry ice. "I've changed the plan."

"What the hell? What's the matter, Buffler? You sick?"

"Do you think I'm sick?" Buffler cracked coldly. He raised his blindfold and moved toward the instruments.

"I never knew you to be sick *down here,*" said the houseman dubiously. "I thought your sickness was something that you got when things didn't go right. Did something in that telephone call upset you? Something about Jewel?"

BUFFLER snarled, "Maybe *I'm* going blind." He bit his words with an icy fury that was on the ragged edge of breaking. "Maybe *I* can't tell pink from green. Maybe *I* can't count windows straight. But by heaven, I can't do any worse than the experts I hire!"

"What the devil?" the houseman barked. "You're dizzy. You're sick as a horse. Get upstairs. I've got one more job here—"

"*I've* got one more job!" Buffler roared.

He snatched the color filters out of a slot and started the big barrel of the ray gun rotating on the turntable. He ripped a command at the houseman.

"Stand back, damn you! *I'm* doing this one; to make sure it won't miss."

The big barrel swung around in my general direction, and the spin of a wheel from Buffler's shaking white fingers brought the elevation down. The puzzled houseman backed away to the corner, as if to humor the old man to the last, but he studied Buffler's operations with the eye of a critical machinist.

Buffler continued to snarl enigmatically. "A little bonus on my pay sheet, for someone who didn't come through with the goods."

Then one of his white hands shot to the switch, and the other suddenly rotated the gun past me toward the next corner.

"Look out!" the houseman screamed.

"I'll do this one, you damned bonehead!" Buffler shrieked.

Then both the mad voices were drowned by the hum of motors and the thunder of purple sparks. The houseman's hands beat at the air in protest, but the invisible line of death turned full on him—

The houseman simply fell, lifeless.

"You're next." Buffler's murderous bulbous eyes turned on me, and I could read the words of his snarling lips, submerged by the thunder of the machine.

Half blinded by the dazzle of sparks, I saw the gleaming barrel start to swing back. I closed my eyes, waited.

The waiting dragged out to full seconds. The sensation—whatever it would be—must be almost upon me. It would be quick, I thought. Perhaps there would be no sensation. Perhaps I wouldn't even know. Why didn't it come? Or *had* it happened? Or would I faint before it struck? I forced my eyes open.

I saw, against the wild array of purple sparks that the barrel had stopped, pointing a few feet to one side of me. Buffler's nervous hands whirled a wheel, and the gun gradually nosed upward—toward the stairway!

For halfway down the stairs were four uniformed men, and back of them Dr. Ramsell.

I couldn't hear their guns. I could only see them blaze away at the humpty-dumpty figure at the death-ray controls. Jonathan Buffler's pear-shaped head was suddenly streaked with red. The black blindfold leaped from his forehead, fluttered above the delta of purple sparks—then *flash!*—and it was transformed to a puff of white smoke.

Buffler fell, his fat white hands clutching his blood-streaked jowls. His lips wrenched in agony. I could not hear his cry, but I could see it in his face.

The officers advanced down the stairs cautiously, making sure they were well in the clear from the death ray. Evidently they had arrived in time to see the houseman go down.

But before anyone reached Jonathan Buffler, he pushed himself up heavily on his elbows, and seemingly with superhuman effort crawled—crawled toward the path of the gun's invisible ray. With one last agonized burst of strength, he rose before the barrel. Then he fell, as the houseman had fallen, completely lifeless…

Almost as soon as the echoes of the motors had died away, my gag was removed, my bonds were slit, and the welcome sting of circulation shot through my wrists and ankles.

FOR the remaining hours of the night, the doctor stayed with me in my bedroom, dressing my wounds and giving me some of the psychological as well as physical care that my condition required. I hadn't realized until it was all over that I had been on the verge of hysteria.

Bit by bit, I told him my story.

When I had finished, the doctor said, "So there was a death's-head among the mirrors..."

"Yes," I conceded. "The only mirrors he really needed for his murder were the ones in Gertrude Becker's office. The rest were all a part of his ruse, so that the ones he needed wouldn't attract undue attention. But he saw to it that they were an individual color, so that his filtered light detector could direct the death ray to the right window."

"And he kept those mirrors swaying," the doctor observed, "so that the ray couldn't miss fire. Those swinging quartz mirrors must have reflected that ray through the whole sweep of the room."

I thought that over for a moment, shuddered. And then one of the most puzzling questions of all came back to my mind.

"But this houseman of Buffler's—he seemed a cross between an inventor and a cold-blooded executioner. Not brutal—just cold as ice. Wonder who the man was."

Dr. Ramsell stroked his chin. "Well, maybe we can check through the Patent Office in Washington. Just in case somebody in the last few years invented a machine even generally similar to the one in the basement. Of course, he might have had a criminal record, and we could check on his fingerprints."

"You may have something there," I said. "He certainly was tough enough. But at any rate, we'll never know the big scheme they were planning. As far as I can judge, this whole thing boils down to this proposition:

"Somewhere in his career, Jonathan Buffler came across this fellow, and the two found they had a lot in common. They got to work on this death ray, which can be focused at either a near or far object, made certain plans for its use—and then Buffler botched up the whole works."

Dr. Ramsell nodded grimly. "Yes, he was better at that than anything else."

"But I'm still at sea on how he got his wires crossed," I said. "It was Becker he was after. She knew he killed his wife, and so held a gun at his head, so to speak. But it was Jewel he killed, eh?"

"Becker can thank Jewel's selfish scheming for that," said Dr. Ramsell, a slight smile back of his lively black eyes.

"Jewel returned from her recent visit with Buffler bearing the news that he had appointed her to be Secretary Number One. She forced Becker to move out at once, and little Jewel took over the Number One office, pink mirrors and all."*

The doctor picked up the pocket mirror that lay on the floor just under my bed.

"Is this your dot-and-dash instrument?"

"Yes. You caught my message?"

"I didn't, but a cruising police car did. The officers caught the reflected dots and dashes from the Tower and phoned me. I came right out. Rather clever of you, Olin," he grinned.

"I take after my great-uncle," I said with a wink. Then, more seriously, I asked,

"Dr. Ramsell, was Jonathan Buffler just a bungling murderer—or was he crazy?"

The doctor laughed lightly. "What do you think?"

----

*The science of light is quite a complex one, and there is much about the nature of light we do not know. However, it is well known that light itself consists of many colors, differing in

wavelength ranging from the infrared (which is invisible) to the ultra-violet (also invisible). Thus, if anything is said to be of a certain color, such as the pink of the mirrors in the murder room, it is pink only because its composition is such that it reflects only the pink rays, of that particular wavelength, and absorbs the others.

It is this principle of light that Buffler employed in singling out his murder room in the tower, thus insuring that the death ray would be reflected only in the desired room, and not in every room of the tower. Since the death ray was pink, or could be set for any other color if desired, the room with the pink mirrors was the only one that did not absorb it and render it harmless.—Ed.

THE END

THE TENANT ON THE 13TH FLOOR

By David Wright O'Brien

Corny jokesters often asked for the 13th floor, but this one actually got off there!

IN MY business I have to put up with a lot. I meet a lot of screwy people and hear a lot of third-rate humor and fifth-rate weather reports. Sometimes it's, "How's business, Mike? Going up?" And other times it's, "Hot today, isn't it, Mike?" Or, "Think the rain'll go on all day?"

All very funny. All very interesting.

Sometimes, when the car is jammed with passengers, I think I'd like to run the elevator straight up through the top of the roof. Just for the hell of it. For you see, that's my racket—running an elevator in the Binx Building. And it is a most monotonous racket indeed. Up and down. Up and down. Lord, how I wish I could go sideways just once!

But that's because I'm probably going crazy. I'm not sure I am, mind you. But fifteen years of going up and down, up and down, for a living *might* have a bad effect on the brain tissues. And if *I'm* not crazy, then *someone* is. I'll let you decide that for yourself.

The first time I saw the little guy was on a dismal March morning. It was raining outside, and people clumped in an out of my car in muddy shoes and soggy clothes, smelling damp and trying to put out my eyes with umbrella points.

The little guy carried an umbrella. He wore a black derby and a high celluloid collar that protruded above the black, wet sheen of the rubber raincoat that hung around him. His feet were encased in a pair of galoshes, and he wore tortoise shell spectacles.

I had never seen him before, and I wouldn't have noticed him then, except for the fact that he nodded cheerfully to me as he stepped into the car. Generally only regular tenants of the building did that.

The car wasn't awfully crowded on this trip. Just about eight passengers including the little guy.

"Ten!" someone called.

"Eight!" someone else said.

"Twenty-one!" said another voice.

I threw the lever forward and the car started up.

"Thirteen, please," said a pleasant voice.

I'd heard that gag so often it wasn't funny any longer. Of course there was no thirteenth floor on the Binx Building. Like plenty of other big office buildings we just skipped the thirteenth floor; twelve, then fourteen, see?

I glared over my shoulder to see who the gagster was. The little guy was the only passenger smiling.

"What did you say?" I demanded.

"Thirteen, please," he answered.

I knew how to fix his clock. I'd done it to other funnymen who'd called for the thirteenth floor. Just ignore them when they asked for the floor they really wanted. Ignore them and ride them all the way up to the top.

I STOPPED at eight and two passengers got out. One got in. Then it was ten. Four passengers got out. I shot past twelve, then fourteen, stopped the car at sixteen and one passenger got out. Twenty was the top floor, and when I stopped the car there I turned around again, ready to give the little guy a so-yuh-thought-yuh-were-smart look.

But he wasn't there. The only passenger was a fat old dame. I blinked.

"Lady," I demanded, "what happened to the little guy who called for thirteen?"

She looked startled, wheeled around.

"Why," she gasped, then she wheeled back to face me, "he was standing right behind me. I'm sure he didn't get out…"

Our eyes met, and she stepped hastily out of the car as if it might suddenly fall from under her. I looked at the back of the empty car where the little guy should have still been standing. No holes in the floor. He hadn't dropped through.

"He *musta* gotten off at one of the stops," I told myself. Running an elevator gets you that way. You begin to worry about such things.

The bell in the other shaft rang. It was my turn to start down again. But I looked very carefully at the blank gray wall between fourteen and twelve on the way down. And for the rest of the day it was somehow uncomfortable every time I'd pass the thirteenth floor that wasn't there. *

I was working the late shift that day, nine-thirty in the morning to seven at night. And at seventeen minutes to seven—you count the minutes that way when you're on the long shift and almost ready to go home—I picked up three of the scrubwomen on the sixteenth floor to take them down to the second.

Most of the offices in the building are closed by five o'clock, so the last two hours on the long shift aren't very busy and the cars are never crowded.

The scrubwomen had their pails and mops and stood near the back of the car chattering to each other as I took them down to the second. It was a quick trip, non-stop from the sixteenth down. Then I stopped the car and they were pulling the pails and mops out. The buzzer on my board flashed to indicate another passenger was waiting up on the twentieth.

I slammed the door and started up.

"All the way down, please," said a pleasant voice.

----

* Modern office buildings do not skip the 13th floor. However, there are many among those buildings more than fifteen years old, which do not have a 13th floor. It is amazing that hardheaded business people are still found who are so superstitious that they number floors in a large building so as to skip a number to which bad luck is generally attached. The truth is that most great tragedies, caused by fires and explosions, have occurred in office buildings, which had no 13th floor. However, in order not to be superstitious on our part, it must be pointed out that modern buildings, possessing a 13th floor, are fireproof, and that factor alone accounts for the disasters' apparent selection of buildings without 13th floors since they are old and not constructed to eliminate fire menace as are the newest skyscrapers.—Ed.

Something at the nape of my neck got very chilly. I knew that voice. I stopped the car with a lurch and turned around.

The little guy stood in the back, smiling at me.

"All the way down, please," he repeated.

I swear that he hadn't gotten on at sixteen with the scrubwomen. And *that* was the only stop I'd made.

"Look," I said, and there was a croak in my voice. "Look, when did you get on?"

He smiled pleasantly. "At thirteen, of course."

Now that he'd told me, I wished he hadn't.

I PUT the car into motion very carefully. My nerves were screaming. We went down to the first floor. The little guy stepped out. I was trying to close my eyes against the sight of him.

"I had to work a little late tonight," he said.

"Did you now?" I answered carefully.

"Yes," he said. "But then, business is so good I shouldn't complain." He stood there, not making any move to walk out of the lobby, obviously making conversation.

"You have an office here?" I asked cautiously.

He smiled in that very happy way of his.

"Oh yes. Oh my yes." He laughed. "I've had an office here for almost twenty-five years now."

I'd been running elevators in the Binx Building for eight years. I'd never seen him until today. And yet he didn't *seem* to be playing the wise-acre.

"That's funny," I said in a sort of strained voice. "I've never seen you until today."

This didn't faze him.

"Of course not," he answered cheerfully. "Today is the first day I've ever used the elevators. Until today I always walked up."

"To the thirteenth floor," I said in a choked voice.

"Yes," he seemed happy to chatter, "thirteen flights of stairs are good exercise. Excellent exercise. Used to keep me in splendid condition. But of course," he gave an apologetic little laugh, "I believe I'm getting a little old for such strenuous exertion now. So today I used the elevator for the first time. I think I'll continue to do so."

This was more than I could take. He was really pulling my leg. I got a little sore. This was all nonsense. What could I have been thinking of?

"So you have an office here?" I asked nastily.

He nodded.

"On the thirteenth floor."

"Where's your firm name on the building directory?" I asked, pointing a finger at the directory board on the wall across from the elevators.

He stepped over to the board and pointed with a thin finger.

"Here," he indicated. "Right here."

I stepped out of the elevator and walked over beside him, squinting up at the spot at which he pointed. It was black and blank. Nothing was there. It was the empty space at the bottom of the "H" section.

"Listen," I snapped. "If you're trying to be wise—" and I glared down at him.

He looked bewilderedly at me.

"It's right there," he said. "Z. Hobson & Company."

But it wasn't, of course. Yet the expression on his face was so sincerely *convincing.* Still it *wasn't* there!

He suddenly looked down at a big watch he'd pulled from his pocket. A watch with a huge, old-fashioned gold chain.

"My," he said. "Oh my, it's getting late. I must hurry, or I'll miss my supper." He smiled apologetically, tapped his black derby. "Goodnight," he said pleasantly.

I watched him walk briskly out of the building. Then I turned and looked at the spot on the directory to which he'd pointed. It was still blank. There wasn't any Z. Hobson & Company there.

WHEN the night man relieved me, ten minutes later, I went straight to the bar next door. I needed a few quick ones. My wife gave me hell when I got home groggy, of course, but I couldn't tell her the reason. I couldn't tell anyone. Up and down. Up and down. Up and down. Maybe I *was* going nuts.

And if I was going batty, the symptoms were still with me the next morning. For the little guy stepped into the elevator again, and again he nodded pleasantly. If the elevator hadn't been so crowded I think I'd have refused to take him up.

And it would have been better for me if I had refused. For the same damned thing happened again. He called for the thirteenth, while a chill ran up my spine. I didn't dare look at him as I made my stops all the way up to the fourteenth. But when I turned around to look at that stop—he wasn't there.

He hadn't gotten off at any of the previous stops. I know. I watched that door like a Junior G-man. But he was gone!

And I took him down, around six o'clock, that evening. Took him down even though I *knew* he hadn't stepped into the car at any stop.

I was in no mood to make light talk with him that night. And I reeled in on my wife's cold dinner for the second night in a row. But I needed the alcoholic fortitude.

Obviously there was no thirteenth. I told myself this for the next two days. But for the next two days the little guy got on and off at the thirteenth floor. I wasn't sleeping nights. I was a wreck.

It was on the third evening, about six o'clock again, when I whipped past the gray wall where the thirteenth floor *wasn't* and I suddenly *felt* him standing in the back of the car.

I looked straight ahead. I didn't dare turn around. My voice must have been almost hysterical as I spoke.

"Look," I quavered. "Hasn't this been going on long enough?"

"Eh?" he said behind me. "I'm afraid I don't quite understand you."

"This thirteenth floor stuff," I blurted crazily. "You know there isn't any thirteenth floor!"

His voice was clearly bewildered as he answered.

"I'm afraid I really don't understand you. My office is on the thirteenth. I get on and off there."

His last sentence was the one I didn't care to face. It was *too* true. I was getting more than frantic.

"But the Binx Building doesn't *have* any thirteenth floor," I wailed.

"Oh," said the little guy, and there was sudden understanding in his voice. "Oh, I see. You mean *actually* it doesn't."

He didn't add anything to that. That seemed to make it perfectly clear. Ha ha. It didn't *actually* have any thirteenth floor. Ha ha ha. Yes, indeed. That made it all right. I felt like gibbering wildly.

He suddenly spoke again.

"But I *do* save rent that way," he reflected.

I GOT the elevator down to the first floor before I lost control completely. I jerked the door open. I couldn't get him out of there soon enough.

He stepped out into the lobby and turned to make some nightly small talk. But I wasn't having any. I slammed the door and shot up as quick as I could. That night I got so drunk I told my wife. It didn't help. She just looked at me. When I reeled off to bed I heard her calling her mother's to find out if they had an extra room for her.

I came to work at the Binx Building the next morning resolved that it would be my last. I would quit as soon as the day was over. Enough was enough. Another day and they'd take me away in a steel-ribbed jacket.

But nine o'clock passed without the appearance of the little guy. Ten o'clock went by and I still hadn't seen him. At eleven he stepped into the elevator. He smiled pleasantly, touching his black derby.

"Have an extra heavy load for you today, Mike," he said.

I didn't answer. But I thought, my God has he got *friends?*

"I'm moving out," he went on. "Have to expand. Business is getting so very good I need new quarters."

I shut my eyes and shook my head hard. But he didn't disappear. Didn't disappear, that is, until the thirteenth floor. At least he must have disappeared. For he was in the car at the twelfth and gone when I made the stop at the fourteenth!

And it was three trips later when I saw him again. I was going down, in an empty car, when suddenly the weight in the elevator was jolted. I noticed quickly that I'd just passed thirteen.

Then I looked over my shoulder.

The little guy was there. And three big filing cabinets and a heavy old fashioned typewriter were also there.

"This is all I have to move," he said, smiling in that friendly dog way. "It's not too heavy. I telephoned for some movers to meet me in the lobby. They'll take it to my new offices."

"Your new offices," I managed to blurt, "will they be on, on, the—"

"On the thirteenth floor?" he finished my sentence. "Of course. The thirteenth is very lucky. I wouldn't have any other floor for my office."

"But there are no thirteenth floors in the business district of this town," I protested groggily.

He smiled again. "Not actually," he conceded. "But I've found one that will do, just a block from here, for a while. It's on the thirteenth," he finished.

AT LAST, thank God, we were down on the first floor. And there, so help me, were two burly, bearded, overall-clad moving men. They stepped into the car and lugged out the filing cabinets and the old typewriter. The little guy gave them a slip of paper and I suppose it had directions on it for delivery.

Then he turned to me, extending his hand.

"Goodbye, Mike," said the little guy beamingly. "It's been pleasant knowing you. If there's ever anything I can do for you, I wish you'd look me up. Here's my card, my, ah, business card."

He handed me a white pasteboard.

There was nothing on either side. I gagged.

"Wha—what's your business?" I managed to gasp.

"I make invisible ink," he said. "Well, goodbye."

He turned then and marched out of the lobby, a little guy in a black derby hat and a high celluloid collar, whistling happily. The boss of the Z. Hobson Company, Invisible Ink.

That afternoon I caught the manager of the Binx Building. I wasn't going to quit, but I did need a vacation. The manager saw the color of my face and felt that I needed one too.

"Starting today?" I begged.

"Starting today," the manager agreed.

I started to turn weakly for the door. Then I stopped for a minute.

"Say," I demanded, "how long have you managed this place?"

The manager looked at me as if I were crazy.

"Fifteen years," he said.

"How long," I asked carefully, "has the Binx Building not had a thirteenth floor?"

The manager thought.

"About ten years," he answered.

"Who," I gulped, "was the last tenant on the thirteenth, before it was changed to the fourteenth?"

The manager frowned. After a minute he said:

"An old duck named Z. Hobson. A little fellow, as I remember, whose business was ah, let me see, oh yes—invisible ink. He died two days before we inaugurated the no thirteenth floor idea. Nice pleasant old duck."

I must have staggered for the door.

The manager called after me.

"Why were you so curious, Mike?"

"He just moved out today," I croaked.

"You take a nice long vacation, Mike," the manager said in sudden anxious solicitation. "I'm sure you'll straighten out."

Maybe he's right. Maybe I will.

I'm still on my vacation though...

THE END

THE SHADOW OF SATURN

By E. Hoffman Price

Magic is directed will, black it may be as is occult surgery.

WHAT I have to say about the Siamese triplets will have nothing at all to do with any linking together of physical bodies. The bond, which connected Dick Wayland, and Benson's wife, Diane, was an invisible one.

Of the three, Wayland was the first I met. His upper eyelids, lurking beneath overhanging brows, betrayed their existence only by the lashes. His eyes had a purpose, more important merely than looking and seeing. Except to a person of considerable self-assurance, they could have been intolerable whenever he chose to make them so. Now, however, they were amiable and winning as his voice.

"Why won't you tell me how long I have to live, Mr. McQuoid?"

"If your health worries you, why not see your doctor instead of an astrologer?"

The man's will drew back like a well trained leopard, to remain poised behind the persuasiveness of smile and eyes. The nose, neither straight nor aquiline, added to his expression of power consciousness.

"There used to be a time," he retorted, "when no doctor worth his salt was ignorant of astrology, and no astrologer ignorant of medicine. Just why won't you tell me how many years I have ahead of me?"

"In the first place, to do so would be a violation of professional ethics." I fingered the letter and the check, which he had sent a few days previously. "In the second place, when you wrote me the minute and hour and date of birth, and the town also, you left out something quite important."

"What was that?"

"You did not tell me that this is another man's birth data, not your own. If only because you tried to trick me, I wouldn't deal with you."

"Do you mean," he demanded, "that you believe you can judge at first sight whether I am older or younger than the date indicates?"

"The horoscope I set up describes a man taller and heavier than you are, Mr. Wayland. He has a squarish face. He is ruddy, he has thick hands and a thick neck, and is probably on the way to being bald. He loves spotlight. You prefer being the power behind the throne. Next time you try to pull a fast one, send data to fit."

Wayland, however, was persistent. He wagged his head appreciatively and countered, "That was to see whether you knew your business. You said, *he*. That happens to be a woman's birth data."

"You never can get your fill, can you? Only a male could have been born when the degree corresponding to that time was rising. This cannot be a woman's birth time. Here is your check. There is no charge. Whatever you are up to, I don't want to deal with you."

"Oh, all right, Mr. McQuoid! There are three of us in this. He and she and I. It is one of those situations."

"And it's important for you and her to outlive him?"

"Yes," he answered. "First time in my life that anything ever has been really important."

Whether I wanted it or not, I had a client—three clients, in fact. Although I did not for a moment feel that Wayland would use pistol or poison to reshape things to his taste, it was clear that something deadly was developing.

"Give me your birth data, and hers."

When he did so, I opened the 1890-1930 ephemeris to his birth month and glanced at the positrons of the planets on his day. Usually one has to draw a map of the heavens, the twelve-spoked Wheel of Fate to see what influences ruled a man. Wayland's stars on the contrary were so conspicuously aspected as to shout from the page. And a glance at the Table of Houses clinched it.

"At your birth," I told him, "the seventh degree of Scorpio was rising."

"What's wrong with *that?*"

I pointed to the wall chart. "Most signs of the zodiac have only one symbol. Yours has four. There is the scorpion, waiting in the dust and ready with his poisonous barb. There is the snake crawling in the grass with his poison. There is the eagle of pride, flying up to stare the sun out of Countenance. Finally there is the Phoenix—reborn man, freed of earth, and become god-like. And judging from your stars, your eagle is still in the dust, playing with snakes and scorpions.

"You are using an invisible weapon, your will power. Like an Australian bushman 'pointing the bone' to will someone to death."

"That's not true!"

"Whether you know it or not, you are practicing black magic. If it weren't for my bare chance of opening your eyes, I'd wash my hands of the entire business, and good riddance! Pick up your check—I can't take any pay."

"Why not? This is important to me."

"If a man asks a lifeguard to give him swimming lessons on his day off duty, payment is in order. But you rarely hear of a lifeguard offering a drowning man swimming lessons at so much an hour. I'll see you when I've studied your chart and hers and his."

Wayland—Benson—Diane—they were Siamese triplets; and Wayland was a blind man with a kit of psychic surgical instruments, trying to cut the invisible bond, so that he and Diane would be free to start a new life together. While the operation might succeed, not one of the three patients could survive.

All this became so clear and so haunting that I broke away from a dinner party right after the coffee and brandy; and on my way home, I followed an impulse and went directly to Wayland's place in the foothills behind Atherton.

The house was on a bald knoll whose base was fringed with oaks. Knowing well the atrocious parking most country places offer, I left my car at the level spot not far from the entrance. The ascent was neither long nor steep, yet the effect was odd. At first I thought that too many cigarettes and too many years sitting at a desk had made me more short-winded than I had realized; but it proved to be another sort of breathlessness, and it was combined with that light-headedness, which one experiences after a swift drive from six or seven thousand feet elevation down to sea level.

It is not so much an actual giddiness as it is a sensing that one's balance is slightly off; that one's own voice sounds like someone else's—probably all this is because the inner ear, which seems to control equilibrium, has not had a chance to readjust itself to the change of pressure.

Ear...inner ear...sound...*sound,* not elevation at all!

Yet there was no more than a suggestion of sound, and that so uncertain as to be no more than premonition that I should presently hear something. Still and all, it played tricks with the equilibrium mechanism, so that I had to exert a conscious effort, however slight, to remain normally balanced.

Presently the sound became audible, yet hearing it was something like seeing an iceberg—in that what is perceived is less than a tenth of all that is actually there. The unheard part of what came from the house was what had the disturbing force. The murmuring, the rustling, the whispering were only the perceptible indication of something beneath the level of hearing.

Wayland was beating a drum. Not a snare drum, not a bass drum, not a tympanum, but something far more primitive. Perhaps remember the travelogue and soundtrack, which Harrison Smith recently brought back from Tibet? Hundreds of yellow-robed lamas gathered to chant to the sunrise.

AUM! Mani padme hum! AUM! Tat Savitur varenyam!

Wayland's drumming was like the chanting of those lamas; and I began to understand as from direct experience why the explorer had insisted that the actual chant gave an effect, which the soundtrack did not have; that the intoning of *mantrams* literally went to one's head, and seemed to wrench the sutures of the skull, and to hammer the nerve center of the solar plexus.

Pain and dizziness became more pronounced. I could not feel the porch flooring under my tread. It was as if gravity had ceased to act. I caught at the jamb, and got a glance through the small pane, slantwise through vestibule and archway and into the living room. Wayland sat on the floor. He had a saddle drum whose wooden shell was no larger than a good-sized mixing bowl. With one hand he beat the head.

Beat is hardly the word. For while he did tap with knuckles and fingertips, and heel of the hand, and slapped with the palm, the strokes were only at times percussive. He varied the impacts by rippling his fingertips as though on the keys of a piano. He made dragging, caressing sweeps. There was only a little sound: a murmuring, a whispering, a muttering, like the persistence of a gong note when the bronze is stilled yet not actually mute.

He swayed and nodded. It was as though he had become a mechanical toy. Wayland was absent: what I saw was his animated frame. The man himself had stepped into another dimension. His will carried on drumbeats, reached out. What I felt was only the eddying backwash of the currents, which he was directing elsewhere.

Wayland was making magic. Magic, stripped of ritual, is nothing more than directed and controlled vibration, the carrier wave of concentrated will, of pure power. Thought, in its plane, is moulded into shape as are iron or clay on the material plane.

I groped, fumbled for the pushbutton. Whoever was receiving the directed impulses of Wayland's drumming was being twisted on a psychic rack. Though I found the button, my fingers acted as though they belonged to someone else. While not ignoring my will, they seemed unable to understand or obey. Rather, my will was groping, hobbled, stumbling.

That beating, that surging, those flashes and whirlpools of light in my own head were the interference waves of a fourth dimensional heterodyne: the illusion of sound and light, images made stronger by twisted nerves.

The geometry of the room was warping out of all relation to reality. It was not only as though I now saw Wayland at once full face and in profile; it was as though, without disturbance of the walls, there was an additional dimension down, which I could see all the way to infinity. Perspective became wholly false. The woman who came down the hyper-dimensional spiral changed rather in figure and feature and expression than in apparent height as she moved from infinite remoteness to step at last into the room.

WHEN the face and form solidified, I recognized Diane Benson. The Ascending Sign of her horoscope had correctly described head shape and carriage, the set of the shoulders, the expression of the dark eyes. I had expected unusual brunette beauty, with Saturn in Libra: Diane went far beyond expectation.

Wayland seemed not to see her, nor she, him. Yet her lips moved, and her eyes, at once haunting and haunted, were fixed as on someone facing her.

Whatever this was, it would be dangerous to interrupt, even if I could. But the hand, which had so long been unable to obey, now acted as though of its own will. Space rearranged itself. The bell snarled in the hallway. Wayland continued his drumming; however, the sound was only a normal one, the curiously stirring appeal of drums. The apparition of Diane had vanished.

I RANG again, and gave the knob a twist and a rattle. The door opened without warning. I lurched headlong across the threshold and into the hall. Wayland yelled, jumped up, and checked himself against a chair.

"Where the devil'd you come from?"

"Walked in. I rang, but it seems your drum kept you from hearing. I must have got impatient and jiggled the door and it wasn't latched. Sorry I startled you."

Though Wayland had not yet wholly returned into himself, he made a characteristic grimace, wry and half-humorous. "Drums always have fascinated me. This one's more relaxing than liquor. You can have your electric organs and the like, I'll take a drum for self-expression."

"This is an odd one," I said, kneeling to get a close look. "Wouldn't be out of place in a museum. Is it something liberated during the war?"

He shook his head. "I picked it up when they auctioned the St. Cyr estate. Junk from the trophy room. Persian armor, Zulu assegai, Tibetan statuette—and this." He reached for the decanter on the tile-topped cocktail table. "Bourbon?"

"Thanks, no. I just broke away from dinner, and followed the impulse to barge in. I had you three people so strongly in mind I couldn't stay in step with sociability this evening."

"Well, now! What did our horoscopes tell you?"

"You're practicing black magic with that drum. If you are not trying to will him to death, you are trying to will her to pack up and run out with you. Pretty mess, you and he, law partners!"

Wayland's face tightened. "How would I be able to do anything of the sort, assuming I were trying to?"

"About one human in every hundred thousand, perhaps one in every million, let's not quibble about numbers, has *will* power. The others aren't able to go beyond mere wishing, hoping. Wish is a firecracker, will is an A-bomb. Wishing is an emotional muddle. Will is pure force. It's the same as electricity, magnetism, gravity, heat, light. It is energy directed and harmonious. That's what you're dabbling with and you're very likely to destroy everyone concerned—yourself, her, and him..."

Wayland's down-droop of the brows, further shading his eyes, told me he had been impressed, so I bored in. "When matter disintegrates it becomes energy. When energy is collected and organized, it becomes matter. The whole material universe is nothing but organized will, and you, you damned fool, are playing with *that*. With a psychic A-bomb. Quit it!"

"You said, black magic."

"Magic is directed will. It is black when directed for your own wishes, even if they are good, as people ordinarily reckon good."

"Aren't you going a bit too far, just looking at the stars?"

"No, I'm not. The way her horoscope is related to yours and to her husband's is such that a danger to one of you is a danger to all three."

And then I told him what I had heard and seen before shock made me give the door a wrench.

Wayland's eyes, probably for the first time in his life, opened wide. "Is that true? Man to man, is it?"

"Could I have cooked it up out of my imagination? And if I were trying to fool you, wouldn't I have picked something more plausible?"

That seemed to satisfy him, for he asked, "How do you explain it? My being able to—to will this, do this."

"If you can accept the idea of reincarnation, at least as something possible—if you can accept the idea of *karma*, the law of cause and effect, the law that every action and every desire sets in motion a train of events—that, life after life, we come back, bound to those we have either loved or hated in previous lives—if that is not too much for you to swallow, I'd risk answering your question. Not with the idea that you should believe it, but that you would not set yourself against it without taking at least a moment's thought."

He gave me an odd look. "I've heard of such things. Hearing a little more won't hurt. But am I to understand that an astrologer can read a man's past lives?"

"To a degree, yes. And the probable trend of his next life. The stars tell all. The only limitation is man's ability to read them. Anyway, you and Benson are law partners, a quite prosaic and matter of fact profession. But you, in your former lives, learned something of the science of vibration. Now you are using it with the self-centeredness you've always had. Though never before have you had the power to go with the selfishness.

"Here is your test—will you be a scorpion, or a Phoenix?"

By way of accepting the challenge, he told me about himself and Diane and Benson. There was nothing novel about the situation, not even in the frills and trimming. Benson and Diane had outlived whatever love they might have had—but he wasn't going to let anyone else have her. It gave him a sense of power to hold put, to command; and Diane would not leave her husband, which infuriated Wayland.

"Chicken-hearted," he summed up. "Nobody'd be hurt, really..."

"She is not what you call chicken-hearted," I told him. "She is simply incapable of changing an innate conviction. That is by no means the same as being stubborn from pride. She was born under fixed signs. In whatsoever pattern such a person is set, she is there to stay. Change is possible, but very slowly, and it has to come from within, never from without. Don't you understand?"

"No. That makes no sense whatever."

"Probably not. Scorpio, your sign, is also a fixed one."

BEFORE that jab had a chance to sink in, a car came up the drive. Wayland exclaimed as though in recognition of its sound. He bounded to the window. After a glance out, he turned on me, exclaiming, "There she is now! Get out, will you? Whatever's brought her here, I don't want her embarrassed—get out! No, Lord, no! Not out the front— Leave by the back—that way—"

His gesture had the force to match the ferocity of his voice. Impatience, resentment at my meddling presence; and, triumph also: he conveyed all these with eye and tone.

I was in the laundry alcove before Wayland opened the front door. I heard her greet him with an inarticulate cry rather than with words. Then a few heel clicks, sharp and jarring, and she was in the living room with Wayland.

Diane was trying to explain her inexplicable urge, and why she had not phoned. She was violently agitated, and scarcely coherent; this, with the echo of distortion of vestibule and hall kept me from catching more than a few words.

"...for a minute I was so dizzy I pulled over to the side of the road...I must have blacked out...no, darling, nothing has gone wrong...I simply had to get out...had to and did, and oh, it was the strangest, craziest thing, heading for your place; but I *had* to."

He said something to the effect that a drink would do her good. While he had himself under better control than she had, more had happened than he was able to understand. I twisted the latch knob, and very carefully opened the door. After this unexpected demonstration of his power to command her will, Wayland would certainly not pay heed to anything I might say to him later.

It seemed, as I skirted the house, that my meddling had done more harm than good, for in telling him what I had seen, I had given him an awareness of a power he had apparently been exercising blindly.

Once in the parking circle, I saw her coupe. I looked into it. She had brought no luggage. But that did not prove that he and she might not leave within the hour, and not to return. This could well be Wayland's long-awaited victory, won by magic.

I WAS at the foot of the grade, and in the deep shadow of the oaks under which I had parked when a long convertible swung into Wayland's drive, tires squealing and scattering gravel. With well over four million cars registered in California, the odds were very much against my guessing correctly whose it was that swooped up the grade and around the curves. But since I, a spectator, had been drawn into the outer fringe of the "sending," it was likely enough that Wayland's drumming had affected Benson; or that Benson had simply trailed his wife.

By the time I returned to the level of the house the visitor was indoors. To avoid a betraying latch click, I had not closed the back door after me. In another moment, I was again in the laundry alcove, and tiptoeing for the front.

"Don't be piggish, Dick," a man was saying. "Diane's life is her own, she's entitled to it, whatever you two have together is your own business. As long as it's kept quiet and private. But when she blows her top and bounces out of the house, jet propelled, after getting rid of some guests by telling them she had a headache, *it's going too far.*"

By now I knew that the speaker *was* Ron Benson. Diane was crying, and insisting that it had not been Wayland's fault; that she had followed an irresistible impulse. And Wayland, seeing no good in discussing magic, got down to a point of his own:

"We're serious, Ron. This went way past the flirtation stage a long time ago. She and I did not have an engagement this evening, and if we had had, I'd certainly not expect her to hustle unexpected callers out of your house. And since that's what she seems to have done, you can put two and two together. You might as well be realistic. The situation is getting under her skin. Break it up, neither is good for the other any more."

As Wayland paused for breath, Benson broke in, "If Diane left me to marry you, you can figure what would happen to our practice. Our clients would lose confidence in us as a team. So quit the sentimental schoolboy stuff and act grown up! She's getting no divorce—" He chuckled affably. "She can't. No more than could I. Everything's too comfortably complicated, you know."

And that was when I left. Their fate seemed now to be so much and so immediately in their own hands that details did not matter. It was not until several days later, when Diane Benson called at my studio, that I learned that nothing had been decided, and that Wayland was more than ever at work, forcing a decision.

She was not as tall as she looked, nor was it the high heels; the illusion came from the way she carried herself. Diane was that uttermost rarity, a woman who knew how to walk. Her hair was all alive, and even though its vital quality might have been the result of skillful processing, no beauty parlor could possibly have given her skin that exceedingly fine texture. Most important, however, were the dark eyes. They told that from living and learning, she had reached full human stature; the other two of the Siamese triplet had not, though their chance was just around the corner of Time.

She summed up what had happened, and except for details told me nothing I did not already know. She concluded, "Dick finally admitted he had been willing me to leave Ron, commanding me to. Though he certainly hadn't intended to have me drive about in a trance, and just on the verge of being blacked out. He promised most faithfully he would not try any such tricks again."

HER features were perfectly under control, with an almost Asiatic serenity—except for the twitch of her eyelids.

"Well?"

"Now he's concentrating on Ron."

"You mean that your husband has begun to take drives like the one that gave you such a shock? Neat way of making you a widow?"

"Oh, Lord, *no*. Nothing like that. Dick has simply been willing Ron to release me."

"And you're not cooperating a bit, when you could make yourself so thoroughly obnoxious in a million dainty feminine ways that your husband would in no time at all be glad to give you to the Indians. Easiest thing on earth, only you've not done it. Why not?"

"Call it a matter of obligation. No one and nothing compelled me to marry Ron. I knew I was wrong at the time, but I went ahead anyway. Because he was good to me, and because I was all in a whirl, looking for escape, and nowhere to go. I didn't love him, but I liked him. He was solid, he had his feet on the ground. Oh, you wouldn't understand what I mean by escape..."

"Wouldn't I? Escape seems to be humanity's career, and first urge."

"I think this must have been escape from myself," she went on. " Or from the giddy crowd I was part of. Nothing seemed especially important, and nothing was. Except getting away."

I pointed to the column of solar arcs on the margin of her chart. "Sun square Venus and Neptune. Saturn crossed midheaven. Say, 1945, in the autumn?" At her nod, I continued, "Escape or rather the attempt to didn't work out at all, and so?"

"Somehow or other, I realized that one can't ever escape from oneself and from what one has made. One has to stick and see it through. If I forced the issue and walked out on Ron, all I'd do would bring Dick grief in one way or another, and we'd probably end by being each other's stumbling blocks, resenting and accusing each other. I'd rather stay and pay my bill, my debt to fate. I have to pay it before I can ever have someone I really love. Idiotic sounding, isn't it? But that's how I feel."

"Did someone tell you what you've just told me, or did you read it, or—?"

"It simply came to me. That you can't run away from what you've made for yourself. It follows you wherever you go. Does that make sense?"

"That," I told her, "is the beginning and the end and the entire substance of Wisdom. You've stated the Law of Karma. You set forces in motion, and now you're at the receiving end until the forces have expended themselves. And what worries you right now is that Dick Wayland is setting fresh forces in motion."

She nodded. "Will you *please* tell Dick that whatever he's doing, holding a thought or whatever he wishes to call it, it is not working out the way he wants it to. Ron is becoming morbid, shaky, and stubborn."

"Why not tell him yourself?"

"He'd only laugh and say I'm chicken-hearted. He insists that he and I belong to each other. That Ron encouraged the flirtation, largely for his own convenience, and now it's up to him to like what he promoted."

"Promoted? So you'd look the other way while he had some other woman on the brain?" I glanced at the chart. "The spring of 1945?"

"That's right. And I was very happy about it all. Taking the easy view of things again. When I could have made a break and been free—ever hear of anything so utterly crazy."

"Pardon my yawn," I said, and gestured toward the filing cabinet. "I've lost count of the number of times I've charted that story. There's not even a bit of novelty about the three of you being so civilized about it all. There is only one thing unusual about you three, and maybe I can convince Dick Wayland."

"What is it?" she asked eagerly.

"It's not necessary to tell you, so I won't. Words may very often set forces in motion, too, you know. The same as acts or desires."

"Suppose Ron went to the mountains for a couple of weeks. That'd break the close association—they've both been working day and night on a case that's wound up now, and a change of pace wouldn't hurt a bit. That's the oddest thing about it all—the way they work together, and really like each other—there isn't any jealousy or animosity, or can you believe that?"

"Just because it's never allowed to happen in fiction, on the ground that it's quite impossible, and that they simply ought to hate each other, doesn't keep it from happening in actual life."

"So you see where that puts me? They're close as brothers."

"Much closer," I told her. "You three. That's what's dangerous. There's nothing I could tell your husband—he's a down-to-earth thinker—but I'll talk to Wayland. He can understand, if he wants to."

"But can't you tell me now what to do, what not to do, how it's going to turn out?"

"No."

"That makes you a queer sort of astrologer." She spoke without petulance; she was merely puzzled. "After all, that's your business, predicting and foreseeing?"

"You're confusing astrology with fortune telling. There is one element which never shows in any horoscope."

"What's that?"

"Will and choice. The stars shape your personality and the pattern of your moods, your peaks of vitality and your depths of depression. But whether your mood will rule you, or you rule it is a matter of choice. There's neither pure predestination nor purely free will—there is rather a blend. You can't escape from the circle of your fate, but within the circle, you have a million choices. Whatever I said to you now would influence you, and since there is no real need of my saying anything, I am not saying it."

"I think I understand," she said, and when Diane left, it seemed that she had actually understood; and the eyelids had quit twitching from tension.

Whether or not Benson's leaving town for awhile would get him beyond the range of Wayland's magic was an open question. He might go into the mountains to set to work with his drum. I began to consider the merits of breaking into his house and burning that diabolical instrument, but ended by discarding the thought. Destroying the drum would not decontaminate Wayland's will, without which no amount of thumping would have any force at all.

When I phoned the office and learned that Benson would be away for a week, I went to see Wayland; and, as before, without first calling him.

He was at it when I arrived. There was that same inaudible undertone of vibration, the same queer and distressing effect, but apparently he had not yet got his will in tune with the rhythm. While the archway opening into the living room had begun to warp, and the walls were approaching a shimmering translucence, there was not yet any opening into higher dimensions.

I rang, and called his name. No answer.

Another jangle, another shout. Concentration broken, Wayland came pouncing for the door. I endured his eyes, and said, "You wanted to know how long Benson had to live, and I wouldn't answer. I may not tell you now, but you have forced me pretty close to telling."

"Come in."

"Get in touch with Mrs. Benson. Let me talk to the two of you at the same time."

"She went with him as far as Modesto—she'll be visiting relatives there while he and two friends from around there are up at the lodge, fishing. If you have a good argument, you don't need her here to team up with you."

176

I spread the three horoscopes on the cocktail table. "In each chart, the malefic planets are so placed, were so placed at the birth of each of you that when the daily motion of the planets—the transits, that is—puts one of you under a disastrous influence, the other two are likewise under it."

"It looks as clear to me as the fine print in an insurance policy is to anyone but an insurance broker."

"All right, take my word for it, then. You three are linked more closely than the Siamese twins were to each other. Except that you're not bound together by flesh and cartilage, but by your karma—by your associations in former lives you are so linked that you cannot be separated. Trying to cut him loose will finish all three.

"She told me how she drove out here, that night, almost in a total blackout."

He nodded. "All right. That cured me of trying to influence her."

"Pouring the power on him can drive him into a fatal accident."

"It needn't," Wayland retorted.

"What you really mean is that as long as you don't shove him off a cliff with your own hand, it's quite all right. I've come to tell you that if you finish him by remote control, by accident as it will appear, you will at the same time finish her, and yourself as well."

He was doing his best not to believe me; at last he said, doggedly, "All I was doing was willing him to release her."

"And that's getting him into such a muddle he'll drive head-on into a collision, or step off a cliff, or forget that a gun is loaded. You've been bringing things to a climax, and the stars are getting closer and closer to the transit that will touch things off. You'll liberate her, all right, and him, and yourself, but not in the way you want."

"I am here. She is in Modesto, with her sister. He and Fred and Dave Sims are up at the lodge, not far from Sonora Pass. How the devil could anything hit us all at once?"

"It need not be all at once in the kind of time and space we know. Though you have been monkeying with time and space of another sort. But skip that. If something happened to him alone, it would kick back at you and her. She'd never again be the same.

She would know that you caused it. And that would be hard to take. If you simply must be rational and materialistic, I'll put it this way, as one of many possibilities—the strain, the tension, the upset, would make you both accident-prones. And the corporations that retain you are constantly in hot water about the accident-prones on their payrolls. Don't tell me you don't fully understand what I mean. Accidents don't simply happen—they are caused by the tangles and confusions in the sub-cellars of the subconscious."

He gave me a twisted smile. "I thought it was the stars?"

"Same thing!"

He said, slowly, "We three are in danger that I am making?"

"You're a butcher boy trying to separate Siamese triplets. There is only one way to break the bond that holds you three together."

"What is that way?"

"Quit driving with that will of yours! Burn that drum. It may not have any real bearing on the case at all. It could not have, unless you had the will to make it serve you. Destroying it would nonetheless be an outward token that you have abandoned occult surgery. That you are accepting things as they *are*. That you have quit trying to rearrange lives. That you have renounced your stubbornness and your arrogance and the importance of your own desires. That you've become a grown-up man.

"Go to that lodge with the drum and burn it, right before him."

"Fine business, with the Sims boys there!"

"Herd them out for a bit of fishing, while you and he supposedly confer on an emergency that's just come up."

Wayland snatched the drum. "Will you go with me?"

"Any time you say."

He glanced at his watch. "Make it now."

I said, "We can take it easy, and be there in time for breakfast. That'll make it natural and easy for the Sims brothers to carry on with their fishing."

"You're afraid to trust me alone with this drum till tomorrow."

"I'm afraid to trust your moods and thinking. Let's go."

WE DROVE through the warmth of the great central valley. A red moon came up through low-hanging haze. Wayland took his time, yet there was constant demand on his skill until we finally got out of the unbroken procession of trucks. He was busy with more than driving. He was thinking, digesting, analyzing, after the fashion of his sign. It was not until the moon was high and white, and valley sultriness replaced by mountain chill that he spoke.

"I'm glad we picked the situation to pieces," he said, abruptly. "One thing though that you skipped."

"Could be more than one, but let's have it."

"If the three of us are so tied together, there is nothing left to reach for. I don't need a certificate of title to Diane. There's nothing left to be had—we already have everything there is. Funny, that's about the way she expressed it, when she and I started. We'd not upset any apple carts, we'd hurt no one. She must have known from the beginning, subconsciously at least, what it's taken me until now to get through my head. I think I've become so used to complicated cases in my practice that anything really simple confuses me."

The eagle, I now knew, had at last begun to use his eyes for some purpose other than trying to stare the sun out of countenance. Wayland's company was no longer disturbing. He had ceased radiating that remorseless and avaricious will. He was becoming human.

We stopped once for gas, and several times for coffee. The wind whining down from snowcaps reaching twelve thousand feet into the moonlight had a biting edge. The thin air at once soothed and stimulated Wayland.

"She was speaking of karma. Fumbling with your words, but somehow, speaking in her own right. It wasn't exactly retribution, or crime and punishment. It seemed bigger than all those."

"It is bigger. Thoughts, desires, cravings set up vibrations. People are drawn to each other, either for love or for hate, because they vibrate in the same wavelength. The only way to break a bond is to change the wavelength of your thoughts and feelings. Once that's done, you make new contacts, there are new attractions, for better or for worse."

This was oversimplifying things; but what checked Wayland's impending query was our coming to a road marker. There we left

179

the paved highway to go laboriously up what was little more than a wagon track.

Above the mumble of the engine, I caught the mutter of distant waterfalls. Once, I heard a far-off rumbling. The previous winter's snows were beginning to shift and slide.

Gray glamour reached in and thinned the darkness of the pines. The gray became an eerie lavender. The headlights, now murky and deceptive, created illusions, through reflection from foliage and granite walls, to make it seem at times that Wayland was about to drive over the edge of a thousand-foot drop. Fatigue made such illusion more disturbingly realistic.

Wayland cursed, booted the brake, and whipped into a skid. There was a grinding sound. As the car slewed over, a fender crumpled. After spinning the wheels in a futile effort to pull out of the ditch, a shallow one, Wayland said, "Well, it could be a lot worse. We're almost there. Ron can tow us out."

It was only then that I noticed the boulder, which because of the deceptive light, Wayland had not observed until he had come within a couple yards of straddling it. A small fragment had wedged under the oil pan. We tugged and heaved until we got the larger obstacle against the bank, and out of the way. It was wet and muddy; apparently it had been dislodged after nightfall. The hot sun, beating down all day, had melted enough snow on the upper slopes to saturate the earth, and release the boulder.

"We could have been right there when, it landed," he observed, as we went on. "Or we could have been stalled a couple miles back."

As we entered a cleared wide space, I glanced across the ravine. The opposite wall reflected a sickly glow. "Whoever's on the way behind us probably has enough clearance, with your car jammed against the bank," I remarked. And then, noticing that the light did not shift, I added, "The reflection of your headlights. Walked off and left them on."

"Count on me for that. Favorite trick."

Though mists obscured the clearing ahead, I could distinguish the dark bulk of two lodges. The roofs had a steep pitch, to keep them from collapsing during the heavy snows. We were at the edge of a small upland meadow, which reached from the rim of the ravine to the nearby foot of the heights that towered over it.

"The first place is Ron's lodge," Wayland said. "Our timing has been a bit too good. I hate to barge in so early, but waiting in this damned mist is no treat."

"Suppose I go back and snap off the lights before the battery's run down," I proposed. "While you rout him out. It'd be better that way, than having me at your heels. At the best, he'll be surprised to see you, and whatever you two have to say will be none the worse for having it between yourselves."

I had scarcely turned when he said, "We forgot the drum. Something else you can tend to."

WHATEVER happened, I told myself, that devil's drum was not going to survive. Engrossed with this thought, I retraced my way as far as the buttress that marked the beginning of the meadow shelf before I noticed the rattle and patter of rock fragments. Then a big chunk thumped down to the springy earth, and rolled to within a few yards of me. A crash helmet would come in handy, it seemed.

I turned and called to Wayland, "Watch out!"

But he had already stopped. Though little more than a dark splotch in the early gray, his posture made it clear that something other than my words had warned him. I heard a deep rumbling. He must have sensed the vibration an instant before I had.

The mists shifted and thinned a little. Far up, the snow-packed slopes reflected the first ruddiness of dawn. An acre or more of the mass shifted, so that of a sudden, it no longer mirrored the glow. The rumbling, deep and sullen, increased in volume; but the sound was like that of the stream, which roared incessantly in the gorge. Anyone lulled to sleep by it could hardly be aroused by the new and ominous undertone.

I did not know the lay of the land; Wayland did. He knew how much or how little space there was between the two lodges, and the steep slope down, which poured a hundred thousand tons of saturated earth sheared off by the pressure of settling snowfields. Surely this must always have been considered a safe spot until now, when a trick of nature had upset all previous estimates. Boulders, freed from the slow-moving mass, thumped down to the meadow. Above, the creeping earth was picking up speed.

The roar was like the soundtrack of a freight train, enormously magnified and in the tempo of a slow-motion film. Instead of ducking for the shelter of the buttress, I yelled, and ran toward Wayland, as though I had to risk doing what I was sure he would not do. Stumbling over a fragment however sent me sprawling.

"Stay away!" he shouted. "I'll wake him."

He raced for the lodge. I had landed afoul of an outcropping of rock. Numbed for a moment, I had difficulty in getting up, and when I did regain my feet, I could do little more than grit my teeth and hobble.

Wayland pivoted, wove, evaded a boulder, which bounced and went crashing into the ravine. He became a barely visible blur in the mists. Dark against the darkness of the cabin, he vanished entirely from sight. He shouted again. For all his heart-breaking effort, he could not have made himself heard.

I yelled till my throat cracked. I took a few steps forward, then stopped. Wayland could not make it. I was sure he had been knocked down. Then I got a glimpse of him; his motion revealed him. He reached the door.

A lag in the ever-deepening rumble allowed me to hear even the rattle of the latch, and his cry, "Ron, get out!"

A late poker game and a comfortable amount of Bourbon...no wonder Benson and his friends had not turned out already. Wayland was kicking, beating at the door. I began backing away from my relatively safe spot. Instinct drove me, though every moment made me feel as if I myself were in the lodge, and as good as doomed, and paralyzed by the knowledge that there was no escape for me.

Lights blazed from the windows.

The seconds dragged eternally.

A long path of light reached out as the door opened. Two figures were outlined by the glow. One was a woman. I caught only the momentary twinkle of white arms, the glint of silk, the gleam of hair—

The light winked out, and the meadow quivered. I could barely distinguish the crash and splintering of the sturdy lodge as it was engulfed by the dark flood and ground to bits by the boulders that were part of the flow.

The edge of the slide moved slowly now, as the pressure behind it subsided. The further lodge still stood, untouched. Benson's had blended into the black mass, which stopped a few yards short of the ravine's lip.

Neither Wayland nor Benson nor that woman, whoever she may have been, could possibly have survived. If by some miracle any shred of life remained in any of them, it would be no blessing either to that survivor, or to anyone who had to see what remained. Nevertheless, I hobbled forward. I had to listen, if only to make sure there was no sheltered pocket from which came a cry for help.

Several trees had survived the dwindling fury of the rush. Timber, squared timber, projected from the slide. I skirted the end, as though the further, the darker side would offer a more promising front. There was now no sound except that of the wind and the stream. Both seemed far away and feeble.

Then, beyond any doubt, there were human voices.

"...so help me, Dick, I never saw anyone look as downright foolish as you did when a woman turned out instead of Dave and Fred—and then you couldn't believe it was Diane!"

That was all I could grapple with for a moment. That anyone, much less all three, could have escaped was too much to be grasped at once; so that while both Wayland and Diane spoke, I could not get what they were saying. The voices seemed far off. My thought was, "I am rather far off myself." Reaction was more of a shock than was having witnessed the actual destruction.

Benson spoke again: "You took the craziest chance, Dick. I'd never have had the nerve. You know—well—everything looks different—I've been stubborn about you two—three *is* a crowd..."

There was a murmuring and a rumbling in my head, as though that devil's drum had begun to sound. I hobbled along the edge of the debris until once more I tuned in on speech. Diane was saying, and with wonder and new life in her voice, "Ron, do you really mean it? It's really the way you want things now?"

"...No, not trading, not paying, it's just that things look different..."

All I saw was three wavering spindles of mist, so much like all the other grayness that I could not have distinguished them had they not been luminous in the manner of phosphorescent flecks in tropical waters, though by no means as bright. There were three vague spindles, and no more speech at all.

After blending into and with each other, they became distinct again, and separate. And by now I understood that I had not actually heard any speech at all; I had perceived thought so strong and vital that it had seemed that there had been spoken words.

Two of the shapes moved closer together and somewhat apart from the other; and then they, as well as the one from which they had separated, thinned into morning mist.

By the time the debris was cleared away, I had learned that since the Sims brothers had at the last minute been unable to join Benson, Diane had changed her plans and had gone with him; wherefore he and she and Wayland had met for the last time under the shadow of Saturn.

During his final few moments, Wayland had risen from among scorpions to become a Phoenix, winning liberation for him and for Diane, and for Benson as well. And it was not until later, when I burned the devil's drum, that it came to me that Benson had also risen above himself, earning his freedom.

THE END

THAT DREADFUL NIGHT

By David Wright O'Brien

When you go on record and say you don't believe in haunted houses, you shouldn't be afraid to spend the night in one...

IT ALL started from the discussion we were having about superstitions. As all such discussions generally do, this one got off on a tangent until we were talking about the terrors lurking in the other world.

Of course I was right up there in front of the conversation, shooting off my mouth at great length and generally letting it be known that there was nothing in existence that could turn my hair to silver because of fright.

"Nothing?" one of our group demanded incredulously.

I found all eyes suddenly focused in my direction, and several expressions of frankly admiring awe.

I cleared my throat.

"Of course not," I told them.

There was a silence. One of those silences, which I should have had sense enough to know meant that everyone present was combing his mind in an effort to hit on something that would force me to back up the bravado of my words.

I got a little uneasy.

"There's nothing," I repeated a little less confidently, "that could frighten me for even an instant."

Nobody said a word. They were still at it. Searching for something to knock me off the roost.

"Think of something," I said. "Think of anything."

I knew that that was precisely what they were all doing, and so I figured I might as well beat them to the punch. It sounded good, anyway.

"Anything in existence?" someone asked.

I nodded nonchalantly. "Anything in the other world," I declared.

The meditation continued. Finally one of the oldest of our group spoke up.

"I remember a place once that darned near scared me solid," he declared. "It was a house."

Everyone supplied the adjective at once.

"A *haunted* house?" they cried.

I had a sudden chill. This was definitely taking a turn I didn't relish.

The old fellow nodded.

"That's what I mean," he said, "a haunted house."

EVERYONE was buzzing with suggestions then. Everyone but me. I just stood there, wondering why, at my age, I'd never gotten sense enough to keep my mouth shut.

Then someone broke in over the buzzing.

"Listen," he said, "who knows a really haunted house in these parts?"

I decided to speak up then before I was completely railroaded.

"Haunted houses," I sneered, "are nothing. Nothing at all." I gave the statement all the scorn I could muster.

The old guy who'd mentioned the haunted house idea in the first place gave me a solemn glance.

"Have you ever been in a haunted house?" he asked me.

Everyone was looking at me again.

"Of course not," I told him. "They're a lot of nonsense. Stuff for superstitious weaklings to shudder about."

He shook his head sadly.

"I *have,*" he declared, and he shuddered, then, as if at the mere recollection of it.

I gave him a tolerant smile and went on with my effort to get the topic off haunted houses.

"Can't anyone think of something tougher?" I begged. "You might as well pick something really stiff or nothing at all."

No one had any suggestions. I was breathing a little easier.

"Good lord," I said smilingly, "surely you ought to be able to think of something."

Sometime I will learn when I have said enough. Sometime I will become smart enough to know when to stop talking. Up until my last bright remark I had been talking them all out of the idea. Now I'd talked them right back into it. At least the old guy, who suddenly shook his head.

"No," he said. "There couldn't be anything worse. I know that for a fact. And if it's so very silly, I'm sure you won't mind taking us up on it."

I looked around the group. The expressions on the faces of all showed that they heartily agreed with the old guy's sentiments.

Definitely, I was in a spot. But nevertheless I had to make one last stab at writhing loose.

"Of course I wouldn't mind," I told them all. "I wouldn't mind a bit. I still say it's silly superstition, and I'm going to prove it. But, of course, finding a place that's supposed to be haunted is another thing to think of."

I looked around. Most of the group were frowning, combing out the old gray matter again in an effort to think of a house that had the reputation of being haunted.

They didn't seem to be getting anywhere, and once again I was all set to breathe easily, when once again the old guy popped back into the center of my trouble.

"There's an old house not so very far from here," he told me. "Everything I've ever heard about it points to the fact that it must be haunted. In fact," and he paused dramatically, "I've heard the story of one some of us might know, who spent a night in there and *never came out again in the state in which he'd entered.*"

Everyone in the group caught the chilling impact of those words. And I think I caught them harder than the rest.

I gulped, and then I realized that the old guy and everyone else in the group had turned to stare at me questioningly.

Of course I forced a smile.

"Stuff and nonsense," I said. "An old wives' tale."

The expression on the face of the old guy didn't change. He just continued to stare at me.

"Perhaps so," he said. "But the person I referred to, who failed to come out of that house as he had entered, was my brother."

I can tell you here and now that that statement didn't help my state of mind any. I looked at the old guy, trying to read from his poker faced expression whether or not he was pulling a fast one.

Then someone said in an awed, trembly voice, "So that's what happened to your brother…"

It wasn't a fast one. I was sure of that, then. And I was even more certain that I wanted nothing else to do with the topic of haunted houses and the suggestion that I spend the night in one. Particularly the one the old guy had pulled out of thin air.

But one glance around the group showed me only too clearly that there would be no backing down now. I'd stuck my neck out much too far. Much, much too far to ever hope to go back on my brave words and retain any respect among them.

I went way down for the smile I finally managed to come up with. And even at that it was a pretty weak effort.

"All right," I said with that hard-to-hold smile. "All right, I'll take you up on that challenge. I'll prove my contention."

What an absolute sap I was—but definitely…

AFTER I'd stepped in over my neck, everyone agreed that there would be no sense in waiting any length of time to have me prove myself. And on the suggestion of the old guy, the following night had been chosen for my demonstration of iron nerves.

Consequently all the group met at the same place the following evening, shortly after ten o'clock.

Everyone was especially festive. It was like a great big picnic— to all but me.

They weren't going to walk as far as the door of the chosen haunted house with me. Oh, no. There were none of them quite willing to do that. But the old guy—there he was again—had volunteered to accompany me as far as a half mile from the place. He was to point it out, and then, no doubt, watch from a distance to make sure I carried out my boast.

Of course I didn't like it. And a day of waiting hadn't helped a bit. My nerves, by the time eleven o'clock rolled by, were getting to a state, no fooling.

And finally, when the old guy stood up and said, "Perhaps we had better be starting toward the house," I felt like yelling in sheer relief.

All the group quite insisted on making a point of personal farewells before I set out with the old guy. It was just as if they thought, or hoped, they'd never see me again in the same condition.

There was little I could do about it, however, so I stood around shaking hands and joking and acting very brave until I'd finished the gauntlet of none-too-well wishers.

And then at last I was walking along beside the old guy, heading for a destination, which anyone with any brains would never set out for.

For companionship I might as well have had no one, for all the solace the old guy provided.

He scarcely spoke at all. And his first words after we'd walked along a while set the tenor of anything he said afterwards.

"There is no moon in the sky tonight," the old guy said gloomily. "It was on just such a moonless night as this that my poor, dear brother entered the house to which I am taking you." He trailed off with a sad sigh.

There was scarcely anything I could say to that. It wasn't the happy sort of stuff I wanted to carry on with, so I didn't answer. But the old guy's words had succeeded in calling my attention to the fact that it was most certainly a dreadful night.

There was no moon, as he had remarked. Nor stars, for that matter. And the lonely, narrow little hillside roadway along which we walked was bordered on both sides by tall, gaunt trees. The wind was busy whistling eerily through the branches of these trees that night.

Now and then I could see the old guy, out of the corner of my eye, glancing dourly up at me to see how I was taking it. It was hard to be sure whether or not he was hoping I'd be in a dither, or just genuinely sorry for the brash venture I was starting.

It was natural, I suppose, trudging along there in the lonesome darkness of the eerie night, to imagine after a while that eyes were peering out at us from behind the trees bordering the road. At any rate, we hadn't gone very far before I was pretty damned sure that strange eyes *were* following us.

If the old guy had the same sensation, he didn't mention it. And it was certainly a cinch that I wasn't going to ask him about the matter.

AFTER a while the roadway along which the old guy was taking me, began a steep and unexpected rise. A minute later and we were standing on the crest of a hill, looking down at a bleak, black mansion on a smaller hill perhaps half a mile off.

"There," the old guy said surreptitiously, "is the haunted house."

My first reaction was an urgent desire to bolt off in the opposite direction posthaste.

Then I was aware that he was watching me narrowly, waiting for any such evidence of change of heart.

"Well, well," I said with as much cheer as I could muster. "Well, well, well. So that's the haunted house, eh?"

"That," said the old guy, "is it."

I laughed a little shakily.

"Well, well," I repeated inanely. "So that's the haunted house, eh?"

"I feel," said the old guy, with an icy stare, "that the fact that that is the haunted house has been fairly well established by now."

I gulped, an action that was getting as frequent as breathing.

"Heh, heh," I stalled. "Big place, isn't it? Thought it would be smaller, somehow."

"It seems also somewhat evident," the old guy declared acidly, "that the house is a large one. Are you going on, or aren't you?"

"On?" I squeaked. "On? Oh, yes. Heh-heh-heh. You mean to the house. How silly. But of course."

"Then why don't you get moving?" the old guy asked.

The wind took that moment to howl weirdly through the trees on either side of us. I wasn't certain, but I had the sensation that those unseen eyes were watching us again.

My heart must have shared that sensation, for it suddenly seemed to take refuge somewhere down in my shoes.

"Well?" the old guy said.

"Well," I answered lamely, "uh, ah, so-long. Thanks for showing me the way. I'll, uh, see you later."

The old guy nodded cryptically. "Perhaps," he admitted. "At any rate I hope so."

"Thank you," I said bitterly. "Thank you so very much."

"I'll be watching from this hill," the old guy said.

"Sure," I answered, "sure. I get the hint. You'll see me enter that place, never fear."

The old guy didn't answer, and I started down the hill road. Never had I felt an impulse before as strong as the desire that made me want to turn for one last glance and a wave of the hand at the old guy. But of course I couldn't do that.

I had another sudden impulse to turn around and set a few dash records in any direction leading away from that ominously waiting mansion ahead.

The utter blackness of the night was getting me, now. And I began to wish for the faintest twinkle of a star, or the smallest ribbon of moonlight.

Instead I got an increased howling of the wind through the trees, and an awfully weak sickness where my stomach should have been.

I WAS less than a quarter of a mile away from the blackly forbidding mansion before I was aware I'd covered that much ground. And now I slowed my pace, proceeding more cautiously.

There was a small, grass covered series of wagon tracks where a road had once been, leading off through the trees and up to the mansion itself.

I hesitated there an instant before turning up it, forcing myself to do so merely from the realization that the old guy back there on the hill was watching every move I made.

It got worse moving along that old side road through the woods surrounding the mansion. Worse than I imagined it ever could be.

Then it was that I saw the light moving up in the third story window of the otherwise darkened mansion. It was the tiniest pinpoint of light, barely distinguishable. But it was there, and it moved, as if from room to room!

What kept me moving on toward that old house after seeing that light, I'll never know. It certainly wasn't courage, for my teeth were chattering louder than a brace of castanets.

At last I was in the weedy clearing, which surrounded the grim old framework mansion. And now, looking up at the third floor again for the first time since I'd seen the moving light, I saw that it was gone.

The ominous old building was black and bleak once more.

There wasn't a sound now, save for the constant, moaning background of the wind through the gaunt trees. Tensely, I crossed the weedy clearing until I stood at last before the small porchway of the front entrance.

"The old guy is watching," I told myself. "I can't back down, now. The old guy is watching. He'll tell the others if I funk out."

I stepped up onto the porchway and stood there by the door, listening intently.

I heard nothing save the moaning of the wind and the kettledrum pounding of my heart.

Closing my eyes firmly, I placed my hand on the cold, round surface of the doorknob.

Gently, ever so gently, I turned it. I found the door opening inward under my pressure. Opening inward, and creaking ever so slightly on its hinges.

OF COURSE I wanted to run like hell again. And of course I wasn't smart enough to do so. I just stood there, the door half open and my hand on the knob.

I stood there, trying to get up courage enough to open my eyes and look into the darkness that lay inside that doorway. My teeth were chattering double time.

Slowly, one at a time, I opened my eyes.

Ahead there was nothing but blackness. Highly uninviting blackness. Distinctly unpromising blackness. Ominously beckoning blackness.

My knees came in on an offbeat to accompany my chattering teeth with a knocking tempo that blended nicely. My pounding heart, of course, filled in the kettledrums to round out my private little rhythm section.

I turned to look longingly back over my shoulder, and was suddenly aware that the moonless night and the black, unfriendly woods were just as terrifying now as the blackness of the mansion yawning before me.

That was probably the only reason I pushed the door even further inward and stepped into the clammy darkness ahead.

Slowly, gropingly, I put my hands out before me and began a cautious exploration of the room in which I now found myself.

I had located a wall and was using it as a directional guide through the darkness while trying to focus my eyes to this new visual change when the door slammed. The door through which I had entered but an instant before...

I froze there, pressed back against the wall in terror, unable to do anything about it as my teeth and knees began knocking in harmony again.

But there wasn't any further sound. There was nothing else to indicate *that something was in the room with me.*

It must have been fully five minutes later, however, before I thawed from my frozen position. And in those five minutes surrounded by darkness and unpleasant *possibilities,* I must have heard a hundred minor creaking noises.

I moved on, then, a little more swiftly, for my eyes were beginning to focus a little better in the darkness and I no longer was forced to fear looming bulky objects—as long as they didn't move.

By now, I was thinking in terms of finding some spot, some corner where I could crouch against the protection of two walls and peer through the darkness for the rest of the night.

THE house was huge, probably large enough to have some eighteen to twenty rooms in all. But they could keep their eighteen or twenty rooms. All I wanted now was one room. A small one. A safe one. On the first floor, near a window, where I could jump if I had to.

By now, I was shaking like a pair of dice in the hand of a palsy victim. And I was just turning down what seemed to be a narrow hallway leading off from the big front room, when I heard the creaking of the floorboards in a room somewhere above me.

Of course I had to recall, at that unfortunate moment, the pinpoint of light I'd seen moving along the third floor when I'd been a quarter mile from the mansion.

This time I didn't breathe.

I stood there frozen, wide-eyed in terror, my lungs so full they threatened to burst. Stood there, listening.

The creaking floorboard noise was not repeated.

"An old house," I told myself. "Settling deeper and deeper into the foundations every day, I suppose."

Quick thinking. Easy explanation. Wishful thinking. Wishful explanation . I forced myself to move on through the darkness, down that narrow little hallway.

And then I heard the floorboards again. This time, followed by footsteps. Slow, measured footsteps. Growing louder with every instant.

And then I realized that I was standing near a wide, railed, gracefully turning staircase, and that the footsteps were moving to the top of the staircase, and then starting down!

There was a small, cramped, dark cave beneath the stairs, and I dived into it immediately. Now, the footsteps were right above my head, still measured, descending the stairs.

I tried to remember prayers to say. Especially prayers to cover situations like this. Prayers to deal with terrors of the unknown. It was no use. My mind was as frozen as my muscles.

The footsteps were now at the bottom of the staircase, and they paused for an instant, indecisively.

I could feel those unknown eyes probing slowly right and left through the blackness—searching.

No sound, at first. And then a creaking floorboard. Had I been seen? Did it know I was hiding here?

My mouth was cottony thick, my tongue dry and swollen from fear. I'm not at all sure that my heart bothered to beat during the next thirty seconds.

Another creaking floorboard broke the indecisive silence. And then the measured footsteps started again, away, off in the opposite direction of the staircase where I crouched limp with terror.

I LISTENED for another minute, as the footsteps grew less and less audible, finally blending into the awful silence. The thing was on the first floor, in some other section of the house. How long it would remain there I could not estimate.

But I felt fairly certain it would be back this way. And the under-staircase might not be a good hiding place twice in a row. A limply exhausted heap, I pulled myself out from under my refuge and stood up, shaking from head to foot.

I think I had the door in mind when I took those first few steps back in the direction from which I'd originally entered. But it made no difference what I had in mind an instant later. For I heard the footsteps, measured ominous, coming back to the room they had but recently deserted.

The under-staircase was out. And I wasn't certain that I'd be able to make the door before the thing re-entered the room. There was no window within leaping distance, either.

I had but one opportunity. Up the stairs—but rapidly.

It was all I could do to scramble fast and keep quiet all at once. But I managed it, gaining the top landing of the stairs before the sound of those footsteps below got much louder.

I found myself in a hallway, now. A hallway off which there were from four to six doors.

Inching along through the darkness, with one ear cocked toward the staircase I'd just ascended, I came to a door that was slightly ajar. The sound of the footsteps downstairs had stopped again. And now I stood there, listening for any noises from the room with the half opened door.

There was only silence.

And then I heard it. Heard it as my spine froze and icy fingers caressed the back of my neck.

Weird, eerie strains of violin music, coming from the floor below!

My knees were suddenly unable to support me, and every muscle was rigid with terror.

Somehow my hand found the knob of the slightly open door. And somehow I managed to drag myself into that room. I slammed the door behind me, but I didn't care. I was looking for a window.

The violin music had stopped with the sound of the slamming of the door. Then it started all over again, spine chilling, eerie.

I stood there quaking in the darkness of that room, my eyes peering through the darkness at my surroundings. It was a bedroom. An old brass fourposter was against the wall in the center of the room, and beyond that was the window.

The moon came out at that instant, throwing a chill blue light into the room and across the old bed.

This time I couldn't control my reaction. I felt my teeth chatter with the clattering noise of crockery bouncing on a shelf in an earthquake. It was loud, betraying, and I couldn't help it.

For there on that old bed, beneath white sheets, a figure stirred, and then two eyes were glaring at me through the semi-darkness!

I WAS unable to stop the moan of terror that escaped my lips. I must have been on the fringe of gibbering lunacy. My teeth never chattered more loudly.

And then the figure, covered completely by the sheets, sat erect in the old bed, emitting a piercing, ghastly screech!

I remember fumbling for, the doorknob. I remember that the sheeted figure was climbing from the bed, gibbering and moaning, and moving toward me.

And then I was yowling madly, tugging at the door, almost knocking myself down as it suddenly swung open.

I raced down the darkened hallway, then, looking over my shoulder only long enough to see that the sheeted figure, still screeching and sobbing and groaning, was in the doorway.

And even as I put my hand on the banister, I heard the violin music below me stop abruptly. There was a deep, ominous gurgle, then, and footsteps moved down there toward the staircase.

Trapped.

I looked back down the hallway, to see the sheeted thing standing there in the darkness, howling and leaping up and down. There was nothing else to do, so I bolted down the hallway in the other direction.

There were more doors, and I rattled the knobs of each of them, seeking any room with a window from which I could leap.

They were all locked. And from behind several there came new hideous moanings and gibberings and ghastly voices.

I was adding to the din now, shrieking bloodily and often, my mind a red haze of hysterical horror.

Looking back but once again, I saw the sheeted figure in the darkness flapping madly around in the hallway at the top of the stairs.

The next five minutes were five eternities of madness.

The entire, ghastly house was alive with screams, shrill cries, gibbering moans, hideous yowlings.

Vaguely, I was aware that I was at the end of the hallway, and that there was no longer any avenue for my escape.

Collapsing limply in a heap in the corner, I continued my terrified screams for assistance.

And then I was aware that my head was knocking against a windowsill directly above me. So great had been my terror that I'd failed to see the window at the end of this hall.

I dragged myself erect, still screaming hoarsely between gibbering moans. Dragged myself erect and struggled, with almost helplessly weak desperation, to raise that window.

At last it opened, and without looking twice, I hurled myself out of it.

THINKING back on it now, I realize I must have landed on my head in that desperate leap. For the next thing I recalled was a damp chill and moist ground, and I was opening my eyes.

I was still next to the house, lying in a clump of weeds.

Groaning, I managed to climb to my feet. Looking up, I saw that dawn was breaking. I must have been lying there unconscious for several hours.

And then I remembered. I looked up once at the grim, bleak old mansion, saw the open window through which I had leaped.

And then I took to my heels.

I was stumbling, dirty, breathless and ragged when I got back out onto the roadway. I'd taken a short cut through a thicket of brambles.

Then I saw the old man up there on the road hill. The old guy had kept his vigil as I thought he would.

It was all I could do to force myself to slow down, but I managed. When I finally came up to him I was breathing a little more easily, but from the look on his face as his eyes appraised me, I knew there would be no fooling him.

He was, in my estimation, no longer the "old guy." He was now the "wise old man."

"You saw them," said the wise old man somberly.

I nodded wearily. "I was a fool to scoff," I admitted.

"No matter," he said. "Now you have learned. And you were both fortunate and brave to stay there until dawn and emerge as you had entered."

I suddenly decided to say nothing about that leap out the window and the hours I'd spent unconscious. I decided not to mention the fact that I'd have been back, screaming madly, if I hadn't knocked myself out in that leap.

We started back down the road, away from the ghastly, haunted old mansion. Both of us were thinking.

"Perhaps you can tell the others," he said after a while, "that there is such a thing as the other world and creatures that exist in it."

I nodded, making a firm resolve to see that the word was spread convincingly. No more would I join the scoffers who professed scorn at the thought of the existence of the other world. No more would I refuse to believe in people. And never again would I volunteer to spend a night in a mansion haunted by human beings.

No, sir. Not this ghost. Not me!

THE END

If you've enjoyed this book, you will not want to miss these terrific titles...

ARMCHAIR SCI-FI & HORROR DOUBLE NOVELS, $12.95 each

D-81   **THE LAST PLEA** by Robert Bloch
THE STATUS CIVILIZATION by Robert Sheckley

D-82   **WOMAN FROM ANOTHER PLANET** by Frank Belknap Long
HOMECALLING by Judith Merril

D-83   **WHEN TWO WORLDS MEET** by Robert Moore Williams
THE MAN WHO HAD NO BRAINS by Jeff Sutton

D-84   **THE SPECTRE OF SUICIDE SWAMP** by E. K. Jarvis
IT'S MAGIC, YOU DOPE! by Jack Sharkey

D-85   **THE STARSHIP FROM SIRIUS** by Rog Phillips
FINAL WEAPON by Everett Cole

D-86   **TREASURE ON THUNDER MOON** by Edmond Hamilton
TRAIL OF THE ASTROGAR by Henry Haase

D-87   **THE VENUS ENIGMA** by Joe Gibson
THE WOMAN IN SKIN 13 by Paul W. Fairman

D-88   **THE MAD ROBOT** by William P. McGivern
THE RUNNING MAN by J. Holly Hunter

D-89   **VENGEANCE OF KYVOR** by Randall Garrett
AT THE EARTH'S CORE by Edgar Rice Burroughs

D-90   **DWELLERS OF THE DEEP** by Don Wilcox
NIGHT OF THE LONG KNIVES by Fritz Leiber

ARMCHAIR SCIENCE FICTION CLASSICS, $12.95 each

C-28   **THE MAN FROM TOMORROW**
by Stanton A. Coblentz

C-29   **THE GREEN MAN OF GRAYPEC**
by Festus Pragnell

C-30   **THE SHAVER MYSTERY, Book Four**
by Richard S. Shaver

ARMCHAIR MASTERS OF SCIENCE FICTION SERIES, $16.95 each

MS-7   **MASTERS OF SCIENCE FICTION AND FANTASY, Vol. Seven**
Lester del Rey, "The Band Played On" and other tales

MS-8   **MASTERS OF SCIENCE FICTION, Vol. Eight**
Milton Lesser, "'A' as in Android" and other tales

If you've enjoyed this book, you will not want to miss these terrific titles…

ARMCHAIR SCI-FI & HORROR DOUBLE NOVELS, $12.95 each

D-91 **THE TIME TRAP** by Henry Kuttner
THE LUNAR LICHEN by Hal Clement

D-92 **SARGASSO OF LOST STARSHIPS** by Poul Anderson
THE ICE QUEEN by Don Wilcox

D-93 **THE PRINCE OF SPACE** by Jack Williamson
POWER by Harl Vincent

D-94 **PLANET OF NO RETURN** by Howard Browne
THE ANNIHILATOR COMES by Ed Earl Repp

D-95 **THE SINISTER INVASION** by Edmond Hamilton
OPERATION TERROR by Murray Leinster

D-96 **TRANSIENT** by Ward Moore
THE WORLD-MOVER by George O. Smith

D-97 **FORTY DAYS HAS SEPTEMBER** by Milton Lesser
THE DEVIL'S PLANET by David Wright O'Brien

D-98 **THE CYBERENE** by Rog Phillips
BADGE OF INFAMY by Lester del Rey

D-99 **THE JUSTICE OF MARTIN BRAND** by Raymond A. Palmer
BRING BACK MY BRAIN by Dwight V. Swain

D-100 **WIDE-OPEN PLANET** by L. Sprague de Camp
AND THEN THE TOWN TOOK OFF by Richard Wilson

ARMCHAIR SCIENCE FICTION CLASSICS, $12.95 each

C-31 **THE GOLDEN GUARDSMEN**
by S. J. Byrne

C-32 **ONE AGAINST THE MOON**
by Donald A. Wollheim

C-33 **HIDDEN CITY**
by Chester S. Geier

ARMCHAIR SCI-FI & HORROR GEMS SERIES, $12.95 each

G-9 **SCIENCE FICTION GEMS, Vol. Five**
Clifford D. Simak and others

G-10 **HORROR GEMS, Vol. Five**
E. Hoffman Price and others

Printed in Great Britain
by Amazon